Praise for S

“Refined and subtle, and at the same time one of the most striking voices in contemporary Dutch literature.”

LIZE SPIT, author of *The Melting*

“A wri[illegible]
there's no need to hammer it home[illegible]

De Volkskrant

“Subtle and refined.”

NRC Handelsblad

“Robben's style is deceptively simple. You don't have to be an adult to read *Summer Brother*, yet Robben's imagery, subtle humor, and surprising plot will connect with the most literate of readers. The novel offers a moving insight into a boyhood that gives pause for reflection.”

De Standaard

“Like no other writer, Robben can empathize with the mind of a child and he imbues the reader with this open and uninhibited outlook as the story unfolds.”

Hebban

“*Summer Brother* is a wry and funny book about a damaged family.”

Algemeen Dagblad

“Lovingly, Robben shows Brian's hapless attempts to deal with pills and full diapers, yet all the while he is working mercilessly towards the inevitable climax.”

VPRO Gids

"A poignant story about loyalty, disloyalty, solidarity, and puberty."
De Limburger

"A truly gutsy novel."
Tzum

"*Summer Brother* is a beautiful, modest novel. As he did with *You Have Me to Love*, Robben will once again win over a young generation of readers with this book. That in itself is praiseworthy."
Elsevier

"Jaap Robben has once again written an overwhelming book."
HMC Dagbladen

"His first novel, *You Have Me to Love*, was well-received, won prizes, and became a sales success. *Summer Brother* is a worthy successor and has all the ingredients to follow the same path. Robben knows how to write simply and magnificently—I kept underlining beautiful sentences in the first chapters."
Trouw

Praise for You Have Me to Love:

"*You Have Me to Love* is an intense and dramatic novel filled with meticulous use of detail and a forensic psychological accuracy. Its power comes from the fierce energy of the narrative structure, the way of handling silence and pain, and the ability to confront the darkest areas of experience with clear-eyed sympathy and care. Jaap Robben handles delicate, dangerous material with subtlety and sympathy, but also with a visionary sense of truth that is masterly and unforgettable."

COLM TÓIBÍN

"I was completely seduced by this novel—it's raw and harrowing and very moving. Robben is a very powerful writer who reminds me very much of Per Petterson."

AIFRIC CAMPBELL

"Beautiful, just beautiful."

GERBRAND BAKKER

"This is a bold, tender and ambivalent narrative, raw and disturbing, with moments of painful beauty; a taut narrative heavy with a convincing sense of dread."

Irish Times

"*You Have Me to Love* explores raw and unsettling psychological territory. It is a story that once read will stick with the reader for a long time."

Literary Review

"Moving between child-like speculation and shocking realism, Robben's novel transports the reader into lives almost beyond imagining in the contemporary world. With echoes of Ian McEwan and Peter Carey, Robben's tale, already a huge success in the Netherlands, is one to savor and discuss."

ALA Booklist

"A small masterpiece."

Harpers Bazaar

"*You Have Me to Love* left me gasping, literally, for air. And groping for understanding. A blindingly good novel about the vulnerability of children and the hard truth of the world they inhabit."
The King's English Bookshop

"A promising novelist has risen. Robben lifts you from your life and sweeps you away, with no chance of escaping."
De Morgen

"An overwhelming debut about lost childhood innocence, *You Have Me to Love* can be favorably compared to Niccolò Ammaniti's *I'm Not Scared* and Ian McEwan's *The Cement Garden*."
Het Parool

"A gripping novel that steadily tightens its hold."
De Volkskrant

"Like a record stuck in its groove, it won't let me go."
European Literature Network

"From the very first sentence it is clear how well debut novelist Jaap Robben writes. His childishly simple yet highly suggestive sentences make *You Have Me to Love* as stark and foreboding as the island on which it is set."
NRC NEXT

"Unbelievable—a beautiful story, light for all its heaviness, written in a clear and powerful style. A coming-of-age tale in which Robben merges grief, simplicity, and isolation in a phenomenal way."
De Telegraaf

SUMMER BROTHER

JAAP ROBBEN

SUMMER BROTHER

Translated from the Dutch
by David Doherty

WORLD EDITIONS
New York, London, Amsterdam

Published in the USA in 2021 by World Editions LLC, New York
Published in the UK in 2021 by World Editions Ltd., London

World Editions
New York/London/Amsterdam

Printed by Zwaan Lenoir, Wormerveer, Netherlands

British Library Cataloguing-in-Publication Data
A catalogue record for this book is available on request from the British Library.

ISBN 978-1-64286-081-8

First published as *Zomervacht* in the Netherlands in 2018 by Uitgeverij De Geus, Amsterdam

This book was published with the support of the Dutch Foundation for Literature

Nederlands letterenfonds
dutch foundation
for literature

Twitter: @WorldEdBooks
Facebook: @WorldEditionsInternationalPublishing
Instagram: @WorldEdBooks
www.worldeditions.co.uk

Book Club Discussion Guides are available on our website.

For my dear son Midas

1

I thought we were just going for a drive. Specks of hay drift past the pickup and blow in through the open windows. It's harvest time but not for us. Rusty heating pipes rattle in the back, along with the shell of a washing machine we picked up yesterday by the side of the road. Dad swerves right and rolls to a halt at the petrol station.

"Want anything?" he asks as he fills the tank. Mondays are okay because Benoit is on the cash desk. His boss won't serve us anymore. Says customers like us cost him money.

A truck piled with hay bales thunders past, flaps a bleached-out canvas banner flogging coffee that's always on special offer round here. The way that stuff smells, you'd swear they ground it up with roofing tiles.

"Hiya," I say to Benoit. A shrill little bell tinkles.

"You two aren't allowed in here," Benoit fuzzes from his glass booth. His mouth is too close to the microphone. "Told you that last time."

I point at his mike and waggle my hand next to my ear like I can't make him out. "I said, you two ..." I shake my head and waggle some more. The sacks of charcoal piled around his booth make it look like he's barricaded himself in. Down the aisle, bunches of flowers are dying by the bucketful. I hang around the fridge packed with energy drinks while Benoit tries to keep tabs on me in the fish-eye mirror below the ceiling. The tinkly doorbell goes nuts again.

"Benoit!" Dad bellows, like they're old chums.

"I was just telling Brian that you ..."

"We'll take one of these, while you're at it." Dad grabs a massive chocolate egg from the bargain bin. "Present for his brother."

"Are we going to see Lucien?"

Dad presses the price tag to the safety glass. "Fifty percent off, don't forget," he says, picking at the big red sticker. "Wait a sec, that can stay on. It's not like his brother will notice."

"Okay, okay," Benoit stammers and rings up the discount.

"Tie it up nice with a bit of blue ribbon, will you? His brother will like that."

"We can't wrap discounted items."

"Red's fine, too."

"Like I said, it's not allowed."

"You want anything else?" Dad shouts over to me.

I shake my head.

"Right then, how much do I owe you?"

Benoit swallows and peers at his cash register. "That comes to thirty-eight twenty-fi—"

"Here you go." Dad scoops a handful of coins from the inside pocket of his leather jacket and clatters them into Benoit's tray. "And not forgetting ..." He fishes a folded tenner from his jeans pocket and makes a show of smoothing it out. "Now wrap that thing up, will you? Nice and fancy, like."

"I need to count the money first."

"It's just that we're in a bit of a hurry."

Benoit nervously starts sorting the coins.

Chocolate has smeared the plastic even before we reach the car. Dad strides ahead, blue ribbon fluttering behind him. "Get a move on, Bry."

"Are we really going to see Lucien?"

Benoit emerges from the shop. "I'm seven euros twenty-five short."

Dad turns around, but keeps backing toward the car. "Sure you counted right?"

"It's short."

"Nah, can't be." Dad pulls his surprised face. "And we need to get a move on, see. His brother's waiting."

"I'm going to have to write this up."

"Steady on, Benny boy. Is this how you treat your loyal customers?" Dad slows his pace. "I'll drop by tomorrow with the rest."

"I won't be here tomorrow."

"Ah-hah," Dad grins. "But you can make up the difference till next week, right?"

As we pull out onto the road, Benoit is still standing by the door. Dad shoots him a friendly wave and tops it off with a thumbs-up. Benoit starts to raise a hand but gives up halfway.

"Why are we going to see Lucien?"

"About time, I reckoned."

My big brother lives in a bed half an hour's drive from our caravan. The last time we saw him was when he turned sixteen and the time before that must have been Christmas-ish. I mostly remember him sleeping. When he finally woke up, all he did was stare at the tinsel that danced and shone above the radiator by his window. We never go on Christmas Day or his exact birthday in case we run into Mum. Even now, I catch myself hoping her car's not parked outside.

Beside the main entrance, the boy with the bulging eyes sits there leering at us. His face is mostly forehead, and dark hair spikes up through the gaps in his leather helmet. He looks unforgiving, like he knows this is our first visit in ages. I always get the jitters when we walk through the door, worried Lucien might be angry we stayed away so long, or afraid something has happened to him and nobody thought to tell us. But mainly because this is more Mum's territory than ours.

The white walls are grubby up to hip height, scuffed and dented by wheelchairs, trolleys, and those beds they're always pushing around. Wheelchairs with all sorts of bits tacked on are parked along the length of the corridor. A bin bag hangs from a trolley piled with trays and plates smeared with food. In a room off to the side, there's a boy lying on a blue mat, howling at the ceiling. His legs are twisted at a weird angle, like they belong to another body and someone stitched them onto his at the last minute. His arms are outstretched to catch whoever might come crashing through the ceiling tiles.

"Bry!" Dad is already at the end of the corridor. "Check this out!" The automatic doors keep wanting to swing shut, but because of where he's standing they jerk back open. Behind him a statue of Our Lady gestures us to slow down, though everyone here moves at a snail's pace.

"Isn't that where Lucien's room is?" A dull wall of plastic sheeting has been stretched across the side corridor. Someone must have opened a door or a window, because the plastic sucks itself hollow with a smack, then rustles back into a bulge. The sound of drilling is coming from the other side. A silhouette pushes the shadow of a wheelbarrow.

"Do you think they moved him? For Christ's sake ... Your mum is supposed to keep us posted." The cellophane around the chocolate egg crinkles in his fist.

"Maybe he's down here somewhere?" We look at names

outside random rooms, someone wails behind a door. "Let's ask at reception."

"Where's our Lucien?" Dad plants the chocolate egg on the counter. "His room's gone and no one said a word to us."

"One moment, please," the woman answers. "Just need to finish typing this up."

Her name tag says she's Esmée and her blouse is home to the kind of breasts Dad's sure to crack a joke about. There's a gleam in his eye already. Esmée hammers the enter key with her index finger, rolls back her chair, and gives us a friendly look.

"We're here to visit Lucien."

"Lucien Chevalier?"

"This is his brother."

"Oh ... a brother," Esmée says, but she doesn't look at me. "And who might you be?"

"The Dad."

"Ah, of course ..."

"Is he still here?"

"He most certainly is. Lucien has been temporarily moved to one-o-six. We've had a bit of a reshuffle due to the renovation work." Before we can ask, she tells us how to get there. "Down this corridor, second corridor on your left, third door on your right."

"Cheers." Dad's eyes dip to her breasts. He must have cracked that joke in his head, because he gives a little chuckle as he taps two fingers to his forehead. "See you later."

The corridors are lined with superheroes whose faces have morphed into passport photos of the residents. "Man, oh man," Dad sighs. "You don't get many of them to the pound."

"Huh?"

"Come off it, Bry. You could pitch a tent in the shade of those tits."

"One-o-one," I read out loud. "Here's one-o-three. Must be down the other end."

"We'll play it by ear," Dad mumbles. "No point hanging around if he's napping."

Lucien's name by the door is decorated with blue and yellow scribbles. One of the nurses must have clamped his fingers around a felt-tip pen.

"Ready?" Dad looks at me, one hand on the door handle. "Bry?"

I nod and he throws open the door as briskly as he once pulled milk teeth from my mouth. The closed blinds flap against the open window. Crêpe-paper birds on strings dangle from the ceiling. Below them lies Lucien. The thick hair on the back of his head is sticking up, uncombable as ever. From the waist down, he is lying flat on the blanket, but his face and his upper body are turned away from us. He's grown closer to the sides of his bed since we saw him last. My brother changes in little things. Thicker eyebrows. Spots along his hairline. Bottom lip sticking out like the rim of a holy-water basin.

"Lucien?" His eyes open to two slits, a yellow breadcrumb of sleep in one corner. Mum would have wiped that away in a flash.

"You're Lucien," I say to remind him of himself. "It's us again." And I tap my chest. "Brian and Dad." I shift along a bit so there's room for the pair of us next to his bed. Even so, Dad hangs back. He licks his lips and coughs without needing to. I take another step so he can stand beside me.

"I'm fine where I am," he says and nudges my hand with the chocolate egg. "For your brother."

I've already taken hold of it, but I'd rather he gave it himself. "You do it," I whisper and try to give it back.

"No, no. You're better at this." His hands disappear into his jacket pockets. Lucien leers at us. I hold the egg up to his face a second, then put it down on his bedside cabinet. Lucien only understands chocolate when he tastes it.

"It's been a few months, hasn't it?" I want to touch him but I don't know how, so my hands stroke the railing of the bed. On the magnetic photo board by his head, Lucien is curling at the edges. It's the one where Mum is crouched beside his wheelchair and her leggings have squished her tummy into two rolls. A ponytail spouts from her head and her hands clutch the same shoulder bag she's had for a thousand years. Above it is a new photo, with Didier. Like all their pictures, he's got his arms round her and she's pressing her cheek to his to show us how much he loves her. "Dee-dee-yaaay," Dad calls him, putting on his la-di-da voice.

Mum always sticks their snapshots in the middle. Peeping out from behind them is a group photo of Lucien with the other residents, at the entrance to a theme park. Everyone is looking at the camera except my brother. The only photo of him smiling is the one where a stranger's hands are holding a guinea pig to his cheek.

I'm down in the right-hand corner with a magnet half over my face. It's the photo Mum had in the little window in her purse. One of my front teeth has just come through and my hair is slicked back and gelled tight. I remember feeling all grown up because it was the day I got my earring put in. I had one of those rattail braids down my back too, but you can't see that in the photo. "Look," I say to Lucien. "That was me." There's a familiar strangeness in talking to him. Mostly because he doesn't say anything back. Grown-ups are better at yakking like this, even if it does sound like they're talking to their dog.

Lucien gawps at the paper birds, which have been swaying gently from the ceiling since we came in.

"How about a little light?" Dad tugs the cord on the blinds. All the windows are rigged so they only open a crack, to stop the residents tumbling out. We can see summer through the window but it still seems miles from Lucien's bed. From the whole building, come to that. The mopped floors smell of outdoor swimming pools.

Lucien scrunches up his eyes in the sudden light. They open, twitch shut, and then open wide again. Hopeful, like he's forgotten why he closed them in the first place.

On the parched field outside the window, two residents are playing tennis but they only get as far as tossing the foam rubber ball. Up it goes and their rackets flail through the air, too late and well wide of the mark. Then they hunt the ball and get ready for a new throw, straight-faced, knees bent. One player has her fists clamped tight around the neck of the racket. The other has put hers down and is throwing the ball with both hands. Whoosh. Missed. Rummage in the bushes.

"Your brother would rather have a nap, by the look of it." Dad gently squeezes Lucien's feet, the only part of him that's under the blanket. A touch without touching. "I'm off for a coffee. Back in a bit." He shambles out the door, a new record. It usually takes him longer to disappear.

"Lucien?" I ask. "Want some chocolate?" The ribbon is wrapped tight around the egg, so I pull it off for him. The rustle of cellophane makes him curious and his head rises from the dent in his pillow. "Look!" My knuckles smash the egg into brown fragments. "This is for you." I hold a blunt shard of chocolate in front of his face. "You like this, don't you?" Lucien starts to rock from side to side and I drop the shard into the cave of his mouth. His crooked teeth are smaller than I remember, but it's probably just his head that's bigger. He sucks, chews, smacks his lips. His forearms rise up from the bed at odd angles and his fingers play slow-mo on invisible piano keys.

"Mah-mah-mmah!" he shouts crossly.

"Want some more?" Teasing, I dangle a new piece in front of his eyes. He opens his mouth so wide I'm afraid it will tear at the corners, so I pop the chocolate in quick. When he lived at home I could understand the sounds he made. Like if there was food on the table and he couldn't reach. Or if he spotted the hoover, which always scared him silly.

"Brian," I say, so he can repeat after me. "Come on, say 'Brian.' Say it and I'll give you another bit." I climb up and sit on the deep windowsill. The heels of my shoes clunk softly against the radiator. "Brian," I repeat. "Braa-yun."

Suddenly he's wobbling so fiercely that the wheels under his bed start to groan. He stretches an arm in my direction and his fingers stir the air. "Do you mean me? Do you remember?" I point to my photo on the board. His face cramps up and he strains to look past me, out of the window. "Do you want to see them playing tennis?"

I turn and nearly fall off the sill. A girl has her cheek pressed to the window pane. "What the ...?" She rolls her other cheek to the glass and leaves a greasy stamp with her nose. Lucien makes a sound I've never heard him make before. He howls. The girl has a ponytail and curtains of black hair that fall over her ears. Her tongue licks slow patches in the haze of pollen on the glass. Then she steps back to admire the result, holding on to the window ledge with both hands. "Do you know her?" It's only now that the girl seems to notice me. She smiles. I can't really tell whether she lives here or she's a visitor like me.

"Is she your girl?"

Lucien is choking with excitement. Red veins pop into the whites of his eyes, his breath comes in gags and gulps.

The girl waves both hands at him. I pat Lucien on the back and he quietens down for a while. She has gone. Lucien coughs, and flecks of applesauce spatter his lips, chin, and shirt. "Easy now. Don't choke." I grab his beaker from the bedside cabinet and push the spout between his lips. His head begins to shake wildly. "Easy, easy." He tries to slap the beaker away from his mouth. Afraid to leave Lucien alone, I hope someone out in the corridor will hear and come in to help. Thankfully, his chest stops heaving. Another bout of coughing. "Are you okay?" He swallows a couple of times and I tilt the beaker of water to his lips. He sucks a mouthful or two, then turns his face from the spout. "Point if you want more," I say and put the beaker on the windowsill where he can see it.

"Was that, like ... your girl?" I peer out in case she's crouching below the window, but all I see is mossy paving slabs and a strip of greenish gravel. "Does she do that a lot?"

No answer, of course.

I hear scuffling out in the corridor and expect to see Dad returning with his coffee, or one of the nurses coming to check on us. The door handle is pointing down, so someone must be on the other side. "Hello?" The girl who licked the window peeps round the door.

"Is that you?"

She giggles and pulls her head back.

"You can come in, you know."

The door flies open and the handle strikes the buffer on the wall. "Here I am!" she cheers, arms half-raised. She looks older than a girl, but she's not really a woman. A kind of "girllady" whose breasts have shown up early. Her skirt is a lampshade and her right foot points inward like it's on a mission to trip up her left. She comes closer and her eyes lock onto mine, as if she's trying to drill through my pupils and see inside my head.

"Brian," I say. "That's my name. What's yours?"

"Thelma."

"Hi, Thelma."

"No-hoh. Thh-elma."

"Thelma?"

"Don't copy me! Thel-ma!" Her fingers scrabble at her waistband and yank her Minnie Mouse top up to her chin. She plucks a name sticker from the black vest underneath. "Look," she grouches. The sticky side is fluffed with black. She presses it to her breast and rubs. "There."

"Selma," I read out loud.

She looks proud.

"Do you live here too?"

Her forehead wrinkles. "I'm nearly new."

"How long have you lived here then?"

"Bigger than a week," Selma says, her voice unexpectedly loud. The words that come from her mouth sound rounder than when I say them.

"Two weeks?"

"Bigger!"

"A month?"

She tilts her head and looks at me like I'm supposed to know the answer. "Before here I lived with Gran."

Lucien has turned as far as he can to face us. "I know him already," she says and clumsily manoeuvres her way past me to the bed. "You think I'm cute, don't you?"

Lucien howls.

"You think I'm cute, don't you?" She takes his face in her hands and squeezes his lips together to make a fish mouth. For a moment I'm afraid she's going to kiss him. His eyelashes flicker anxiously as she runs her thumbs under his eyes.

"I don't think he likes that," I say.

"Does too," she replies.

Now Selma's thumbs are gliding over Lucien's closed eyelids. The muscles in his neck tense up. He looks like he wants to shake his face free of her hands. But at the same time the cramp melts from his fingers and they go from gnarly twigs to looking pretty normal. Selma lets go suddenly and his head falls back into the pillow.

"Huh-hmmm. Huh-hmm." He smiles a big banana grin.

"He's my brother," I say.

Selma turns to look at me and plants her fists on her hips. All the while Lucien is trying to wobble and hum her hands back to his face.

"No," Selma snaps. "Work to do." With one hand on the bed rail and the other on my shoulder, she edges past me.

"Will you be coming back?"

She scuff-steps out of the room and heads down the corridor. Lucien cranes his neck to watch her go.

"She's gone," I say. "Want some more chocolate?" Lucien slumps back, his restless fingers claw the sheet.

"Want me to do what she did?" I take his face in my hands and squeeze his cheeks until he pouts. I can feel his molars grind between my palms. Maybe I'm being too careful. I run my thumbs along his eye sockets and keep on stroking. When I let him go, his head snaps back. But he doesn't smile the way he did for Selma.

Out in the corridor, she is nowhere to be seen. Dad's probably hanging around the smoking area.

"Just the man I'm looking for," he says as soon as he sees me. "I was about to head your way."

"Lucien is sleeping again."

"Oh … not much point then." He nods toward the coffee machine. "Want one?" I shake my head. A baldy old man is sitting in the corner, rubbing finger and thumb together like he's trying to coax sparks from his skin. His long beard is trimmed in a semicircle and the fingernails of his other hand *rat-tat-tat* on the tabletop. He must be able to read, because a card propped up in front of him says *JACQUES YOU'RE ALLOWED ONE CIGARETTE EVERY HOUR ON THE HOUR*. His fold-up alarm clock says four minutes past. The coffee machine splutters and falls silent. Dad jabs the blue button until the thing starts humming again. "Penny-pinching bastards have set it so you can't get a decent cup." His coffee overflows. "Hah! That's more like it!"

A nurse walks by and I zip out into the corridor. "Zoubida!" Her plastic clogs squeak as she spins round.

"Hey, Brian! Haven't seen you in a while." Her testy little smile is for Dad.

Zoubida is my favourite nurse. "I thought you didn't work here anymore."

"Oh, there's no getting rid of me." She rubs a hand over her tummy. "I've just become a mum …"

"Good for you," Dad says. "Hope you know what you're letting yourself in for." He thumps me on the shoulder.

"A bit late to reconsider …"

It takes Dad a second to twig that Zoubida is joking too. When it comes, his laugh booms down the corridor, so loud that everyone turns to look. Zoubida slips me a wink.

"Must be getting on," she says. And, like every time she sees me, she gives my split earlobe a gentle tug, as if there's something she can do about it. "Makes you look tough, you know," she says. "See you later."

I feel a blush rising as I tag along behind Dad toward the exit.

"Okay then. That was that." He raises a hand to the receptionist but she's staring at her computer screen.

2

The sun is high in the sky. Our little shadows have to scuttle to keep up with us. In a corner of the car park, workmen squat in the shade of their vans. One glugs down a bottle of water, pours the last mouthful over the neck of the guy beside him. A man next to them claps white clouds from his hands and tears a chunk of bread from a loaf that's lying between them on a plastic bag.

"May I trouble you for a moment?" It doesn't dawn right off that the voice is talking to us. "Mr. Chevalier?" A man with a ring binder in his left hand is bustling up behind us.

"Who's asking?"

"I beg your pardon?"

"Who might you be?"

The man has an extra chin below his chin. And another one below that. "Santos is the name," he puffs, extending a hand to Dad by way of greeting. "I recently took over as unit manager here."

"Aha, the unit manager ..."

"I understood from reception that Lucien's father was paying him a visit." It sounds like he's talking about someone else.

"Yes, well ... we were just ... uh ..." Dad clicks his key fob to unlock the doors to the pickup but we're not close enough to make the lights flash impatiently.

"I'll get right to the point. It's about Lucien."

"Then it's his mother you need to speak to."

"We have indeed contacted your wife to …"

"Ex-wife."

Dad crosses his arms, and his leather sleeves creak at the elbows.

"Excuse me. Of course. Your ex-partner."

"If it's cash you're after, she's the one to see."

"It's regarding another matter."

"Yeah? Well, you can see her about that too."

Rubble thunders down a chute across the way and booms in the skip below. "It's just that from Lucien's dossier I understand you share parental authority."

"Listen here," Dad says. "We divided our boys nice and even, like." He leans in close to Santos. "She got Lucien. I got Brian. Her choice."

"It concerns the renovations taking place this summer," Santos continues warily. "Since your ex-partner is on honeymoon and therefore not in a position to …"

"Honeymoon?"

"Is Mum getting married?"

"Um … Yes, I believe so …" Santos flips open the ring binder and snaps it shut immediately. "That's the information I have here."

"To Didier?" I ask. "So the wedding's been and gone?"

"I would imagine so." Santos shields his chest with the binder. "As I understand it, they are on a four-week honeymoon."

"Four weeks!" Dad laughs with a bunch of oh-ho-hos, like he does when someone gets hit in the face by a swing on *America's Funniest Home Videos.*

"My apologies, I assumed that both of you would have been informed."

"So, she's off sunning herself on a beach somewhere and Lucien's left to stew in his own juice."

"That's not quite how I would put it," Santos says.

"Did she put you up to this?"

"No, not at all. My question concerns the renovations. I'm sure you yourself must be aware of the pressing need to modernize our facilities." Santos breathes easier as he launches into his spiel. "The layout of the building dates from the time of the monastery, and nowadays we are more a hospital than a residential community. We had hoped to complete the work in May but, despite careful planning, there have inevitably been a few hiccups along the way. Temporary accommodation has been arranged for our more mobile residents, in collaboration with local partner organizations. But given the shortage of beds in the region, space is at a premium. So, my question to you is: would you be willing to care for Lucien at home this summer?"

"Whoa-ho-ho!" Dad holds up his hands. "We pop in here every now and again. The boy barely knows who we are. And now we're his carers for the summer? Things are tight as it is. Two dogs. Brian here. Myself. And in case you were wondering ..." He zips up his jacket, half opens it again, sniffs. "I am a working man."

"I see." The unit manager tacks on a neutral smile. "Well then, that's settled."

"Roping in parents to dig you out of a hole." Dad twirls his car keys around his finger. "That's what you get when you bring in cheap labour."

"Let me assure you, that is far from being the case," Santos protests. "These are skilled craftsmen doing an excellent job. The contractor fully appreciates the urgency of the situation. Hence the fund for parents willing to help out." He glances at his watch. "Thank you for your time, Mr. Chevalier. I will pursue the other avenues available." He takes his leave with a barely perceptible nod. "Oh yes, and since Lucien's mother is not contactable at present and we are unable to inform her of any alternative arrangements, would you mind if we kept you abreast of Lucien's situation?"

"Come again?"

"Would you like to know when we have found a place for Lucien?"

"Yeah-yeah-yeah," Dad says. "Of course I would."

Santos pulls a pen from his shirt pocket and scribbles on a Post-It note crammed with other scribbles.

"How much is in there, if you don't mind me asking?"

"In where?"

"That fund of yours. The contractor's fund."

Santos flips open the binder and sticks the yellow note to the inside cover. "Many parents have had to take unpaid leave or give up their holidays in order to have their child at home. In light of the unforeseen expenses that often arise, the contractor has agreed to provide financial recompense."

Santos turns to leave again and Dad asks "So how much do they pay?"

"It's important to stress that this is a reimbursement, an allowance if you will."

"And how much would that be, then?"

"I'm afraid I don't have the exact amount to hand. It depends on the length of the stay."

"A rough estimate will do."

"A little over two hundred and forty euros, if memory serves."

"Per?"

"Excuse me?"

"Per month?"

"No, per week." Santos points in the direction of the entrance. "And now if you don't mind, I really need to be getting on."

"The best care for my son, that's the most important thing, right?"

"That is always our top priority," Santos nods. "It's what our team works day and night to achieve."

Dad thrusts his hands in his pockets, then takes them out and crosses his arms again. "And if we *were* to take him for a while?"

"That's very kind of you. But there are still a number of external options I can explore on Lucien's behalf."

"A month should be doable."

Santos looks a little dizzy. "But you indicated that you don't have the room. And then there's your work. And the fact that Lucien's main bond is with his mother."

"I don't show up here as often as I used to, but that's her doing. Can't let Lucien miss out on that score now, can we?"

"I couldn't agree more. A child should never bear the brunt of a parental conflict."

"At the end of the day, I *am* his dad, right? And this would be good for my boys, now, wouldn't it?" Out of nowhere Dad grabs me by the neck and yanks me toward him. His knuckles ruffle my hair. "This one here's got the whole summer off. What could be better for Lucien than that?" I squirm out of his grip.

"If I may be frank," says Santos taking a firmer tone, then hesitating. "The financial support I mentioned ... may in no way form a motive for deciding to look after Lucien at home. And, umm ..." He runs out of words.

"Lucien is my son! And Bry's on holiday. Care and attention guaranteed."

"But what about your work? Your son needs someone at his side constantly. Not to mention the domestic limitations you outlined ..."

"You took me by surprise. What kind of dad doesn't

have a bed for his own kid? I'd sleep out in the garden if I had to. And wouldn't it be great for my boys to spend time with each other again?"

Santos and Dad stand there, each waiting for the other one to speak.

"So? Are we agreed?"

Santos blanks Dad's half of a handshake and fiddles with his papers. "I will have to consult on this internally. There are a few formalities to sort out first." His neat, pink fingers pluck a sheet of paper from the binder. He scans the front, then turns it over. "Is your current telephone number in our system?"

Dad recites the number and looks on as Santos jots it down.

"Is the last number a seven or a one?" Dad asks.

"Didn't you say seven?"

"*This* is a seven." Dad pulls the pen from his hand and scrawls a great big seven over the final digit. "Just ask for Chevalier."

"Very well." Now Santos does take the hand Dad offers him and shakes it briefly. "We'll be in touch."

Dad plays it cool as we exit the car park and indicates as we turn onto the main road. At the next junction, he even eases up to let someone in. "What's a couple of weeks?" he says softly, though there's no one else to hear. "It'll be good for the two of you, eh? And how much hassle can it be? Your brother's in bed all day. Spoon a tub of applesauce into him every couple of hours, double helpings if he's hungry. A little drink from his beaker now and then. They'll draw us up a schedule. We can stick him under the shower if his nappy is full. Probably shits regular as clockwork, just sit him on the pot and let gravity do the rest. It's not like he's going anywhere. I'll sort out a TV by his bed to keep him occupied the rest of the time and, hey presto, another day gone. Quick wipe with a facecloth, brush his little gnashers and then beddy-byes. Nothing to it, right?"

"Hmm-hhh."

A pizza in the middle of the road turns out to be a rabbit. Birds fly up from its flattened insides as we get closer. The crows stay pecking the longest and are first back on the road once we've passed. If the rabbit's only taken a knock, Dad usually brakes. That's a sign for me to get out and check for insects crawling around its eyes. If there aren't too many, I grab its ears or its hind legs and sling it into the back of the van. As soon as we're home, it goes straight into the freezer for the dogs.

Every mile or so we overtake a belching tractor or a ramshackle truck that's missing a licence plate. All bound for barns in Saint Arnaque or the next village along. Leaning towers of hay bales bob and weave on rattling trailers. Dad parps his horn twice before we overtake. Behind the wheel of one of the trucks is a boy my age, too edgy to look to the side when we draw level.

"We'll show your mother a thing or two."

"What?"

"Show her we can manage, the three of us. That I'm a decent father." His free hand trails across the empty place on the front seat made for three.

"Did you know Mum was going to marry Didier?"

"If I'd known, you would have heard long ago."

My mother got married without me knowing. Maybe I was sat in the pickup at the petrol station fiddling with the radio. Maybe she said "I do" as I was biking home from school. Or jumping into the stream. Or reading a comic.

There's a groan of rubber as I grab the handle on the door and wind the window down.

"Isn't that right?" Dad yells as the wind rushes past my ears.

"Yeah!" I shout back, though I've no idea what he's on about.

His knuckles slam into my left shoulder. "Bry?" Another thump. Same way as he belts a vending machine until a free can rolls out the bottom. He'll keep on thumping until an answer rolls out of my mouth. "True enough, eh?" Thump.

"You betcha!" I bawl.

"You betcha," Dad repeats and nods along with his own words. He goes on talking, but with my head stuck out the window I can't hear a thing.

3

The flapping sole of my right shoe gobbles sand with every step. Dad has dropped me off so I can head to the caravan and fry us up some eggs while he drives down the road for chips. There's rustling up ahead, so I keep still. It's a scruffy sparrow tossing leaves about. Bathroom tiles peek out of the rubble under the bushes, where someone has dumped bundles of advertising leaflets. The prickly shrubs are hung with shreds of blue bin bag, its contents carried off on the wind. Across the stream, up through the broom bushes, and that's me home. From the top of the slope, I can smell the bottle bank that stands where the main road skirts the rutted track to our turf.

A strange car is parked outside our rusty gate. The man on the driver's side looks down at his lap when my eyes catch his. I stroll on past. He opens his door and gets out. "Excuse me," he calls. "I'm looking for Maurice."

"He's not home."

White-and-blue checked shirt, crease in his trousers, and a braided leather belt. Pointy nose and thinning grey-black hair that looks like it's been puffed up somehow. Don't get many of his kind round here.

"He does live here, doesn't he?"

"Depends."

"Beg your pardon?"

"Depends what you want him for."

"I understood he has a caravan for rent nearby." He

holds up the card we stuck on the supermarket notice-board.

"You're not supposed to take that."

"Oh, sorry." He looks at the card like he's only just noticed he's holding it. "I didn't have anything to write on. I'll be sure to put it back."

"Unless you rent the caravan. Then you won't have to."

"It would only be temporary."

"Temporary ..." I repeat. The pause you leave is more important than what you say. That's one of Dad's. I clock two removal boxes on the passenger's side. The deep black of a television gleams between the seats. This gentleman's in a bind. He can pay full whack.

"How long do you want it for?"

"That would depend on what it is you're offering."

I shrug and feign a yawn to stretch the silence.

"A couple of days ..." the man says and shoots me a nervous look. "That would be enough."

"A couple of days?"

"Longer would be more convenient. A few weeks, if possible. It's all been a bit sudden."

"A few weeks, if possible ..." I raise my eyebrows.

Repeating stuff is important too, Dad says. Makes them think you've answered and it's their turn to talk. "More use than anything you'll learn at school. Follow my lead and you can clinch any deal. That's what it's all about. If you're hard up for cash, first thing you do is talk the price down. That way you can fend for yourself if your old man snuffs it." Dad likes asking questions and then giving the answer. "Always ask yourself: would you come and live here for the view? Of course you wouldn't. Anyone who turns up here is out of options." His story is in my head now, word for word. "We're talking people with problems. No roof over their head and a good reason to steer clear of hotels and bungalow parks ..." Dad has his tactics with tenants: leaving silences that need filling, mulling things over, making them think it's all tricky-tricky-tricky. Looking around, playing for time. "Patience, patience," he says, like it's something I don't have. "The sooner they open their mouth, the more rent you can get out of them."

By this time, we've walked a good way into the yard. "A month, maybe," our gent says.

"A month, you say?" I narrow my eyes and stare out across our turf with its old workmen's huts, caravans, shipping containers, and the big iron shed that Jean and Brown Henri use as a garage. The rivets up the sides have nearly disappeared behind stacks of firewood, topped by sheets of corrugated iron that are weighed down by stones. Jean used to do the odd scrapyard run when we first moved here, but his Piaggio three-wheeler has spent the last two winters over by the fence with nettles growing up around its soft, cracked tyres.

"Tricky, tricky," I say. We only rent the one caravan but I try to look like I'm weighing up a ton of options, shake my head nice and slow. "Very tricky."

Our gent's eyes stray to the cage in front of our caravan, and Rico and Rita just about bark themselves inside out. They take turns jumping up and snapping at the bars above them. Not keen on visitors, those two.

This visitor crosses his arms tight across his chest. His eyes are on me but his mind is on the dog cage the whole time.

"And Maurice?"

"What about him?"

"Should I wait for him? Perhaps he'll know whether there's something available?"

"Maurice is my dad."

"And roughly what time do you think your father will be back?" I take a good look at his wristwatch. A gold hand the width of a hair glides past the seconds.

"He'll be a while yet."

"Shall I wait in the car? Or is there no point hanging around?"

"A month, you say?"

"If possible."

"Come with me. What's your name?"

"Emile," he says, a little awkwardly. An angle grinder screeches in the garage. You can't see Henri, just the fireworks sparking up the gloom.

"I'm Brian."

"Are there any other children living here?"

"Not really. How come?"

"No reason."

"Turned sixteen the other week," I lie myself three years older. "No kids round here."

"School holidays?"

"Yeah, just started."

"And where do you live?"

"There." I point over my shoulder. "You got someone?" I ask to beat his next question. "Or are you on your own, like?"

"That's all a bit ..." Emile raises one shoulder. "It's all been a bit sudden." For the first time he looks me straight in the eye, gives a shy smile. "Still, at least I have my fish."

"Fish?"

"Nothing special, a small aquarium." He shows me how small with the space between his hands.

"Angelfish?"

"No, nothing that fancy."

"You've got an aquarium in your car?"

"Don't worry, the fish can take it. In this heat it will be a while before the water cools, especially in the car. They should be all right," he says, mainly to convince himself.

"Can I see them?"

"First, shouldn't we …?" He points to the caravan for rent, standing with its back to an empty concrete swimming pool. "Is that the one?" Green gunk crawling up the sides. Stickers from theme parks and holiday islands, faded and peeling at the edges. Frayed little curtains at the windows.

"Is it occupied?"

"Not right now. We keep it free for people who need something temporary."

"What kind of people? If you don't mind me asking."

"Different."

"Different how?"

"Different from you." Dad didn't tell me what to do with other people's pauses. "A while back we had one of them Arafats with a headscarf for a wife and two kids in tow. They lasted a fortnight."

Emile nods absently.

"The guy before that turned out to be a tax dodger. Did a bunk one night, left his coffee maker and everything. Dirty underpants on the floor, right where he dropped them."

"And?"

"Never seen again."

"Oh."

"That was a year ago. We cleared out all his crap. Kept the coffee maker though."

"I've brought my own."

I show him how to open the door. The air that swamps us is thick and warm, the place has been shut up too long. "Take a look around if you want."

With one foot on the aluminium threshold he pokes

his head in, looks left, then right. There's a bald patch the size of a beermat on the top of his head.

"You'd see more with the light on." An insulation strip drops off the side and I kick it under the caravan.

"It's only temporary," he says, more to himself than to me. Emile shuts the door and then opens it again. Fiddles with the knob on the lock. "Is there a key?"

"It only locks from the inside."

"Oh."

"But no one ever comes here except us."

Emile looks out across the yard.

"Do you want to rent it or not?"

He nods a "yes" that might be a "maybe" and could still be downgraded to "no."

"It's got aircon." Emile tries the lock again and looks at it from the inside. "My Dad will need to tinker with it. The aircon, I mean. Just minor repairs, like." I point out the unit beside the storage box.

"And your father won't have a problem with my aquarium?"

"Can't see why."

"Should I wait till he comes? Or can I discuss the rent with you?"

"Hundred a week," I blurt out.

"Oooh ..."

"No deposit." I'm not really sure what a deposit is, but it's what Dad always says. "And you pay up front."

"That's a bit steep." His eyes settle on my torn earlobe.

"I used to have an earring."

He nods, but it's like I've caught him out.

"You can park over there. Any problems, just come and see us."

"Uh ..."

"You won't find cheaper round here."

It's not really our caravan. It belongs to two brothers who used to run a scrapyard here, the same guys who started building the swimming pool behind the caravan. Now the pool's just a concrete pit with a carpet of dried-up gunge at the bottom. We've been renting out the caravan ever since the scrap merchants got banged up. I heard Henri say they used it whenever they had a girl over. Jean and Brown Henri have a share in the caravan, or that's what they told us when we arrived two years ago. Dad didn't have the money for that, but he gets a cut as long as he brings in the tenants, deals with any hassle, and sorts out any repairs that need doing. Plus he collects the rent and divvies up the cash.

4

On the table there's a torn bag of chips from Mandy the Nail's. Its real name is The Snack Palace, but Armand, the owner, has a thumbnail half an inch long. When you order a hot dog, he digs his nail into the steaming skin and runs it the length of the sausage. Then you choose from three sauces and he squirts a sad little dribble along the split.

"What kept you?" Dad chews from his easy chair. He grabs a couple of chips and drags them through the mayonnaise. "I thought you were going to fry us some eggs."

I give him the coolest look I can muster.

"What?"

My lips are sealed.

"What is it?"

Silence. His eyes are already narrowing. I can't spin this out much longer.

"What's the look for?" Dad wipes his greasy fingers on his jeans and goes to get out of his chair. "Fuck's sake, Bry! Answer me!"

Quick as you like, I toss four twenties onto the Formica tabletop.

"For the first week." I try not to sound too chuffed with myself. "And the tenant's moving in straight away." Dad looks at me, then back at the money, chewing all the while.

"Well, that explains the car at the gate." He counts the

notes again, like he can't quite believe it. "This is for one week?"

"He didn't even haggle."

Dad pulls aside the curtain behind him, but you can't see the caravan from there. "Don't tell me it's another Arafat clan? We can't have kids here again."

"No, no. This one's alone. Well, just about."

"Just about?"

"He's got an aquarium."

"An aquarium?"

"Oh, and he wants the aircon fixed."

"Well, we can take a look at that in the morning." Dad shifts up so I can sit on the arm of the chair. He slides a hot dog in my direction and tears the bag of chips all the way open. Picking up the four twenties, he spreads them like a hand of cards and fans his face. "Nice job, Brian my boy."

The fifth twenty-euro note is glowing in my pocket.

5

To get the last stubby screw out of the aircon, I have to twist so hard that my thumb cramps up. Dad leans against the storage box of Emile's caravan and coughs his lungs awake. "Don't lose any!" His voice wheezes and wavers. "Important little buggers, they are."

The casing comes loose at last and I lift it off. Emile came out to introduce himself to Dad but as soon as he saw that Rico and Rita were with us, he nipped back into the caravan.

"Well spotted, Bry," Dad whispers.

"What?"

"You know ..." He checks that the door of the caravan is shut. "Getting this guy to pay full whack. Did you see that watch? And those shoes?"

"Of course I did." I sit down in the spiky grass and wiggle my bum until the blades stop pricking through my swimming trunks.

"Hand-stitched by a bunch of fucking elves." Dad spins the fan one way then the other and kneels down beside me. "Thirteen-millimetre wrench."

I rummage in his plastic shopping bag of tools. "This one?"

Dad checks the number and sets to work on a stubborn bolt. I tie a new knot in the cord of my swimming trunks and brush a couple of dried-up earwigs out of the aircon casing so Dad can't have a go at me for leaving everything to him.

The dogs take turns trotting over to the concrete swimming pool behind the caravan. A yard or so from the edge they freeze, crane their necks, and peer into the pit, one paw off the ground. Snuffling back across the grass, they poke their noses into the aircon casing, sneeze, and shake away the cobwebs. The swimming pool is big enough to hide two Renault vans. You can still see the tyre tracks if you know what you're looking for. White paint flakes from the concrete, the broken ladder has keeled over. Pine twigs are shooting out of the latest cracks, the old ones were plastered over a while back. Two of the walls have been painted a sloppy ocean-blue and a job lot of tiles are stacked in a corner, waiting for someone with the will to smarten up the pool and fill it with water.

"They can smell it, you know," Dad says.

"What, that you took a leak back there?"

"Jean says they used to hold dog fights in that pool."

"Honest?"

"They used to come from all over to watch and place bets. Lit the place up with construction lamps. Sometimes they chucked in a fox. Or a badger."

"Couldn't they climb out?"

"Easy enough to kick them back in." Dad shakes his head. "The blood and blind panic have soaked into the concrete. Those mutts of ours can still smell it." Dad rubs Rita between the ears while her rough paws slide down his calf. "Ask our new tenant for a bowl of water, will you?" The dogs both look up at me.

I knock on the door and yank it open without waiting for an answer. Rita squeezes past my legs and shoots into the caravan.

"I need some water for the dogs."

"Could you please take that ... dog outside?" She has already bounced onto the seat opposite Emile.

"Here!" Rita slides off the seat on command but then jumps up with her front paws on the draining board. "Sorry," I shrug, "she slipped past me."

A plate clatters into the sink as she gulps down a scrap of leftover food.

"Could you get that animal out of here?"

I drag Rita out by her collar. Rico is at the door, tail wagging, ready for his turn.

Emile gets to his feet. "Water, you said?"

"I'll get it." I know the place better than Emile and reach into a corner cupboard for a bowl. It slowly fills with the stream of lukewarm water from the tap. A long piss would be quicker. Emile's aquarium is on the table, two tea towels draped over the top.

"Is your aquarium busted?"

"No. Just letting my fish acclimatize."

"Shame. I'd love to see them swimming."

"You're welcome to come back another time."

Next to the aquarium is a puzzle book and a mobile phone, the kind I've only ever seen in adverts. "Is that the latest model?" I ask.

Emile runs his finger over the keys and the screen glows green. He stares at it, then slides the puzzle book over the top.

"Does it do all kinds of new stuff?"

"That's what they say," he smiles. "All I've done so far is talk to answering machines."

Emile looks at the bowl, now overflowing with water. "Will you be able to fix the air conditioning?"

"I think so."

Emile nudges the puzzle book so it's straighter than it was. "Should I offer you something to drink? Coffee maybe?"

Rico and Rita guzzle the water before I've even let go of the bowl. The aircon is spinning and humming again. "Just as well it's a sturdy little caravan or this thing would blow it clean away," Dad says proudly, gathering his tools in the plastic bag. "Don't get too close, Bry. That fan will lop off your foreskin before you know it. Leave you with a helmet and no hoodie."

I hate it when he talks about my dick.

"Cosy chat?"

"How do you mean?"

"I heard you two talking in there. Anything I should know?"

"Not really."

"Like what?"

"Like his fish need a rest."

Dad scratches the baggy arse of his jeans, puts the casing back on the aircon, and nods at the screws so I'll hand them to him.

"He asked if we wanted coffee."

"Now there's an offer we can't refuse."

Only the light above the sink is on. Dad is sitting next to me at the table and Emile is standing by the draining board. It looks like he's come to visit us.

"Hmm, this is quite something." Dad has lifted up a tea towel and is peering into the dark aquarium. Fish flit past. A little brown monster is cleaning the glass with its suction mouth.

"Flashy little buggers." Dad taps a nail against the tank. "Safety glass?"

"Not that I know," Emile mumbles. "Might be."

"We could do with one of these, eh Bry? Beats the TV any day."

"What can I do for you?" Emile asks.

"Um … you asked us in for coffee?" Dad shoots me a quizzical look. "Right?"

I nod.

While Emile pours, Dad sizes up the caravan. "So … made yourself at home, I see."

"Uh, kind of …" Emile sits down opposite us. I get the impression he would rather we drank our coffee outside but doesn't know how to tell us. "Shouldn't we be heading off?" I ask Dad.

"The gentleman's just served us coffee." A thump on my shoulder. "Don't be so rude. Decent brew, by the way."

There's a smart shirt lying on Emile's bed, and his coffee maker is installed on the kitchen counter. Between us lies the puzzle book, curling at the edges. Emile follows my gaze. "I haven't got around to unpacking the rest."

"Want us to help?" I ask.

"I'd rather keep things simple for the time being."

"Simple …" Dad repeats. Drops of spilled coffee hiss between the coffee pot and the hot plate. I shift in my seat to straighten up my swimming trunks and they both look at me.

"Nice cool breeze in here," Dad says.

"Yes, indeed," Emile nods. He catches Dad staring at the packet of biscuits and says, "I'm not having one but, please, help yourself."

"All right, just the one."

Dad takes a biscuit from the packet. "And? Settling in nicely?"

"Uh, yes, fine. I've only been here one night."

Dad examines the biscuit as if he's wondering which side deserves his second bite. "And what brought you here, like?"

"Pfff. It's kind of complicated."

"Didn't see it coming?"

"Not really, no."

"Had to up sticks all of a sudden? Aquarium and all."

"It takes a bit of explaining."

"No one moves here for the view."

"Goodness, well I ... I have some things to straighten out." He nudges a few crumbs together with his fingertip and deposits them next to his cup.

"Yeah, yeah," Dad nods, as if he knows exactly what Emile's getting at. There's a ticking sound at the caravan door. Rico is standing guard, tail swishing.

"The whole thing is ..." Emile's head shakes away a thought. "Rather complex."

He turns the packet of biscuits toward me.

"Whoa-ho." Dad puts his hand over the opening. "It's time we left you in peace."

"Is there anything else we need to arrange?" Emile asks.

"Looks like the two of you worked everything out yesterday." He lands another punch on my shoulder. "Any questions, just ask our Brian here."

Ask Brian? Dad never leaves this kind of stuff to me.

"And as for collecting the rent ..." His knuckles reconnect with my shoulder. "Agreed?"

"Fine," says Emile, as if he was about to recommend me for the job, too.

"Sorted!" Dad goes to whack my shoulder again, but I stand up so I'm out of reach.

I step outside and the heat hugs me like a fat, sweaty stranger.

"Oh yeah," Dad says, with one foot on the doorstep. "Almost forgot the bill. Let's call it twenty p.p."

"Twenty p.p.?"

"It took the two of us to get her up and running."

"You mean the air conditioning?"

Dad steps back into the caravan, Emile shuffles backward out of the light. "To be frank, that strikes me as rather pricey."

"Running costs included. That thing guzzles electricity. Flick the switch and our TV goes on the blink." Rico tries to squeeze past me and I pull him back by his collar. "Keep those mutts away from the tenant, Bry."

"I'm doing my best!"

Dad shuts the door but I can hear their muffled voices clear enough.

"I was under the impression that ... because the rent ... that this was included."

"I get it, I get it. But your rent only covers the caravan, see. The aircon's an added extra. Summer only, so there's no monthly payment. But if you decide to make use of it, we have to charge you a little something. Didn't Brian explain?"

No answer.

"A one-off payment, like." The door swings open. I jump back and act like I wasn't listening. "Forty is a bargain, isn't that right, Bry?"

"Yeah, fifty's the usual."

The corners of his mouth give a little twitch. That was exactly what he wanted to hear.

"All right." Emile turns toward the kitchen cupboards. "Would you mind waiting outside for a moment?"

"Not at all." Dad hops swiftly off the step. "Any technical problems within two weeks, we'll sort them free of charge."

The dogs rub against our legs like they're trying to wipe the heat from their coats. They lick the empty water bowl and shove it across the grass ahead of them, growling at each other.

Emile opens the door again and hands Dad the cash.

"Much obliged," he says and zips the notes away in his breast pocket. "Oh, one last thing ..." He points in the direction of Henri's garage. "I'd steer clear of those two, if I were you."

"Why is that?"

"Just keep your distance, that's all. They're a different breed to you and me."

6

“This is one tenant we need to handle with care.”

“Why did you tell him to watch out for Jean and Brown Henri?”

“Our Emile is a walking ATM, Bry.” Dad leans in close. “And we need to be the only ones with access. Got it?”

We trudge along behind our shadows. “Here you go.” Dad pulls out a well-worn tenner and stuffs it into the pocket of my swimming trunks. “A little summer bonus.”

I heave a secret sigh of relief that Emile didn’t mention how much rent he’s paying.

“What do you think is up?”

“What, with our tenant?”

We both look back at the caravan.

“How should I know?” The curtains are closed as if no one’s inside. “Maybe he’s a banker who’s done a runner with a suitcase full of cash. Or a loser who never left home till one day he snapped and smothered his senile old mum with a pillow.”

“You really think that?”

“The gentleman’s lips are sealed. So are ours.” Dad pats his breast pocket. “An arrangement for which the gentleman is willing to pay.”

“Where are you off to?”

Instead of heading for our caravan, Dad strolls over to Jean and Brown Henri’s garage. “Just dropping off the rent.” Inside, metal clatters on concrete. Swallows swoop in through the open doors.

"Good morning!" Dad's voice echoes through the space.

"Maurice ...!" Jean looks up, startled. Open boxes are piled all around him. White plastic bottles with blue tops on his left. Identical bottles on his right, only labelled. A regular job from one of Brown Henri's brothers. A brand-new Mercedes is gleaming on the hydraulic lift, but Henri is nowhere in sight.

"Hey, Brian! Holidays started already?" Jean asks.

"Since Friday."

"Nice one." He takes a blank bottle and plucks an oval sticker from a sheet.

"What kind of shipment you got this time?" I ask.

"It *was* Romanian mayo." Jean turns the bottle in his firm grip, slaps the sticker on the back, and thumbs away the air bubbles. "But now it's organic mayonnaise. From Picardy." The next bottle is ready and waiting in his other hand.

"How are things ..." He gasps for breath. "... with the girls?"

"Can't complain."

"Yeah, yeah. There speaks a boy ..." He pauses, inhales again. "... who hasn't found himself a girl yet." Clear plastic tubes run from his nostrils to a bigger tube that winds behind his ear and connects to a machine that puffs every few seconds, like it's blowing air into something leaky.

"How many bottles to go?"

"Two pallets, been ... at it since Saturday."

"Maurice!" Brown Henri emerges from the toilet. "Long time, no see. Count my tools there, will you Jean?" Their laughter is a duet. The only way for Dad not to flounder is to come up with a wisecrack of his own. But Jean beats him to it. "No need. All your tools are ... over at his place already." They roar. Dad chews on a remark to hit back with. Happy with his banter, Jean fiddles with a molehill of a birthmark below his chin.

"Jesus, Jean!" Dad bursts out.

"What?" Laughing sucks more breath out of Jean than talking.

"When are you going to let me burn off that ugly lump of yours? One *tssst* with the soldering iron will do it." Jean's hand shoots back to his neck like he's afraid it's happened already.

"I'm always telling him that ..." Henri yells. "But till Jean finds himself a woman, he's got to have something to play with."

Now Henri and Dad are the chuckle brothers, and Jean is left to stroke his molehill like it's a sad little creature in need of comfort. "Brian, if you want something to drink ..." He motions toward the fridge. They always keep a can of energy drink in the veg compartment for me. Dad stretches contentedly. Cracking a joke always frees him to take up more space. Henri sniggers to a halt. "By the way, have we got ourselves a new tenant?"

"Indeed we do," Dad says. "Arrived yesterday."

"Haven't seen him out in the yard," Jean says. "What's he like?"

"Nothing out of the ordinary. Had to pack up and leave, sharpish like." Dad rakes his front teeth over the stubble below his bottom lip. "Bust up with the missus is my guess."

Jean leans back on his chair to get a view of the caravan.

Rico is snuffling around the table with the ferret cage. "Maurice, get that dog away from there," says Henri.

"Here!" Dad whistles Rico to his side, points at a spot under his chair, and presses the dog's head to the concrete floor until he whimpers. Rita looks up, but only stretches and settles back down in a stripe of sunlight.

"Can I feed the ferrets?" I ask.

"There's still some of ... that dried chicken."

The two ferrets are up on their back legs, quivering, sniffing, and shoving each other aside as if there's only one spot in the mesh they can poke their pink noses through.

I find a dirty knife, slice off a few strips of meat, and drop them into the cage. The ferrets go from restless stoles to furry whirlwinds.

"Careful with that knife," Brown Henri calls over as he's about to slide back under the Mercedes. "It's hard to count to ten when you're down to nine fingers." He holds up both hands—the right one is a pinkie short. If I stare too long at his missing finger, Henri always issues some kind of warning. "Never grab the wrong end of your angle grinder, son ... Never fall behind with your payments ... Never think of a woman when you're working at the saw bench." A new one every time. They could be the ten commandments of our old scrapyard. Dad's commandments always start with "never" too, and usually end with "your mum." But he still has all his fingers.

"Hey, Maurice ..." Jean nudges Dad. "When were you thinking ... of paying the rent?"

"Oh right," says Dad, and tosses a bunch of Emile's banknotes onto the table. "There you go."

"Well, I'll be." Jean starts counting.

"How much is it?" Brown Henri asks and goes on tinkering with the car.

"A hundred and ten!" Jean shouts.

"Is that all?" Henri asks.

"If my money's not good enough for you, I'd just as soon take it back."

"It means you're still four hundred euros behind."

"And the tenant?" Jean asks.

"What about him?"

"Is he living here rent free?"

"All in good time, all in good time."

"And what time's that then?"

Dad's tongue flashes across his lips.

"End of the week."

"End of the week," Jean echoes.

"Tenants have been damn slow at paying since you started collecting the rent," Brown Henri says.

"He's a little low on cash at the minute. No need to play hardball just yet."

Dad turns to look at the shelf units that line the wall. One is home to a bunch of shiny exhaust pipes. He shakes his head disapprovingly, as if he's an expert and everything he sees is a pile of junk.

"Leave the new guy alone for a while," Dad says.

"How come?"

"The gentleman needs a little privacy. Nothing wrong with that now, is there?"

"As long as he's no trouble," Henri says. "On the run from God knows what. I don't want this place swarming with coppers."

"A loner like that," Jean raises his eyebrows knowingly. "Curtains closed all day. I mean ..."

"Got any spark plugs?" I ask, to steer the conversation away from Emile.

"Spark plugs?"

"For my scooter."

"Long or short socket?"

"Short." Dad says it for me.

"I can take a look ... out the back in a sec."

"Hundred and ten," says Henri, shaking his head. "And the rest?"

"I told you—soon."

"Is that right?"

"Yeah, that's right."

"It's been the same story for the past two months."

From the way his cheek is trembling, I can tell Dad's trying really hard to keep something inside.

"Or should we cut off the electric again? That sometimes jogs your memory."

"Lucien might be coming home soon," I say to change the subject.

Now all eyes are on me.

"Who's Lucien?"

"Nobody ..." Dad tries to gloss it over with a slight shake of his head.

"My brother."

"And he's coming here?"

"Maybe. Just for a bit."

"And how long is a bit?"

Before I can answer, Dad cuts me off at the pass.

"A week, max. Two at a pinch."

"Fuck's sake, Maurice. This is no place for kids."

"The boy's got nowhere to go. And his mum won't take him. It's only temporary."

"Bry here was supposed to be temporary, too." Henri slides out from under the Mercedes.

"What do you mean I was temporary?"

"Stay out of this!" Dad bellows. Rico and Rita spring to attention, hackles up, ears pointed.

"You're a good lad, Brian ... But this is no place for you. And now your dad's ... bringing in another one."

"You're not bringing in anyone, Maurice!" Henri snorts.

"Then screw the lot of you!" Dad grabs his tool bag from the concrete floor and storms off. The dogs scamper after him, panting with excitement.

The rent lies crumpled on the table.

Jean levers himself out of his garden chair, steers his oxygen tank carefully around the stacks of boxes. He beckons me through to the back of the garage.

"Short socket ..." Those few steps leave Jean even shorter of breath. "That's what you said ... right?"

He pulls open a drawer.

"Why did Henri say that?"

"What?"

"That I'm temporary."

"Ah ..." As if to tease him, the machine puffs too little oxygen into his lungs. "Here." He hands me two small boxes.

"One's enough."

"And one ... for spare."

"Thanks, Jean."

He gives me a thumbs-up.

"Did Dad really say that?"

"Forget it ..."

"I was never temporary."

"Course not."

"So why did he say it?"

"That's something ..." He pauses to give his breath a run-up. "Between your dad and us." He runs a clumsy hand over my forearm. His hands mostly hang like slack and stumpy tools from his wrists. I didn't know they could touch.

"How much do I owe you?"

He gestures to me to let it go.

"Tell me how much they cost."

"Free of charge."

"Is this enough?" I pull out the grubby tenner.

"Too much."

"I still owe you for that headlight."

Jean chuckles. "Are you sure Maurice ... is your dad?"

He takes the tenner, folds it in half, and presses it back into my palm. "Start saving for ... a girlfriend."

"So how come I was temporary?"

"What are you on about?" Dad knows damn well what I'm on about. He's hunched in front of the dark television screen in his leather easy chair, elbows on knees.

"I've always been with you, haven't I?"

"Bry," Dad says, so softly it takes me by surprise. "I had to say that or they'd never have rented us this place. We'd have had to live in that shitty Taunus van. Hang around in car parks. Is that what you wanted? They would have taken you off me in a heartbeat."

That wasn't what I wanted.

"Here," I say, and give him back his tenner.

"No, no. I'm not taking money from my own kid."

I'm relieved he's letting me keep it.

"How are you going to get Lucien here?"

"Leave that to me."

"But they don't want him here."

"Ah, but what are they going to do about it? Well?"

"How should I know?"

"Lucien's coming," Dad says, like it's me who's trying to stop him. "And once they clap eyes on him, they won't dare send him away. Wanna bet?"

7

Dad has something to discuss with Santos in his office, so I go on ahead to see my brother. Down the corridor, I run into Selma pushing a trolley stacked with towels. Her face is tight with concentration.

"Hiya," I say. Her eyes are fixed on the pile of towels in front of her, willing it not to topple over.

"Hiya," I say again, a little louder this time.

"Don't talk," she says flatly. She stops, takes a towel from the pile with both hands, places it neatly on a table in a little kitchen, and returns to her trolley.

"I'm Lucien's brother, remember?"

"Don't talk. I'm working."

"You're working?"

Her shoulders slump in time with an irritated sigh. "Don't ta-halk."

"Okay, suit yourself."

Lucien no longer has the room to himself. Henkelmann's bed is parked alongside his. The last time I saw Henkelmann was when we still visited with Mum. Back then he lurked under an empty table in the family room. I never wanted us to sit anywhere near him, though he only ever bit himself. Crocodile skin on the insides of his wrists and elbows. And in the folds between his index fingers and thumbs.

Now he's lying perfectly still in bed, staring at the little Christmas tree with luminous needles that slowly change colour. His wrists are velcroed to the bed rail.

"You've got a neighbour," I say to Lucien. Little cuts have appeared around his mouth. I can hear the soft humming noise he always makes when he's restless. "Henkelmann won't harm you. He only bites himself."

Someone has given Lucien a box. Judging by the state it's in, he's been gnawing on it for a while. "That's not for eating," I say, tugging at the cardboard. Lucien raises his arm to guard the box. A wet shred of cardboard is stuck to his teeth. "It's for your own good." But he won't let go.

Henkelmann lets out a kind of creak. His toothless mouth opens so wide that I can see all the way to the back. It looks like the inside of a shell, his extended tongue is the fleshy creature that lives inside. Lucien scratches nervously at the corners of his mouth.

Carefully, I take his hand but he pulls it free immediately. I grab it again and squeeze his wrist until my knuckles turn white. You can inflict a lot of pain on Lucien before he feels it.

I stroke between his pinkie and his ring finger the way Mum used to. I keep stroking and feel tendons pulling at the crooked bones beneath his dry skin. "Mum got married, did you know? Does Didier visit too, sometimes?" I stroke between his other fingers, until his eyes open and close more slowly. Now I don't have to squeeze as tight to hold his hand.

"So-o-o," says a deep voice at the door. We both jump. "Time for some exercise." A man with hair curly as telephone wire steers a wheelchair into the room. "I'll just park this here." He's so tall he has to stoop to reach the handles. "Oh, hello," he says when he notices me. "I've come to kidnap Lucien."

First he goes over to the other bed. "Fancy a game?"

Henkelmann cramps up instantly, his body so tense it

rises from the mattress. His wrist straps take the strain.

"All right then. Just the one." Curly holds a finger above Henkelmann's open mouth and teases him, bringing it a fraction closer then pulling it away again. "Ah," he says. "Playing the waiting game today? Been practising behind my back?"

Henkelmann stares at the ceiling. The finger circles above his face and passes his mouth again. Round and round. Then *snap*! Henkelmann roars with laughter.

Curly shakes his finger as if it hurts. "Man, that was quick!" Then he comes over to us. "And who have we got here?"

"I'm Brian, Lucien's brother."

"Thibaut, Lucien's physiotherapist. I'm taking your brother for a walk."

"Can he still walk?"

"He's still got it in him." He lowers the bed rail. "If I had the time, we could definitely make more progress. As things stand, the most I can do is keep him mobile." Thibaut lets Lucien's scrawny calf muscles glide through his hands. "The drugs don't exactly help."

"What do you mean?"

"You know, all the pills he has to take."

"Aren't they doing him good?"

"Of course they are. Sure. But, as a physio, I mainly notice how they affect his motor skills." He can see I don't quite get it. "Some pills make you less able to move around." He gently lifts Lucien's feet and starts turning them this way and that. "So, let's wake these fellas up first." Lucien gives a cranky groan.

"Is it okay to bend his ankles that far?"

"These are movements he should be able to make himself. I'm reminding his feet what they can do."

Thibaut feels Lucien's knees and starts to massage

them, then lifts his feet high in the air and makes him pedal. A couple of farts gurgle in Lucien's pants. Thibaut lets go and Lucien tries to carry on pedalling but he can't do it on his own.

"Right, then." In one easy movement he turns Lucien so that his legs are dangling over the side of the bed, slides shoes onto his feet, and velcroes them tight. "Here we go." Lucien clamps both hands around Thibaut's hairy forearm as it pulls him slowly from the bed and holds him steady.

Lucien flexes his knees a few times as if to make sure the floor can take his weight.

"I'll drop him off in half an hour. Will you still be here?"

"I think so."

At every step, Lucien lifts his foot way too high, only to put it down an inch or so in front of the other.

"That's the way," Thibaut says, shuffling backward toward the door. Lucien mashes a couple of panicky steps on the spot. "Come on. You're doing great."

Thibaut winks at me and swings the door open a little further. From the corridor I hear, "Now that foot! Yes. And now this one. No, this one."

It feels weird being left behind in the room.

Henkelmann lies there leering at me. I remember when he had teeth, only he wouldn't let anyone brush them, so he kept getting infections and cavities. They had to give him an anaesthetic before the dentist could get anywhere near him. One day they decided to pull all his teeth out in one go, but his gums became so hard that he could still bite.

"Do you want to play that game with me?" I stand beside his bed and lay a cautious finger on his arm. I thought his crocodile skin would be tough as tree bark, but it's unexpectedly soft and warm. Velcro creaks around his wrists.

I'm not sure I dare. My fingers are trembling inside. I hold out my arm, and his chest swells to hold his breath. I circle my finger above his face, then tap his mouth quick as I can. *Snap*! Just missed. My heart is thudding behind my eyes. "That was fast!" Henkelmann laughs so loud that his bed wobbles and clinks. "Want another go?"

His body stiffens. My fingertip lands between his eyebrows and follows the slope to the tip of his nose. It's one of the few places where his skin is smooth. Even before I tap his mouth ... *Snap*! Just missed. Henkelmann roars again, but tenses up the second I move away.

"Okay then, just one more."

"Will you come?" Selma is standing in the doorway.

"Come?"

"To my room."

"Are you finished work?"

She nods so deep her chin almost touches her chest.

"I'm waiting here till Lucien comes back."

"Pleeeaaase." She tilts her head the way other girls do when they want to look cute. "My room is one up ..." She points at the ceiling. "Fifteen minutes."

"Fifteen minutes?"

"Till the long hand gets there." She points at her right temple, closes her left eye, and peers at the clock above the door.

"And then?"

"Boys can come in for fifteen minutes. Door open." Out of nowhere, she grabs my hand and swings it to and fro. "And you're boys."

"Okay," I say, and pull her behind me like a water skier. "This way?" We head for the stairs and her belly jerks with every wave of laughter.

I let go of Selma and she waddles up ahead of me. Her

backside sticks out as she plants both feet on each stair before moving on to the next. Every few stairs she looks back to check I'm still there. "Keep behind me," she puffs, holding out her arm like a barrier.

A card beside her door bears her name and a lopsided sun. "Here's where I live." You can pick out the things that belong to her at a glance. The rest look like the stuff in every other room. The table and chairs are from the rec room, her cupboard is identical to Lucien's. A row of dolls along the top stare into space.

"Door open with boys," she says firmly, making sure the handle connects with the buffer on the wall. "It's the rules."

The cuddly monkey on her bed is big enough to wrap its arms around her. Beside him sit three dolls in smocks, dummies stuck in their baby mouths. "Look!" She points to the wash basin. "My makeup."

"Oh, yes."

"Look!" The makeup bag is so crammed that the zip won't close. "Look!" A capless tube of toothpaste, flecked with white. Necklaces, scarves, and tiaras hang from the towel rail. "Look!" And, when I don't turn around quick enough, "Loo-hook!" At the foot of her bed, a poster of a couple on a scooter. "I want to ride on the back. With him." The boy is leaning forward to go faster and looking over his shoulder at the girl. She has one arm around his waist, long hair streaming from under her helmet. Lipstick smile, perfect teeth, free hand holding down her skirt while the wind tries to peek underneath.

"Look." Selma puts on a sun visor. The Disneyland Paris logo has almost rubbed off.

"Have you been there?"

"With Gran." Her face clouds over. "After Grandad died."

"That's sad."

"Huh?"

"Sad for your grandad. That he's dead."

She points at a photo of herself as a little kid in diving mask and swimming trunks. "Then I was long, long ago."

"What do you mean?"

"A ve-e-ery long way on the bus. It was holidays."

"What country was it?"

"It was …" She bites her lip. "The beach."

"Do you visit Lucien every day?"

Her smile warps her face. "Lucien thinks I'm cute."

"Do you always stroke his face?"

"Always!" She sounds like I've accused her of something. "His mum showed me."

"His mum? That's my mum too! Have you met her?" For the first time in ages, Mum feels close, almost like she's in the room with us. "What did she say?"

Selma gawps at me.

"Does she visit often?"

Selma just smiles.

"Did she tell you anything?"

"Lucien thinks I'm cute."

"Is that all? Didn't she say anything about me?"

The same smile answers every question.

"Can you turn it on?" She touches the video recorder. For a second, I wonder if she was kidding. I never meet anyone who knows my mother.

Selma presses a videotape into my hands. I slide it into the opening and press play. She starts clapping. I go to turn on the TV too. "No!" she snaps. "I can do that." She points at the red button on the remote but stops just short of pressing it.

Then she drags me over to her cupboard and whips out a bra. "Look, look, look!" she shouts, though I'm already looking.

"Put that away." I can feel my cheeks turning red and I don't want them to.

Selma laughs and drapes the bra around her neck like a feather boa, moving to music only she can hear. She mimes into an invisible microphone while the fingers of her other hand tickle the air. Her breasts and her belly sway along under her top. There are more bras in her cupboard, all of them big and white. She hoists the bra above her head like she's at a football match and it's a scarf with the name of her team on it.

"Put it away, will you?" I don't want anyone walking past to see me standing here while she's doing this. "I've got a scooter, too." I nod at the poster on the side of her cupboard.

"Really?" Selma asks. "Really you have?" The bra hangs slack in her right hand and finally drops to the floor.

"I'm still working on it. I have to fit a new spark plug."

"Have you got helmuts?"

"Helmuts?"

She raps her knuckles gently on the side of my head. "For if you fall, dafty."

"I like to ride without."

I sit down on her bed. The bra is lying in the middle of the floor. As Selma flumps down next to me, the mattress dips and I slide a little closer to her. The tip of her right shoe traces circles on the faded linoleum. Her ears are small and round. All at once I understand why people say ears look like shells.

"You're my first visit," she says softly.

"Really?"

Selma nods and tucks loose strands of hair behind her ear.

"What about your mum?"

"Gran is my mum."

"But she can't be."

"My mum wasn't we-ell. And I had to live with Gra-an." She draws out the last word of every sentence, as if she's told me time and again and she's sick of repeating herself. "Longer and then longer."

"And your real mum and dad?"

She shrugs.

"Are they dead?"

"No," she whispers, like we're on a secret mission. "They're a bit ..." She points at her head and makes circles with her finger. "That's why I lived with Gran and Grandad. And then Grandad died," she huffs, like it was a really stupid thing to do.

"Gran was my mum this long." She holds up nine fingers.

"Why don't you live with her anymore?"

"She went to an old fox home."

"An old fox home?" I chuckle.

"Don't copy me." Without looking, she picks up a doll behind her and combs her fingers through its matted hair.

"Does that mean your gran can't come and visit?"

"Want a drink?"

She jumps up and the doll lands in my lap.

"Here I get to choose." She holds a tumbler under the tap. When it's full, she drinks it down in one go. Then she fills it again. She holds the tumbler in front of her face with both hands, to make sure she doesn't spill any. "Here you go."

"Thanks." I never drink water. Water's for dogs. Selma has left a bite of lipstick on the other side of the rim. I take a swallow.

Sitting on the edge of the bed, I look up at Selma. Girls don't normally get this close to boys like me. She looks into my eyes, for two seconds, then three. From this angle you can't really tell she lives in a place like this. Maybe a little, something about her nose. But then noses always look weird if you look at them long enough.

"What's your favourite drink?" I ask for the sake of something to say.

"Energy drink."

"Honest?"

"My fave-rits."

"Mine too."

She shuffles a little closer. So close that no one could fit between us. My heart is pounding in my throat. There's not a sound from the corridor. If I stand up now, our faces will touch. Little lines appear next to her eyes. She leans toward me. I shrink back and water sloshes onto my lap. The air smells of shampoo, her hair tickles my cheek. A giggle, a smack of the lips, and she whispers, "Tonight we're having lasan-yaa!"

8

Halfway across the car park, Dad puts a tube of rolled-up papers to his mouth and blares at me to get a move on.

"What have you got there?"

He shows me the papers. "Boy-oh-boy-oh-boy. You wouldn't believe the crap I had to fill in …" *AGREEMENT* in big fat letters at the top of the first page. In the space below Dad's name there's a squiggly signature. I didn't even know he had one.

"Have we got enough room?" Dad recites. "Is the shower wheelchair accessible? Which party is liable. When he has to take what pill. When he has to eat. As if I don't know my own son. That Santos bloke even wanted to send someone round to take a look."

"To look at what?"

"To pay us a house call," Dad sniggers. "See if anything needs adapting."

"So it's going ahead then?"

"What do you mean?"

"Lucien's really coming home?"

"What do *you* think?"

"When?"

"Soon. First we need to pick up one of those special beds for him. And a wheelchair." Dad unlocks the doors.

"But … but …"

We get in.

"… isn't Lucien better off here?"

"Course not. He lived at home with us for years, didn't

he? And after that we picked him up and dropped him off at weekends. Now he'll be staying a bit longer, that's all." Dad tosses the papers in my lap.

"Or do you think your old man's not up to it?"

I shake my head.

"Well then. Lucien is my son, too. And I have every right to do what I want with him."

"Have they paid you the money yet?"

"End of the month."

"Not till then?"

Dad parps his horn three times. I nearly jump out of my skin. "We're going to have a fine old time together, Bry." I expect a thump on the shoulder but it doesn't come. "Deal?"

I nod.

"Just the three of us."

I don't say a word about Selma or tell him she spoke to Mum. I don't even want to think about the jokes he'd crack if he knew I'd been talking to a girl from this place.

I flick through the papers for a bit. I can read most of the words, but I don't really get what they say. It's a while before I notice that Dad's turned off in the direction of our old flat.

"Just a quick look," he says.

The flat's from when the four of us still lived together. Dad bumps the car onto the pavement and keeps the engine running. I recognize everything immediately. Even the boys playing football across the road, though they all have different faces now.

"Well, well," Dad mumbles, and shakes his head. "Honeymoon ..." There's a smell of threadbare carpets from his hair as he leans across and peers up at the building. As if our old life might be waiting behind the front door and all we have to do is figure out where we left the key. “That’s the house where the two of you were made, son.”

Nothing has changed. Except the red railings that ran along our gangway have been painted dark blue. When Lucien would start pinching us, Mum used to let him walk up and down out there. I usually walked in front of him, kicking a football.

Our tiled paradise. That’s what Dad used to call it. When your floors are tiled from wall to wall, you’re not just any old loser, he’d say. “Tiles everywhere. Did you look behind the toilet?” he asked Gran when she came to visit. Her last visit, as it turned out.

She sat talking to Mum for a long time, then let herself be helped into her grey coat.

“Do you think I’m kidding?” Dad asked.

“I don’t think anything, Maurice,” said Gran, checking the contents of her handbag. She wanted to be driven home.

“There are even tiles under the kitchen cupboards.”

“Ah.”

Gran’s response to everything Dad said sounded like a sigh.

“Don’t you believe me?” Dad got down on his knees and began ripping out the skirting boards under the kitchen units. A dusty swirl of cobwebs. “Look.” He pressed his cheek to the floor. “All the way to the wall.”

“Could you take me home now, Maurice?”

Gran kissed her palm and rubbed it over my head. “It’s true,” I said to her. “Look.” I lay down too. Greasy balls of fluff, dried-up macaroni that had fallen down the back of the cooker, a scrap of old newspaper. “Wow!” I shouted. “Wall to wall. Not everyone can say that, eh Dad?”

He was already halfway to the lift. Mum hugged Gran by

the open door. Her stocking heels lifted out of her shoes.

"You're Lucien's mother. I can't make that choice for you," Gran said, glasses knocked sideways and pressed against her face. Her wrinkled hands patted Mum's back, the way they do in judo when someone has to let go. Mum asked a question I couldn't catch. "He's his child, too," Gran answered. "Whether you like it or not."

Humming restlessly, Lucien walked up to them, dragging his fingernails across the wallpaper. You could tell how much he'd grown by how high the scratches were. A flap of sticking plaster hung in front of his eye. "Mum!" I shouted. "Lucien's been picking at his eyebrow again!" He had hit his head on the edge of the coffee table days before. I had pushed him, but nobody saw.

It was mostly me Lucien pinched. Mum said it was my own fault because I was too rough with him. Either that or I was supposed to know better. One time she was sitting right there on the couch when Lucien went for me. She picked me up, parked my bum on the dining table, and stroked the red patch that would later turn blue. "You know your brother can't help it, don't you?" It sounded like our little secret. "Your mum saw what happened. Lucien didn't mean it."

"It hurts," I squeaked.

"Well, your mum might have just the thing for that." She disappeared into the kitchen and I heard the scrape of a freezer drawer.

"What do we have here?" She pressed the ice lolly gently against the red patch. "Is it helping yet?"

"A little bit."

"When it stops hurting, you can eat what's left." I counted back from fifty in my head so it wouldn't look like the pain had stopped all of a sudden.

By then, Lucien was lying on the rug in front of the

couch. With outstretched arms and crooked fingers, he was clawing at the air trying to catch the light from the ceiling lamp. He had forgotten all about pinching me. You could eat a whole ice lolly in front of him without him wanting one too.

9

A policeman standing in the middle of the road signals for us to stop. His car is tucked out of sight on the shoulder.

"What does he want? Were you over the limit?"

"Trap shut," Dad says as we come to a halt. "Let me do the talking."

The copper slaps the side of the pickup, then appears at the open window on the driver's side.

"Well, if it isn't our old friend Maurice," he says, removing his tough-guy sunglasses.

"Yves," Dad replies, eyes fixed straight ahead.

I don't think I've seen this copper before. He checks out the stuff in the back of the truck, casting a beady eye over the scrap iron without touching anything. Then he wants to see our papers. I open the glove compartment and hand them to Dad. "So, here we are again, Maurice ..." Chirping crickets, the creak of spruce bark. "Had a few phone calls about you recently." He *tap-tap-taps* on the wing mirror. "Drove off without paying at the petrol station. A spot of bother down the pub."

Dad shakes his head dismissively.

"False accusations as usual?"

"I paid Benoit."

"He didn't seem to think so. Not the amount he was due in any case."

"Don't you have criminals to catch?"

"Why do you think I pulled you over?" the copper grins.

"Licence plate registered in your name now, is it?"

"Yeah, of course."

"So if I make a little call, it will all check out?" He turns as if to walk over to his car.

"Any day now," Dad mumbles. "Admin cock-up. I'm getting it sorted."

"Cock-up's your middle name, Maurice."

"Meaning?"

"Meaning these things always seem to take a wrong turn where you're concerned."

"They don't know their arse from their elbow down at that post office."

"And there's still that unpaid fine, Maurice. It's not even thirty euros. Wait till the warning notice hits the doormat and it'll only cost you more."

Dad's picking foam rubber from a tear in the front seat.

"Do you hear me, Maurice?"

Dad nods, eyes still fixed on the road.

I root around in my pocket. "Here!" I hand the copper all the money I have. "Now will you leave my dad alone?"

"Bry!" Dad barks.

"Letting the little lad cough up for your fines nowadays?"

"Do you want my money or not?" I ask.

Officer Yves lifts the pointy beret from his head, runs his fingers through his hair, puts the beret back on.

"Last chance, Maurice. Next time we run into each other, that paperwork better be in order."

Dad gives a nod I can barely see.

"And you can sort things out down at the petrol station yourself." Yves takes a step back and waves us on. Dad starts the engine, accelerating so fast that the wheels spin before they grip the road.

"That'll shut him up for a while," I say, expecting a thump on the shoulder.

"Feel good did it? Shitting on me like that?"

I don't know why he's so angry.

"Acting the big shot, rubbing your old man's face in the dirt? Well?"

"I was only trying to help you out."

"Where did you get that money?"

"Saved up."

"Piss off." He shoves my face so hard that my head cracks off the window.

A high-pitched drone starts up in my ears. I can see from his lips Dad is screaming at me while he stares at the road ahead. Makes no difference if I answer. The wobble-headed dog on the dashboard is already nodding at every word he splutters.

10

The sun sinks behind a mountain range of clouds. The yelp of a vixen stabs the air. Little lights dot the wooded hill that fills our horizon. Every night they light up in the same places, but during the day you'd never know people live there. Hunched on a crate, Dad snaffles a handful of sunflower seeds from a paper bag. He traps one between his teeth, cracks it open, and blows the skin away.

"Bry?" It's the first thing he's said to me since this afternoon.

"What?"

"Go and see if our Emile is still awake."

"How come?"

"So you can collect the rent."

"Hasn't he paid already?"

"For this week, yeah."

"So?"

"Rent is paid in advance, Bry. It's the way of the world. And Wednesday is collection day."

"Wednesday?"

There's a fierce bark from the dog cage, then a whine. Rico's tail sweeps the concrete floor. He can't stop himself sniffing Rita's hole, keeps on and on until she snaps at him.

"Can't we take that load of scrap in the pickup to the yard tomorrow, see how much we get for it?"

"Are you going to sort things out with the tenant? Or do I have to do it, after all?"

"No, it's okay," I reply.

Rita snarls at Rico. He runs himself round in a circle and settles in his corner with his nose between the bars of their cage.

Emile's curtains are edged in bluish light. "I've come for the rent." I practise saying it to myself, then knock on his door and take a step back the way they do outside hotel rooms in films. The TV and a wall clock are still waiting on the back seat of his car, along with two removal boxes. The top one says *LOUISE* in thick black marker. "I've come for the rent!" I shout.

The door to the caravan inches open. Emile's eyes are puffy with sleep. "The rent?"

"Next week's rent."

"But this is only my third night."

"Were you asleep?"

"No. Not really."

"Rent's always paid in advance. We collect on Wednesday."

"Oh."

"I told you that when you arrived."

I keep looking at him for as long as I can.

"Don't you have the money on you?"

"Yes, yes I do. But ..."

"And you said I could see your fish tank, remember?"

He presses his lips into a curve that falls short of a smile. "Oh, right. My aquarium." Emile half closes the door. For a moment I think he's going to reappear with a tank of sloshing water in his arms. But then he says "Come in. They've just been fed."

He has breathed all the air in the caravan in and out a few times. Or that's what it smells like. The blue light from the aquarium casts a haze over everything.

"What's that buzzing noise?"

"It's the water pump."

There's a tottery tower in the sink, knives and forks wedged between piled-up plates. He's barely eaten his spaghetti.

"Go on, get closer if you like." Emile opens the hatch of a wall cupboard, takes out a bulging leather folder, and glances over his shoulder at me. I turn back to the aquarium quick as I can.

"Doesn't it make you want to piss?"

"Sorry?"

"The water bubbling non-stop like that."

"These days it makes me feel calm." Little blue-red fish dart through the water, attacking the coloured flakes that spin around. An orange fish with leopard spots thinks he's travelled miles, but he's only swimming against the current of the water filter. A tiny worm of poo dangles from an invisible hole under his quivering tail fin. As soon as it floats loose, a blue-red stripy fish snaps it from under his pal's nose. Only to spit it out again in bits. "They don't like the taste of shit," I say.

"Sorry?"

"Never mind."

Emile swivels his hips around the corner of the table and sits on the bench opposite me, wide enough to seat one and a half. Our knees touch under the table. He doesn't say anything. The blue aquarium light shades his cheeks paler, carves deeper lines under his eyes. We both look at the water plants waving, the colours flashing past.

"Beautiful," I say, and point at all the fish at once.

"Thank you," he says, as if he painted them himself. "Sometimes I sit and watch them for hours and don't even notice the time."

"Is that why you stay inside all day? Or do you just like the smell of your own sweat?"

"No," he chuckles. "It's definitely not that. In the morning I tell myself I'm going to go out. But I never seem to make it through the door. Then evening falls and that's that." His hands are flat on the table. Fingernails neatly clipped, no scabs or scars. Could those hands press a pillow to a mother's face?

"Is it because of Louise?"

Panic in his eyes. "How do you ...? Is she ...?" He tugs at the curtain, then sweeps aside the net curtain behind that. "How did she find me?" Without even taking a proper look, he turns back to me. "Does she want to talk?" I leave him dangling a little longer but he doesn't let anything slip.

"I saw her name on the box. In your car."

"On the box." He peers out past the curtain again. "So she's not here?"

"Don't you want her to find you?"

"Gosh," he hesitates. "Yes, of course I do. But I suspect it's the last thing she wants."

"How come?"

"Here." He slides two fifties across the table at me. "The rent."

I'm almost out the door before I realize. "Shit."

"What?"

"Could you make it five twenties instead?"

11

I promised Dad I'd go and sit with Lucien, but I make sure I pass by Selma's room first. "Brian!" she cheers as soon as she sees me. "Are you on a visit?"

"If you like."

"You're tall!" she shouts approvingly. Her compliments are always about things I can do nothing about, but they make me feel good anyway. For the first time I notice that her eyes are mostly green, with a fleck of brown in the right one.

"You've got brown in your eyes."

"Oh," she says and tries to rub it away. "Gone?"

"No, no. It's *in* your eye. And it looks really nice."

She rubs again. "Gone now?"

I don't really know what to say. She grabs me by the wrist and swings my arm wildly to and fro. "Pull," she commands and leans away from me.

"Do you want to water ski?" A determined frown and the tip of her tongue between her lips tell me that's what she wants. "Hold on tight," I say and haul her in a circle around the room. The way she's leaning, I can see the crack between her breasts.

"You're strong!" she shouts. I take her round again.

She falls back breathless on the bed but clings to my wrist so I've no choice but to sit down beside her. I poke her in the ribs and her laughter bounces around the room.

"I hate tickles," she gasps.

Selma pulls a doll onto her lap, strokes it absently, and lets it fall.

"You're ve-ery tall," she says and stands up.

She goes on looking at me, so I say "Thank you."

Selma sways from side to side with her hands on her hips. "Nino's very tall, too."

"Nino?"

A ladybird flies in through the top window. It lands on the sill and starts crawling up the window pane.

"Who's Nino?"

"Ladeeee-biiird!" Selma claps her hands. Before the bug can tuck its wings back under its spots, she tries to pick it off the glass. "C'mere you," she mumbles, pressing her cheek to the pane. "Got her!" She brushes the ladybird into her cupped hand. "Look!" she beams, gazing at the crumpled little mess of black legs, spotted wing cases, and snotty insides. "For you."

"It's dead."

"It's not!" She jiggles the little corpse across the palm of her hand. Tries to stroke it back to life.

"Her flying days are over."

"Ladybirdie?"

"I think she really is dead."

"Isutmafault?" Panic clumps her words together.

"What?"

"Mafault?"

"Maybe she was very old."

Selma starts to nod along. "Maybe she was ve-ery old."

"Give her to me."

But Selma has already wiped her hand on her jeans. "She was very old," she says as if she's explaining it to me. "I could tell easy."

We sit side by side on the edge of her bed. "I can't stay long. My dad is getting things sorted for Lucien. He's coming home with us." Our hands are resting shyly next to each other. I want to take hold of hers but I don't know what to do with it after that.

"Snip," says Selma, brightening up all of a sudden.

"What do you mean?"

She points at my face. "Do you mean this?" I tug at my torn earlobe. Now that I'm touching it, her hands are itching to do the same. "Snip-snap." She moves a little closer and fingers my earlobe softly, stroking the little hairs you can feel but not see. It's the first time someone's fingers have touched me like that. She traces the rim of my ear until her fingertip arrives back at my earlobe. It sends pinpricks through my body along the thinnest of electric wires.

Selma sighs and lets go. Black grains of makeup clog her eyelashes. Her pupils are wide. We smile. A lawnmower is raising hell below the window, so we couldn't hear each other even if we had something to say. Selma looks at my mouth like she wants to take a bite but doesn't know where to start. She leans in slowly. I feel her breath. Hear her lips part. Then she presses her mouth next to mine. The corners touch for a second and Selma slides away from me.

My tongue tingles. I'm already sorry it's over.

"Bry?" A shout from the belly of the building.

"Shit. That's my dad. I've got to go. Don't tell anyone I was here with you."

"Bry!" Closer this time.

"Bye," I say to Selma.

A little smile appears on her lips.

I dash into the corridor. Dad is halfway up the stairs, but he doesn't notice me until the automatic doors swing open. "What's up?" I shout.

"Fuck's sake, Bry, where the hell were you?"

"I needed a piss."

"Up here? There are toilets outside Lucien's room."

"Someone was in there."

"Left me to load up on my own as usual."

A girl in a wheelchair sails past us, working a lever with her chin. "Hello mister," she says in an unexpectedly clear voice. Her mouth would be impossible to kiss even if you wanted to.

"Come on, let's get home and set things up. The truck's already full."

"Can we stop by Lucien?"

"You'll be seeing enough of him over the next few weeks."

"Just for a minute?"

Henkelmann is staring at his luminous little Christmas tree. He tenses as soon as we enter the room. It looks like he's holding his breath, but his chest still swells and sinks. He has the eyes of a crocodile before it strikes. Dad walks over to Lucien's bed. My brother's legs are pulled up in front of him and his face is turned to the window.

"Do you remember this guy?"

Dad shakes his head.

"It's Henkelmann, the one who always bit himself."

"Your mum was better with names."

I tap Henkelmann's forearm, like hitting a random letter on a keyboard.

"I know a game he likes."

"Leave the guy alone, Bry. I thought you wanted to say hello to your brother?"

I walk over to his bed. Lucien is asleep. Molars grinding. Eyelids and fingers twitching, like our dogs when they dream. "Are we taking him home with us now?"

"Oh no. Our little prince will be arriving by taxi."

"Taxi?"

"One of those minibuses. They're dropping him off tomorrow around noon."

"You're coming home," I say, and hope he'll open his eyes for a second.

"Let him sleep," Dad whispers.

As we're leaving, I hear the velcro around Henkelmann's wrists creak. "You want to play our game, don't you?"

"Leave him be."

"But Henkelmann likes our little game. Watch." I place a fingertip between his eyebrows, run it down to the tip of his nose and let it fly off like a ski jumper. A tremor in his chin.

"You wanted to bite, eh ...?"

"Leave it, Bry."

My teasing finger circles above his face. *Snap*! The wet of his mouth hits my hand and I fall back. My neck slams into the shelf on the wall. Henkelmann shudders and roars.

"Huh," Dad says. "Some game."

"He's not normally that quick. Have you been practising with Thibaut?"

Henkelmann holds his breath again, hoping for another go.

"Uh-uh." I try to rub the pain from my neck. "That's enough for one day."

12

The back of our truck is groaning under the weight of a huge bed, mattress wrapped in see-through plastic.

"Bra-yun. Braaaa-yun!"

Dad's round the driver's side hunting for his keys. Luckily he hasn't heard her blaring my name.

"Bra-yun!" Selma is leading a parade of two. A boy trails behind her, his hand on her shoulder. "Quicker, Nino. Quicker." The boy is working hard to keep up. I signal her to stop shouting. "Bra-yuuuun!" she cheers, like I'm a prize she's won.

Dad sniggers. "What's with the welcome committee?"

"Open up." I rattle the handle on my side.

"Easy does it, pal. No need to wreck the door."

"Bra-yun!"

"One of the locals by the look of her."

"Could be. How should I know?"

"Look!" Selma points at her face. She's all made up, a mask drawn by a kid who can't colour inside the lines.

Dad winks.

"Oh, yeah ..." I act like it's just dawned on me. "That's Selma. She comes to see Lucien sometimes. Now open the door." Dad jangles his keys.

"I'm Lucien's brother," I tell Selma.

She tilts her head.

"And Lucien is coming home, so we won't be back here."

Selma doesn't understand. Now that Dad is looking at her too, I notice there's something not right about her eyes. Every *S* that comes out of her mouth sounds thicker, tongue wet against her teeth. She's a girl you can't cuddle because she'll leave a stain and everyone will know what you've been up to.

"Kithy, kithy," she whispers, way too loud. "Kithy, kithy."

"Shut your face."

Selma bats her black eyelashes.

Dad climbs into the pickup.

"Look at me." I grab her hand for a second. "Lucien's coming home tomorrow, so I won't be here for a while." The roar of the engine jolts us apart.

"I'll come back soon," I promise. "For you."

Selma turns on her heels. The boy is still attached and traipses off behind her.

Dad blasts the horn twice, short and sharp. All the residents toddling around the grounds look in our direction. Except Selma. Hands over her ears, she stamps up the wheelchair ramp to the main entrance.

To my relief, Dad doesn't say anything about her on the drive back. There's a plastic bag on my lap and a weird-looking toilet seat at my feet. A huge pack of nappies is wedged between us on the seat.

I flip down the sun flap to look at myself in the mirror. As casually as possible, I examine my lips. They don't look any different.

For once I'm happy to hear Dad droning on about loading the truck single-handed.

13

"Catch!" A sausage pillow flies in my direction. "And take this inside too, while you're at it."

He hands me a green ring binder with *LUCIEN* on the spine in block capitals. I flip it open and leaf through random pages, glance at a table. "What's this for?"

"Instruction manual. For if he malfunctions. What pills to give him and when, what he likes and doesn't like, phone numbers at the home. That kind of thing."

"How did you get that bed onto the truck?"

"A couple of lads from the home helped out. Retards, like, but strong ..." He clicks his tongue in admiration. "You should've seen the muscles on them."

"So you didn't load the truck all by yourself?"

Dad hands me a bag. "Sure you can manage? Or is it too heavy for you?"

The bag is nearly full to the top with boxes and bottles of pills.

"Does Lucien have to take all these?"

Dad's already inside the caravan. I follow him in, lugging the stuff he's given me. "Where should I put it?"

"Your room."

"What do you mean my room?"

"Where else?"

"Uh ... your room maybe?"

"Bry ..." he says, and that's that.

Lucien's things look out of place among mine. It's hard to imagine that my brother will actually be here soon. Sharing this room with me.

"Can't he sleep over by the TV?" I ask Dad as he comes in with the pack of nappies and a bedpan.

"And who'd keep an eye on him there?"

"We would. The two of us."

He tosses the nappies on my bed.

"Clear a shelf in your cupboard for those, will you?"

"Would you look at this!" Dad has rolled an extension cord outside. The bed is still on the truck and he's lying on it, remote control in hand. A little motor under the mattress is humming away. "Fit for a king!" He lowers the top half of the bed while the foot end is still up in the air. "You got to give this a go." He budges up. I put one foot on the back wheel and heave myself onto the truck. "Not with those mucky feet." He kicks me in the shins. "Shoes off. There's a fifty-euro deposit on this thing, man. It's all got to go back spick and span."

"But it's covered in plastic."

"Yeah, well we're keeping the plastic clean too."

I lie down beside him. "Here." He hands me the remote and points at the top button. "Go on, press." Dad closes his eyes. The hairs on his forearm tickle mine. I press the button and the motor beneath us starts to hum. "Ah, this is the life," Dad groans as I fold us double. "Now pick something else from the menu."

First I leave our legs up in the air, then switch it round. I close my eyes and imagine it's Selma I'm lying next to.

I fold us double again.

From there, I lower us until we're lying flat out. That's what me and Selma like best. Dad too. He lies there beside me, contented. When he opens his eyes and sees me looking at him, he doesn't crack a joke or slam his fist against my shoulder. I almost want to hug him.

"How are we going to get this thing inside?"

"Never mind that, Bry. Fold us double one more time."

Two wheels on the pickup, the other two in the grass. Whatever we try, we can't get the bed off the truck.

Brown Henri must have seen us struggling and ambles over to see what's going on. "Not a word about your brother," Dad says. Jean is tagging along behind with his oxygen tank.

"Bought yourselves a hospital bed?"

"Yeah, something like that," Dad answers. "We're going to leave it out here next to the fridge."

"Expecting an accident?"

"Can't be too careful." Dad drags a few pallets aside, even though they're not in the way. "Give us a hand, will you? That thing's too heavy for Bry."

Jean peers at the stuff on the front seat of the pickup.

"What's all this for?"

"We're starting a hospital," I say so they'll lay off interrogating Dad.

"Are you now?" says Jean. "Can't say I'd fancy my chances as a patient."

"It's for people with a death wish," I say.

Everybody chuckles.

"The bed comes from a wholesaler." My father's eyes flash from Jean to Henri and back again. "He was looking to get rid of it, sharpish like, so I took it off his hands for a couple of tenners."

"Tenners?" Brown Henri inspects the underside of the bed like he does with his cars. "Bloody cheap."

"That's what I thought. Sell it on at a tasty profit."

"So we'll be waiting even longer for our money?"

"You'll get it soon enough."

"And the tenant's rent?"

"I'm working on it."

"How about we pay him a house call? Or you chuck him out if he refuses to cough up?"

"Give him a bit longer, eh?"

Henri clambers onto the truck and lifts the head of the bed. I lift our end along with Dad. Jean looks on.

"That's it, that's it," Dad groans. "This way. A little more." Rita crouches in our way and earns herself a swift kick up the arse. "A little further and we're clear!" Dad shouts. "Down, down, down."

Jean sizes up the door. "How do you plan to get that thing inside?"

"I don't."

"So what are you going to do with it?"

"It's an outdoor bed." Dad fetches two half-litre cans of beer from the fridge. "Thanks for your trouble, gents." He hands one to Henri and tosses the other over to Jean. "One for the road. I'd ask you to stay, but me and Bry have got things to do."

Jean bumps the toe of his shoe against one of the wheels on the bed. Henri tries to read the sheet of paper under the plastic that's wrapped around the mattress.

"And who'll be sleeping in this bed?" asks Jean. Dad nips into the caravan. "I asked you a question, Maurice."

"Told you already," comes the offhand answer through the kitchen window. "We're selling it on."

The two of them exchange glances.

"Brian?" Henri asks.

"What?"

"Is this bed for that brother of yours?"

"Nah, course not." I shake my head for as long as it takes them to believe me. "You heard my dad, didn't you?"

Once the pair of them leave, Dad appears in the doorway. "Do you think it might rain?"

"How should I know?"

To be sure we drape a length of farmer's tarpaulin over the bed. It crinkles in the breeze. Dad straps it down with two bungee cords and secures them to the frame.

"What are you going to say when they see Lucien on the bed?"

A big orange bee bumbles around us slowly. Rico snaps and it buzzes into a hole in the ground.

"Once they clap eyes on that brother of yours, they won't dare say a thing. Trust your old man."

14

With an old shirt of Mum's, I'm trying to get a shine on the rims on my scooter. Rusty spatters rip the cloth and leave a cut in my finger.

"Hello." Out of nowhere, Emile is standing at my elbow.

"Do you always creep up on people?"

"Sorry, I didn't mean to startle you."

The sun's so bright I can't look straight at him. "Dad's not here." I stand up. "He'll be back in an hour." A wasp hovers over the can of energy drink between my feet, sipping at the yellow drops around the opening. I shoo it away, carefully so as not to get stung. "Got a problem?"

"No, no." His eyes take in the bed. "Like you said, I can't stay inside all day."

"The bed's for my brother. He's arriving today."

"Your brother?"

Emile examines the grip you can pull yourself up on. "Is he rehabilitating?"

"What?"

"Recovering ... from an accident."

"He was born that way."

"What's the matter with him?"

"I don't think it's got a name. Something went wrong inside my mum's belly."

Emile looks at the pallets, the sagging coffee table Dad once used as a ramp for his motocross bike, the chunks of scrap metal with blades of grass shooting up around them.

"He's only staying a couple of weeks."

"I thought you were an only child."

"I kind of am. He's more of a long-distance brother."

"Well," Emile gestures toward the gate, "I think I'll take a walk. Nice talking to you."

"What about you?"

"How do you mean?"

"Just wondering," I shrug, not exactly sure what I mean. "Do you have kids?"

That smile pops onto his face again. The little smile that softens what he says. Or apologizes in advance for what he's going to say. "Uh ... no."

"Didn't Louise want any?"

"She did. Yes, certainly she did. But you don't always get what you want. Perhaps it's for the best."

"Why do you always smile when you say stuff?"

His face turns red. "Is that ... Do I do that? Yes, I suppose I do. Some people stutter when they're nervous. This is my nervous tic." He does his best to hold his lips steady.

"Does that mean you're nervous now?"

"Not because of you." The smile's back again. "It's just ..."

"Did Louise call yet?"

"No."

"Can't you try her on another number?"

"I must have tried every number in the country."

"Are you two married?"

He nods. I want to tell him about Selma, but I don't know where to start.

"Can't you call one of Louise's friends?"

"You're asking an awful lot of questions." Emile crosses his arms.

"Don't you like questions?"

"Questions are fine, only ... I'm not sure who's asking."

"I am."

"Yes, but we don't really know each other."

I squat beside my scooter. There's a glimmer of grease on the axle where I haven't polished yet. Black ridges are burning under my nails, so I wrap the shirt tighter around my fingers and buff the metal clean. Emile remains standing.

"You ask good questions, you know." His toes shift under the dusty tips of his shoes. "To be honest, I've tried to contact her through a friend and through her parents, but they must be able to see who's calling."

"Either that or she's never home."

"Yeah, could be that," he chuckles.

I'm itching to fit a new spark plug, though Dad said I can't do it without him.

The axles are shining again. I pick up the spark plug from the hot saddle and play with it. Emile can see I'm not exactly sure where it should go.

"Below that cable." And when I pull on the wrong one: "No, that one with the connector."

"Do you know about this stuff?"

"I was young once."

I dig a wrench from the jumble of tools in Dad's plastic bag. It doesn't fit.

"You might be better off with an extended socket wrench." His voice is so quiet it's less like something he said and more like a thought that occurred to me. "Number twenty-one, if I remember rightly."

"Just what I was looking for."

The old spark plug loosens easily. I fit the new one like I knew what I was doing all along. Emile doesn't say anything, so I don't know if I'm doing it right. I hold still a second. "Like this?" I ask at last.

"Fine. You could use the wrench to tighten it."

"Did you have one yourself?"

"In my day everyone rode one of these. I was interested in the technical side but most of the time it stood idle in the shed. I wasn't really the scooter type ... that's tight enough."

I must be overdoing it with the wrench.

"With a bit of luck, she should start again now."

"All I need is petrol."

"Not unimportant," he laughs.

I gather up the tools in the bag.

"Can I ask *you* something?" Emile asks.

"How do you mean?"

"Well, you've been asking me all kinds of questions."

"Um ... fair enough."

Emile takes a look around. "You live here alone with your father?"

"Uh-huh."

"So where is your mother? I mean, if your brother's going to be here too."

"She's on honeymoon."

"Oh ..." he says excitedly, as if I've just told him it's my birthday.

"I don't know the guy she's with."

"Oh."

"Only saw him when he dropped Mum off one time. His name is Didier."

"That's a shame."

"I'm not bothered."

"Honestly?"

"Mum says Didier chose her, not everything that came with her. That Lucien was already a present he hadn't bargained for. Didier thought one kid was enough, so I live here with Dad."

"Oh, that's ..." But Emile doesn't say what that is.

"Mum had all kinds of people. Her family and that. And

Lucien. And now Didier. Dad had no one but me."

"And you've lived here ever since?"

"Pretty much."

A sparrow lands right beside us and starts cleaning itself in a pool of sand.

"Then your father's a lucky man."

"How come?"

"To have you. As his son."

All I can do is shrug. Little wrinkles next to his eyes change his smile.

"I'll be off then. Have fun."

"Fun?"

Emile nods at the bed. "With your brother."

15

"It just wasn't doable." That was Mum's standard answer when asked why Lucien wasn't living at home anymore. "Not with Brian around. And not for Maurice either." That's what she said to other mothers we met in the supermarket. Sometimes before they even asked.

Lucien's bedroom was supposed to remain unchanged, for when he came to stay at the weekend. In the meantime our clothes rack moved in, then the hoover. Lucien's bed was soon home to a mound of washing that needed ironing. Beside it stood the box our new TV came in.

I thought living there would change him. That maybe he'd get better. But standing by his bed every Sunday, I saw that everything about him stayed the same.

Mum seemed to spend most of her time waiting for someone who never came home. She called constantly to ask how he was doing. I don't think I missed Lucien. He just wasn't there. It wasn't like he'd disappeared, more like someone had switched him off. Put him to sleep. Like he dozed off after every visit and dreamt of us all week long. And on Sundays, right before we pulled into the car park, a nurse would wake him up.

I knew it wasn't true. He often had cuts on his hands that I had never seen before. Or a new scratch on his face. One time his thumbnail was blue. So Lucien was sometimes awake without us.

Mum was sparing with her bedtime kisses, as if she didn't want to give me too much of what Lucien was missing. That's why we visited him as often as we could. When he had been there a couple of weeks, we took him for a day out at the reservoir.

I had to stay in the car while Mum went in to get Lucien, because that would be quickest. Dad went with her to push the wheelchair. The building looked a bit like a school. "A school where no one learns anything," Dad said. There were a few residents standing around the entrance. I knew they existed but apart from Lucien I had never seen one before. To me they were all half-dinosaur, each one so different that they must be the last of their kind.

"Here he comes," I said out loud to myself as Lucien was wheeled to the car. Walking would have taken too long. Seeing him again, I realized I'd missed him. I began to tug impatiently on the door handle, but the child lock was on.

"You sit in front," Mum said. Quick as I could, I squeezed between the seats. Dad lifted Lucien onto the back seat while Mum kept her hand on his head to make sure he didn't bump it.

"Hiya," I said.

"Ku-wa-waa," he replied, as if I had said something to annoy him. "Ku-wa-waa!"

"Hey there, love. Mum's going to sit with you." She slid onto the back seat beside him, took his hand, and stroked the skin between his pinkie and his ring finger, but he didn't want her to. "Ku-wa-waaah!" Mum licked her fingertips and tried to smooth down a stubborn tuft of hair. She bent to kiss him but Lucien twisted as far away from her as he could. "Isn't this special," she beamed. "The four of us together again."

"The four of us together," I repeated. "Eh, Dad?"

"The four of us," he said.

We had all said it, so it felt like a pact.

"Hmm-hhh, hmm-hhh." Lucien nodded with every hum, as if he was agreeing with us. That tuft of hair was already sticking up again.

Our little beach at the old quarry looked nothing like the holiday brochures. The sand was hard and greyish, and when I tried to dig it hurt under my nails. A sandcastle was out of the question. On our beach all you could really do was scoop a few shallow holes. The sand was speckled with duck shit. Trails of greenish black flecked with white, as if a bunch of elves had started colouring them in and scampered off when they heard us coming. The splats of shit were hard to avoid but I knew better than to complain, because Mum would just fold up the towels and we'd head straight home. A diver had vanished in the reservoir once. I always thought it was eerie how the smooth surface never let you see how deep the water went.

The clouds made it goose-bump cold, but when the sun came out it was hot enough to make your skin prickle. Lucien's skinny arms put up a fight as Mum pulled a T-shirt over his head.

"Maybe he wants a drink!" I shouted. Mum lifted one of Lucien's legs and pulled a pair of swimming trunks over his nappy, though he never went in deeper than his ankles. She examined the insides of his elbows and knees. Looked closely at the hollow of his neck.

It was a while before Dad came to sit with us. Something under the bonnet of the car needed topping up. He arrived carrying a couple of cans of beer in a plastic bag. He never held a bag by its handles, but clenched in his fist like he was afraid something might escape. That's how my father held onto everything that was his.

Lucien rooted about under the trees. I was standing where the green water reached to just under my swimming trunks. My willy didn't want me to go deeper. I kneaded the cold sludge between my toes and shivered. Instead of footprints, my feet left little black clouds that billowed in the water.

Dad lay on his belly next to the towels Mum had spread out and leaned on his elbows to take a beer from his bag. Mum turned to see where Lucien was. "He's over by the trees!" I shouted. He had one hand in front of his eyes. Maybe my brother thought we couldn't see him if he couldn't see us. He took his hand away and laughed out loud.

"You can lie back and sunbathe, Mum!" I yelled. "I'll keep an eye on Lucien."

"No need to shout, Brian."

"Leave the boy alone," Dad snapped.

I felt something sharp under my foot. A shark's tooth maybe. I tried to pick it up with my toes but lost my grip. Mum pulled the neck of her wide blouse down over her shoulders, examined her skin, and turned again to look at Lucien. "He's playing!" I shouted. She lay down. Dad looked at her sideways when she closed her eyes for a minute. I ducked underwater. The closer you got to the bottom, the greener it became. I could barely see my pale hands waving in front of my face and even with my lips pressed together I could taste the water. "I saw a fish!" I shouted when I came up for air. "It was this big!" I spread my arms. "I nearly caught it but it got spooked and swam off."

Dad gave me a thumbs-up.

"And I think I saw that diver too. Maybe."

Mum was looking at Lucien again. He had found a branch and was fighting something in the air. Sometimes he hit a tree by accident. He would make a rubbish knight, except when he got angry. Then he could bite you or smash a coffee maker. Or wreck the spin-dryer in the bathroom.

Dad fiddled with the back of Mum's blouse. She shifted to one side and pushed his hand away.

"Go on, take it off," he said. "There's no one around."

Mum shot another look at Lucien. "Hands off my bra, Maurice."

"Oh, woman ..."

"Mum doesn't like that!" I shouted.

Dad crushed his beer can and swapped it for a fresh one from his bag.

"Go and swim with the boy."

He turned his head away and looked toward the other side of the quarry. That was his answer.

"I'm fine, Mum."

Dad raised his full can in my direction.

Lucien was humming and swaying his hips in a kind of dance. With his head thrown all the way back, he looked up at the light that flickered through the pine needles. A dinosaur cry came out of his mouth.

"He likes it here!" I shouted.

"Yes," Mum nodded. "He likes it here."

Dad strolled over to the climbing frame with his beer. There, he flattened the second can and let it fall in the sand. He rolled his shoulders a few times, then gripped the highest bar. Slowly he pulled himself up until his chin was jutting over the top. He eased back down and did it two more times. I clapped for him.

Mum was lying on her towel with her face in the sun. Lucien thrashed and whacked his branch in every direction but he didn't hurt himself.

Everything seemed just fine.

A family appeared and sat themselves down further along. When a second family arrived and the kids charged down to the water with an inflatable dinghy, Mum started gathering our stuff together, keeping one eye on Lucien and another on the intruders. They had noticed my brother and the kids were staring at him. If I imagined Lucien was half-brother, half-dinosaur, I felt less ashamed of what people thought of him. Then it was pretty cool that he was mine.

"Get out of the water, Brian," Mum shouted, once she had packed everything away. "I won't ask you again."

Mum wanted to take Lucien back to ours before we took him back to the home. So he wouldn't forget what our house was like. But Dad said it would only make him want to stay and he wouldn't understand that from now on he belonged somewhere else.

On the last part of the drive back, Lucien bumped his head softly against the window. Travelling by car always made him sleepy. He was humming like he couldn't remember the words to the song in his head.

"Will you help your dad take Lucien back in?" Mum was on the back seat with the door open. "Will you do that for your mum?"

"All right."

The two of us were done in no time. Dad had the tyres on the wheelchair screeching around the corners. I caught a glimpse of Henkelmann as we dashed past his room. His elbows were all bandaged up, probably to stop him gnawing at his skin until it bled. Down the corridor, Big Camiel stood waiting. "Hello there, sir. Hello there, sir." He blocked our path with his huge hand hovering in the air. All you had to do was high-five him and he'd let you pass. Dad gave him one too and we left Camiel gazing at his open palm.

At the time, Lucien shared a room with Lizzy. She had short, black, spiky hair. Her mum was blond, but Lizzy looked like she could have been Chinese. I had never seen her dad. Lizzy could do a bit more than Lucien—clap along to a song, hold her own beaker, and point at a table or a strawberry on a laminated card if she wanted to say *table* or *something red*. She was too small for an ordinary wheelchair, so they drove her around in a baby buggy. There were two bright red rims under her eyes where her eyelids drooped, and I was afraid she might cry blood if she was sad. Dad said only statues of Our Lady did that, not spastics like Lizzy. "Watch your mouth," Mum snapped, and made me promise never to say anything like that around Lizzy's mother.

When we wheeled Lucien in, Lizzy's mother looked up from her magazine. "Isn't Milou with you?"

"She stayed in the car," Dad sighed. "This is the part she doesn't like."

"I understand." She flicked through a page or two. Dad zipped his leather jacket up to his chin, then half opened it again. "Everything okay? With you, I mean?"

"Yes, sure," she smiled. "Lizzy had a good day."

Lucien lived in the same bed back then, only parked by a different window. With our photos on the magnet board beside him, and a plastic dinosaur I had given him as a present. His view was a poster of the Ninja Turtles. Not because he liked them, but because we both had Ninja Turtle pyjamas. Crêpe-paper birds dangled from the ceiling, left over from the kid that lived in this bed before him.

"Lucien's nappy is full," I whispered to Dad. Even through his trousers I could see it hanging heavy between his legs. Mostly piss, I reckoned, because I couldn't smell anything. "Dad?"

"If it's full now, it'll be full when the nurses make their rounds. That's what they're paid for." Once he had lifted Lucien onto his bed and covered him clumsily with the blanket, we stood there for a moment.

"Have a good week's sleep." Lucien was already rocking his head from left to right on the pillow. I knew he would rock away until he fell asleep.

"Come on." Dad gently patted the bumps in the blanket. "Let's tell reception we've delivered your brother." He winked at Lizzy's mother.

Mum was still sitting on the back seat. Her hands seemed to be comforting one another. Dad always grumbled about it not being a taxi if Mum sat in the back while he drove. But now he studied her face in the rearview mirror and started the engine before I had fastened my seat belt.

"Everything go okay?" Mum asked in a feeble voice.

"The usual," Dad said.

"So will Lucien go back to sleep all week?"

Mum held a crumpled hanky in her fist. I couldn't tell from her eyes whether she'd been crying or not. "Do you want to stroke my fingers the way you do Lucien's?" I asked and held out my hand.

"You can stroke your own fingers," Mum said under her breath. I tilted toward her when we rounded a sharp bend. Then tipped upright as the car straightened up again.

I tried to make my fingers as gnarly and crooked as Lucien's. But I couldn't keep it up. And when I stroked the skin between them I mainly just noticed it was me doing it.

I spotted a toy dinosaur under the seat in front of me. He had wings, so that made him a glide-o-saurus. I nudged him toward me with my feet. There was a plastic line running down his belly with tiny words I didn't understand, though I could read the separate letters. His feet had three crooked toes that were too small to stroke.

Because he asked me to, I let the dinosaur look out the window and I pointed out the things we saw. Concrete lamppost, concrete lamppost, dented crash barrier. Tin cans in the grass. A bridge over another road. A carpet store. A mountain in the distance that wasn't a mountain at all but a big pile of rubble that steamed after it rained. A busted car tyre at the side of the road. A truck without a trailer. Bushes. McDonald's cartons. All this was new to the glide-o-saurus.

"We're going fast, aren't we?" I whispered.

He nodded.

"That's because my dad wants to get home quick."

We had just passed the railway crossing. I remember because Mum took my hand, laid it on her thigh, and started stroking the folds between all my fingers.

16

"Don't swat them," says Dad, though it's the first thing he does whenever a wasp goes near his mouth. The closer we get to the bottle bank, the more fiercely they zigzag in front of our faces. The broom bushes are full of pods. I pluck one, squeeze the peas out, and stroke the corner of my mouth with the fuzzy shell. It feels good but it doesn't tingle. We reach the top of the rutted track to our turf. Dad thinks it's best to wait here for the minibus that's bringing Lucien, so Jean and Brown Henri can't strike up a conversation with the driver.

"Not long now till my boys are back together." Dad shakes a loose stone from his flip-flop and rubs his hands together.

"Did you know our tenant can't have kids?"

"Huh?" Dad looks at me. "What are you on about?"

"Even though he wanted to. And so did she."

"What?"

"He told me."

"When?"

"He dropped by when you were out."

"And he tells you stuff like that?"

"With Louise."

"Who the hell's she?"

"His wife. But she won't call him back."

"Our cash machine has a wife?"

It feels good to feed Dad a story for once. Even if there's not much to it.

"So why did Louise kick him out?"

"How should I know?"

"Our tenant tells you everything by the sound of things."

"All I did was ask. And he answered."

"You asked?"

I nod.

"I asked too and all the guy said was 'compli-bloody-cated.'"

"Emile doesn't like questions."

"He doesn't seem to mind yours."

"He likes to know who's asking." I want to tell him Emile said Dad's lucky to have me, but I can't explain why he said it.

"Anything else to report? Was there a problem?"

The word *Mum* crops up too often in anything else I might say, so I shake my head.

"So that's it?"

I can't work out if he thinks it was too much or not enough.

"He was nice, that's all."

"Nice ..." Dad repeats.

A Renault minibus appears out of nowhere, feeling its way around the bend. "Just act casual, like we happen to be standing here, okay?" Dad strides out into the middle of the road, signals to the driver that he's in the right place and where to turn. Heads at the windows wobble and jolt in time to the bumps and potholes in the road. You can hear the rust groan on the straining suspension. Lucien is right at the back of the bus. A girl with a squashed face gives me the evil eye. I hoped Selma might have come along to see Lucien off. While Dad was sorting things out with the driver, I could have taken her over to our fridge for something to drink. That wouldn't have been weird, just nice. Everyone's thirsty when it's warm. And Lucien would get all excited and wobble like mad in his wheelchair so Dad would think Selma was his girl. Standing by the fridge, little stripes of shadow from the blinds would fall across her face. Rico would make her giggle by licking salt from the back of her knees. I would wait for the right moment and say sorry for being so unkind to her. I'd tell her I didn't have a choice and that I really wouldn't mind if we kissed properly. Selma would smile and hand me her empty tumbler because she'd want another drink first. Meanwhile Dad would be over by the minibus filling in form after form. And Selma would be allowed to stay as long as we promised to drive her back later. We'd go for chips at Mandy the Nail's.

"Turn first!" Dad shouts to the driver and mimes a semi-circle to show him how. He extends a friendly hand through the driver's open window and gives Lucien a thumbs-up. Dad and the driver start talking but I can't hear what they're saying.

The minibus reverses and its double flashing lights come on. Dad slaps the dusty back doors and rattles the handle but of course they're still locked.

"Chevalier?" The thin, beardy driver gets out and walks to the back of the bus, slow and stiff, like there's a steel rod up his back.

"We were expecting you half an hour ago."

"I couldn't see any house numbers." He flicks his head back to dodge a wasp. "Where exactly is your place?"

"Down the way," Dad says and points to the back doors of the bus, which are still locked. "When you didn't appear we decided to walk up to meet you."

"I'm supposed to drop the client off at the front door."

"You've still got plenty of deliveries to make by the look

of it." And when there's no answer, Dad says, "The road's been dug up further down, so you'd struggle getting that bus through."

As soon as the back doors open, every head turns to peer around its headrest. Every head except Lucien's. A linen bag is knotted to the handle of his wheelchair. I help Dad lift out the metal ramp. While the driver clicks Lucien's wheelchair loose, Dad steps back until he's standing beside me. "There's your brother."

The minibus waits ages before setting off again. In among the roots of his dark hair, Lucien's scalp is deathly pale, almost luminous. His calves tense as he tugs impatiently on the straps around the footrests. The sun stings and he tries to wipe it out of his eyes like it's shampoo. His face turns this way and that, but the blinding light finds him wherever he looks. A truckload of tree trunks thunders past and the minibus finally pulls out onto the road.

"Right then," Dad says. We both look at Lucien. It's only now—in a borrowed wheelchair, in the middle of our rutted track, without his bed around him—that I see how small he really is. His polo shirt is buttoned tight at the neck but hangs loose around his shoulders. His scrawny legs look bent out of shape. "Feffe," he mumbles.

In the linen bag I discover a toilet bag, six little tubs of applesauce, and the beaker he drinks from. I hope there might be something from Selma, a note maybe.

"Let's get him into the shade," Dad says.

Lucien twists as far as his seat belt will allow.

The smaller front wheels swing sideways at every clump of grass and get stuck in the tyre tracks in the hardened mud. Swearing, Dad spins the wheelchair around, tilts it back and drags Lucien along behind him. All the time he's got one eye on Jean and Henri's garage.

In the strip of shade by the caravan, Rico and Rita are lying with their mouths wide open, heads rising and falling to the rhythm of their panting. They see us coming but they're too lazy to get up and take a sniff at Lucien.

Dad parks the wheelchair next to the bed, with its back to the caravan. "Let him take in the view." Lucien rubs his cheek on his shoulder. "Give him a chance to acclimatize."

"Feffe, feffe." It sounds like a message the nurses have told him to pass on to us. For days I imagined Lucien being here, but I always pictured him in bed, sleeping. He never really did much else.

"Shouldn't there be a letter somewhere?"

Dad shakes his head like he doesn't understand. "A letter?"

"To tell us what to do." I have another grabble around in Lucien's bag. Nope, nothing from Selma. "Should I look in that file they gave us?"

"Knock yourself out."

I'm glad of the chance to do something, hopeful that someone has written down what's supposed to happen next. The file is on the cupboard by the TV.

"Got it!" I shout from inside. Through the window I can see the back of Lucien's head and that tuft of hair sticking up. Dad drums his fingers against his pursed lips, wrinkles his nose. Suddenly a wasp is hovering in front of Lucien's face. "Look out," I warn, but Dad has already chased it away.

"Maybe it's best if he just sits for a while," Dad says to me. "Or has a drink of something."

"Yeah," I say, looking at the table that lists Lucien's medicines. "There's something about that in the file."

"Feffe, feffe, feffe."

A gummy, grey nest is tucked beneath the roof edge. We've lifted Lucien onto the bed. He rocks from side to side, rubs his eyes with the inside of his forearm. A pair of swallows swoop around us, taking turns to dive for home. But with Lucien here, they keep veering off at the last minute.

Dad's busy moving things, dragging them from one place to another. Dark patches of earth appear in the grass in front of the caravan, along with ants' nests full of little shiny white eggs. I'm ordered to pour a kettle of boiling water over them. As Dad stands there taking a breather, he glances over at the garage and then back at Lucien. A little smile appears on his face when he realizes I've clocked him.

I can't take my eyes off Lucien. The way he lies there rocking endlessly in his bed while a strange new life goes on around him.

When Rico and Rita yawn, Lucien hears them. He works his way up onto his elbows and sticks his chin over the side of the bed to take a look. "Moo-wah-wah."

"Meet Rico and Rita. They're yours too, now. Kind of."

"Moo-wah-wah."

"Rita's the one without a tail." Now that Lucien is distracted, I try to give him something to drink. But he clamps his lips together and twists his mouth away without taking his eyes off the dogs.

Sitting on the doorstep of the caravan, I flick through Lucien's instruction manual and stop again at the table of medicines. I try to mouth their impossible names, work out how many pills he has to take and when. The boxes and bottles in the bag contain five different kinds. The table says nothing about why he has to take them, just sums up their side effects. Drowsiness tops every list. I count two mentions of reduced muscle strength.

And a warning that Lucien is not allowed to drive a motor vehicle. There's a chance of one in a hundred thousand that three of the five medicines could kill you. The phone number of the home is on the front page. Did Selma have a phone in her room? I can't remember. We never had to call Lucien. There's probably a group phone in every section.

"Come here!" Dad calls from behind the caravan. I help him carry two pallets that still look halfway decent round the front. My bed is going to be Lucien's indoor bed and Dad wants to knock something together to stop him falling out. For as long as my brother's here, I'm relegated to a mattress on the floor.

"What do the instructions say?" Dad asks, nodding at the file.

"There's a list of medicines we have to give him. Some of them can kill you."

Dad tries to read it upside down. "It's all poison in the end."

"Poison?"

"One pill cures your earache but gives you a pain in your knee. So they give you a powder for your knee but that makes you dizzy and gives you blisters on your tongue, so you need another two pills to sort that out."

"Lucien's got five."

"Could be worse."

"He has to take them every day. That's a lot of pills in a year."

"Your mum agreed all this with the home. That was her business. At first she went off the deep end about them pumping your brother full of pills, but when he started acting up around her she said 'yes' to any crap that was going." While he's talking, Dad holds one of the pallets at an angle and sticks the plug of his jigsaw in the extension cord. "Pop these on your brother's head, will you?" Dad chucks a pair of ear protectors my way. Lucien shrinks deeper into the pillow when I clamp them over his ears, shakes his head as the jagged wail of the saw rips through the air around us. When Dad's finished, I hear Lucien humming softly to himself.

"Do you know what they gave him that time with my ear?"

"Something to calm him down."

I hold up the file.

"Pff ..." He runs a pinkie caked in sawdust down the list. "Could be any of them."

"How do the doctors know where Lucien hurts?"

"I don't know."

"Then does he really need all these pills?"

"Bry, do I look like a doctor to you? We give your brother whatever's on the list."

Rico and Rita take cover in the shade under the bed, rubbing and twisting their backs against the slats on the underside of the mattress. Lucien hauls himself up and leans as far over the bed rail as he can, catches the occasional glimpse of Rico's swishing tail.

"Bry?"

"Hmm."

"I'm off out," Dad says, eyes fixed on the garage. "Forty minutes max."

"Where you off to?"

"To fetch some applesauce. Can't have your brother going hungry."

"And what about him?"

"He stays here with you."

"With me? No way. What am I supposed to do with him?"

"Just ... nothing at all. Let him watch the dogs. Make sure he doesn't swallow any wasps. Maybe give him something to drink. If he gets restless, stroke his hands a bit. It's not like you can do much wrong."

"And if something happens?"

"An hour tops, Brian. I'll be back before you know it."

Dad drives off and I go inside to put the file back where I found it. Everything looks so familiar in the caravan that I have trouble imagining Lucien lives with us now. I look out through the little window above the sink—he's still there.

Among last year's dog-eared school notebooks, I dig out a comic I haven't read in a while and settle down in Dad's easy chair. I catch my own reflection in the dark of the television screen, then decide to take another quick look through the window. Lucien is lying there peacefully enough. Back to the chair. Thirty-two minutes past three. I read the first few pages of my comic, though I know every speech bubble by heart. Three thirty-five, thirty-six. Outside, the high wall of poplars rustles. Swallows whistle and click. Three thirty-eight. I get absorbed in my comic again.

"Quarter to four!" I've left Lucien alone too long. I dash outside. He's still lying there. A flat little wasp hovers above his face, quivering with curiosity. It zips off to the side then back to his nose, hangs in the air above his forehead, then vanishes.

"Want a drink?"

Lucien's right arm is sticking out between the bars of the bed rail. Rico and Rita take turns licking his hand. "Hhhhhh," he sighs, and his mouth becomes one long yawn. "Watch it," I say. "They bite, you know." But Rico and Rita go on licking his fingers like an endless ice cream, without so much as a growl. Sometimes they lick at the same time, but mostly one waits patiently for the other to turn away.

Jean emerges from the garage, parks his oxygen tank and pulls out his lighter. From the way he stops in mid flow, I can tell he's spotted Lucien. He shouts something over his shoulder.

Henri appears, wiping his mucky paws on an old tea towel. I can see them mouthing off to one another. When I raise my hand, only Jean waves back before they disappear inside again.

17

"Hey Brian, take a look at this!" Dad yells excitedly. He's standing at the truck, leaning in past the steering wheel. "A welcome-home present for your brother." He pulls out a battered cardboard box with a banana on the side.

Beaming with pride, he holds it out to me. Towers of Duplo, built by the kid who used to own them. Toy cars, bashed about until the paint began to peel. A solitary domino tile. Dried-out needles from a Christmas tree are piled deep in the corners. "Not a bad haul, eh?"

I shrug. "What happened to the applesauce?"

"All in good time. This was a stroke of unexpected luck. Remember how you loved this stuff when you were a kid?"

What I remember most was Mum knotting our Duplo blocks in a pillow case and popping them in the washing machine. I never saw the need. Lucien had already sucked them clean. His toothmarks were all over my blocks.

Dad sidles up to me. "Anything happen while I was away?"

"What? With Lucien, you mean?"

He nods over at the garage. "Any visitors?"

"Jean came out for a smoke. He shouted to Henri and they both ogled us for a while."

"That was all?"

I nod.

"See! What did I tell you?" Dad looks pleased with himself. "They're all talk. Now your brother's here, they don't dare lift a finger." Lucien slams his foot against the banana box and sends the Duplo rattling. Rico and Rita think the noise means food and snuffle the foot of the bed.

"Fuckin' hell!" Dad yells. "Jesus!"

"What?"

"Have you seen the state of your brother? This cheek's fine ..." He grabs Lucien by the chin and turns his other cheek toward me. "But look." Half of his face is bright red, so red that the downy hairs on his cheek stand out like gold fuzz. Dad turns Lucien's head from side to side so I can see the difference, then let's go. "You might have put up a parasol or something."

"You said I couldn't do anything wrong."

"That's when your brother was still in the shade."

Lucien presses his sunburned cheek deep into the pillow. The insides of his arms are red too.

"What now?" We'll have to call the home. Maybe Selma will pick up the phone. No, of course she won't.

"Let's get him into the shade first." Dad is already halfway to the swimming pool behind Emile's caravan. Lucien licks the corners of his mouth.

I take his chin carefully between finger and thumb, and turn his head to take another look at the difference. His neck, the rims of his ear, and one side of his forehead are glowing. I press a white patch on his skin with my pinkie. It turns bright red again as soon as I let go. "Sorry, bro," I say. "I need to look out for you more." I hold his face still and run my thumbs under his eyes. "You like this, don't you? That's how Selma does it."

"Huu-huu-huu!"

"Selma," I say again. Lucien wobbles, starts to twist and crane his neck to see over my shoulder. "Hey, settle down. Selma's not here."

Dad comes back with a party tent that's been lying in

the weeds and the mud since last year. "Never chuck anything out," he shouts triumphantly. He's carrying the tent by two legs while the other two jerk through the grass behind him.

Lucien frowns at the flapping white roof unfolding above him. Long-legged spiders creep out of the creases. "Don't be scared," I whisper to him. "Now you won't get sunburned anymore." We brush away the cobwebs and fumble with the guy ropes. One of them won't reach all the way to the caravan, so I tie it to the bed. When I pull the other one tight, I can just fasten it to one of the bars of the dog cage. Dad rolls the rim of an old car wheel ahead of him with his foot, lets it topple beside the bed, and ties the final rope to that. "Right then ..."

We shake the legs of the tent and dried mud shimmies down the plastic. We brush the stray crumbs from Lucien's sheet.

"Oh, yeah," Dad says brightly. "Nearly forgot." He walks over to the back of the pickup. "Close your eyes."

I hear a dull thud on the grass, then rustling and a command for the dogs to stay away. When he lets me look, I open my eyes to see a six-foot stretch of Astroturf rolled out beside the bed. "Our half-cooked lobster will want for nothing."

"Where did you get that?"

"It was going begging. Sweet price."

"What else you got back there?"

"Can't I treat my boys once in a while?"

"Yeah, but ..."

"Kick off those flip-flops," he commands cheerfully. "Take a little walk."

It feels soft beneath my feet.

"And?" A thump on my shoulder.

"Yeah, feels good."

"Well then."

"We need to put something on Lucien's cheek. Want me to call and ask if they know what's best?"

"If who knows what's best?"

"The number in Lucien's file. In case there's a problem."

"Are you mad?" he barks, as if I've got the phone in my hand. "What's that you say, sir? Lucien's been home one afternoon and already he's got a faceful of blisters? Why, that won't do. The minibus will be round to pick him up directly." Dad grabs the bar at the foot of the bed and lifts it a little way off the ground. Lucien is too busy glowering at the plastic above his head to notice. His right cheek looks fiercely ashamed of itself.

"Full-fat yoghurt," Dad says. "Works like a charm."

18

The light that creeps into the bedroom with me makes his crooked, curled-up legs look even paler. Lucien has kicked off the covers. Dad's pallets have made a fortress of what used to be my bed. Quiet as I can, I tiptoe to the mattress on the floor. My shadow ripples over Lucien's body. His breath is moist, his eyes stay shut.

I let my swimming trunks drop to the floor and kick them away, then kneel down and pull the empty duvet cover over me. Even that's too warm. Dad's silhouette fills the open door. "Can I turn out the light?"

"Sure," I say. "Sleep tight."

"You too. Both of you."

A few moments later everything goes black. I hear Dad shut the door to his room and listen to the familiar rummaging around his bed. The clink of his belt buckle, the kicking off of his boots. Night racers skid round a bend in the distance and tear full-throttle onto the bridge.

I snap awake to the sound of someone being strangled. Two minutes to three. I feel my way along the cord to switch on the bedside lamp. Lucien scrunches his eyes in the glare. Three fingers are jammed into his mouth, pinkie and thumb sticking out either side. "What are you doing?" I pull his arm aside so that I can peer down his throat. He tries to bring his fingers back to his face. "Don't," I say. "You'll choke if you don't watch out."

"Nga-nga-nga." The contents of his beaker have stained

the mattress pink. The yoghurt mask on his cheek has burst and smeared into his hair.

"Do you want a drink?" There's still a little left in the bottom of his beaker. His tongue reaches for the spout. "Here, drink this up for now."

The bedroom door slams open. "Jesus, Dad. What are you doing?"

"I heard someone choking, and I thought ..." A long yawn, hollow scratching by his crotch. "... maybe he had you by the throat."

"He's thirsty."

"Go back to sleep," he mumbles, mainly to himself, and leaves us alone. Lucien slurps air from his empty beaker.

"More?"

He jerks his shoulder toward his ear because he thinks I'm going to tickle him, but I'm only trying to straighten his pillow. "I'll get you a refill." The tip of a cigarette glows in the dark of our little bathroom. A trickle of piss hits the bowl, then the sound of pumping until the toilet flushes.

"Try and get some sleep," I whisper to Lucien once I've given him some fresh water. I stroke between his pinkie and his ring finger. I don't know if it's helping, but he closes his eyes.

"Calmed down a bit in here?" Dad's sleepy head peers round the door.

"I think so."

"What was up?"

"Thirsty."

"You can bunk up with me, you know."

"With you?"

"If he's keeping you awake. With that choking of his."

"I'm okay."

“Or you could try and kip on the bed outside. Mosquitoes might eat you alive though.”
“He’s already nodded off.”

The night is fading to light blue. The hoarse cackle of a pheasant sounds below our window. It wakes Lucien too. His pyjama top has crept up, baring part of his belly. His nappy is lopsided. I lean across and rattle the window. The pheasant makes a show of flurrying off and settling down a yard or two further along. Those dopey birds can’t fly, only they don’t seem to know it. There’s something la-di-da about them, as if someone dreamt them up—a posh lady poet caked in makeup.

A construction lamp is shining down on the big steel doors of Brown Henri’s garage. Rita barks. Then Rico. Then Rita again. “Shhh!” I hiss at them to keep quiet and toss one of my flip-flops at their cage, but I’m too late. A distant dog barks back. Lucien’s eyes open and glint in the bluish light. “Moo-wah-wah.”

“Yeah, it’s the dogs.”

I can’t tell if he’s cold or not, but I pull the covers over his legs just to be sure.

19

I find a pen and write Selma's number on the inside of my arm. Lucien has been rocking away since he woke up. Dad's gone out in the hope of earning some easy money. It will be at least another week before Lucien's allowance starts coming in. I'm in luck—while I was in the shower Dad stuck a fresh nappy on him.

Footsteps by the door. The puff of an oxygen tank. "Brian?"

"What is it?"

"Where are you?"

"In my room." I can't remember Jean ever coming in here before. He's got Henri in tow.

"Is that him?" Jean pants, clinging to the doorpost of my bedroom.

I nod. Jean and Henri both do their best not to look at Lucien. "What's your brother's ... name again?"

"Lucien."

"What's up with him?" Henri asks, as if Lucien's not supposed to hear.

"Sunburn. They didn't tell us he's not used to the sun."

"I mean, was he born that way?"

"I think so. Something in Mum's belly. Nothing she could have done."

"And Maurice has left you alone ... with your brother?" Jean takes a look around my room.

"There's not much I can do wrong."

The oxygen tank hisses. Jean shakes his head.

"How long's he staying?"

"You'll need to ask Dad. He'll be back this afternoon."

Their eyes dart back and forth and I can tell they've agreed on something. "Here you go," Jean says and pulls two cans of energy drink from his trouser pockets. Still cold.

"Thanks," I say, and wonder what's coming next.

"I thought you might like it."

"Hey, Brian," Henri interrupts. "How long did you say your brother was staying?"

"Don't know."

"One week? Two weeks?"

"You heard me. I don't know."

Henri pushes Jean aside and grabs me by the arm.

"Ow," I yelp. "Let go of me."

"Don't hurt the boy," Jean says.

"How long is your brother here for?"

"I. Don't. Know."

"Yes, you do." Henri pinches my arm and twists.

"You're hurting me."

"There's more where that came from."

I look at Jean for help, but he's fiddling anxiously with the mole on his neck. I try to squirm loose but Henri only tightens his grip. "How long's your brother here for?"

"Just tell him." Jean runs his hand over my shoulder. "We won't let on to your dad."

"A month, maybe."

"A month?" They exchange a brief glance. "See! What did I tell you?" Henri's grip slackens and I pull myself free.

"For fuck's sake," Jean growls.

Without another word, Henri storms out of my room and exits the caravan.

"Sorry, Brian. But this is no place for a kid, especially

not a kid like him." Jean must mean it or he would never have crammed so many words into one breath. "And your dad knows that full well."

"Don't tell him I told you."

Jean taps me on the cheek. "You're the only one who can give yourself away. Keep your mouth shut. We'll do the same."

20

Lucien sucks on the wet facecloth I've given him. I feed him one of the little tubs of applesauce and follow it up with a few chunks of bread. Henri and Jean have really gone—I checked twice.

"Do you want to take a walk?"

He stops rocking.

"The way you did with that Thibaut guy." I lift his right foot from the mattress. It's warm and dry. I expect it to be soft and pliable but it's all knots and bones. His tendons are tight, the corners of his toenails sharp.

I start by turning his ankle every which way. Lucien hums but he doesn't seem to feel me touching him. It's as if the foot in my hands isn't really his and they accidentally clicked someone else's leg into his hip before they loaded him into the minibus. I dig my thumbnail into his little toe. Lucien goes on humming. I dig deeper and he tries to pull his foot away. "Sorry." I move his ankle in every direction, push until it won't go any further, then push a little more. "I'm reminding your feet what they can do." Thibaut's words sound weird coming from my mouth, but it feels like I'm doing it right.

All the while, Lucien sucks on the facecloth and rubs his forearm over the ridges on the wallpaper. "I'm going to teach your feet to walk like they used to. Promise."

Once I've done both ankles, I run my thumbs over the soft skin of his soles. His toes fan out. "They're awake now, too." Then I brush away the sand and the black fuzz.

I don't remember Thibaut doing that, but I guess it can't do any harm.

Then I knead his calves. His legs are so thin and bony, I'm not really sure what to do with them. Skin is all that seems to be holding his kneecaps in place. When I try to pin one down between finger and thumb, it shoots away like a bar of soap that's been washed smooth. I start to worry I'm going to break something.

His thighs are easier to knead. Lucien starts to shudder a little.

"Now we're going to cycle." I climb onto the bed. "Come on. Pedal, pedal." By tickling the back of his knee, I get one leg to bend, then do the same with his other knee. In a reflex he almost kicks me in the face. "Watch out!" He rams his feet against my chest and his head hits the headboard, snapping forward.

"Careful or you'll break your neck." But Lucien's feet keep on pushing. I climb off the bed. "Okay then, let's walk."

By tugging on his arms, I manage to raise his upper body from the bed. Then I slide one arm under his knees to lift his legs. It's no good—his bum stays anchored to the mattress. He makes a grab for my face. I'm not going to be able to do this alone.

"Lie there, I'll be right back."

Emile holds the door to his caravan open a crack. "Can't you get your father to help you?"

"He's away. Working."

There's no way I can ask Henri or Jean, so that just leaves Emile.

"All you have to do is help me carry him outside."

"All right. It'll give me a chance to meet him."

Meet him? A spot of heavy lifting's all I'm asking for.

"Is he much older than you?"
"Three years. He's sixteen." A pair of storks circle the electricity pylons in the distance. "Has Louise ...?"
"No."
"You don't even know what I was going to ask."
"Yes I do. And the answer is no."
"Oh."
"Every time the phone didn't ring, it was her."
"Huh?"
"It's a line from a song."
"You're good with words."
"I studied English. That's how I ended up teaching."
"That makes it sound like you took a wrong turn."
"You're not far wrong."
"So you're a teacher?"
"Indeed I am, my boy."

Lucien has got hold of a corner of the curtain. Emile is lingering by my desk. I don't know what's so fascinating about my notebooks and comics. Or my cupboard with its open doors and empty shelves. Or the clothes I've worn, waiting in heaps on the floor until they're clean enough to put on again.
"So, you're Brian's brother?" Emile strokes Lucien's calf briefly. "Pleased to meet you."
"He can't talk."
"Can he understand me?"
"Kind of."
Without taking a moment to get used to him, Emile slides his arm under Lucien's armpits.
"Or would you rather take this end?"
"No, no. I'm fine."
Lucien's knees bend easily. He stares intently at Emile, absorbing this new face. "The tighter you hold him, the less scared he is."

"Okay," Emile says.

I count to three and we lift him off the bed. Lucien gives himself over to us without hesitation, as if he senses we've never done this before and he has to cooperate. Taking care not to bump into anything, we carry him out of my bedroom.

As we pass the kitchen counter he lunges for the cups. "Whoa," Emile shouts. Lucien's other hand trails past the framed photo of my gran on the wall. "Look out." Too late. The portrait comes clattering toward us. Gran with her huge glasses. Skin sucked tight around her jaws and cheekbones. Her mouth a crease of disapproval, because she knew we would let her fall one day. Glass shatters across the floor.

Startled, Lucien jerks and yells, "Feffe, feffe, feffe!"

"Apologies," Emile says. "I didn't see it in time. Couldn't get my hand free."

Once we're outside, we put Lucien down with his feet on the Astroturf. Over in their cage, Rico and Rita perk up. "Right," Emile says. "Where do you want him? On the bed?"

"We're going for a walk. He's supposed to practise." I hold out my arm to Lucien, and he latches onto it all by himself. His feet mash up and down on the spot.

"Can you manage without help?"

"Yeah, I'll be fine."

"Are you sure?"

"I can do this on my own. He's my brother."

I want Emile to bugger off, but as soon as he walks away it feels like something's missing. "Do you want something to drink?" I call out.

"No thanks."

Lucien claws the neck of my T-shirt and his other hand

tugs at my hair. "Let go of me. Let go!" Emile runs back over and grabs Lucien by the wrist. His grip loosens.

"Ngang-ngang-ngang."

A few loose hairs blow from Lucien's fingers, his feet stamp the Astroturf.

"He nearly had you by the throat."

"You can go. I'll be all right from here."

Emile still has a firm hold on Lucien, who tries to sit down on an invisible chair.

"Take my arm," I tell him. "The way you did Thibaut's."

He doesn't respond, so I hold my arm right below his paws and clamp them around it. Emile lets go.

"First this foot." I'll show Emile I've got this sorted. "Now that foot." I tap his toes with my flip-flop.

"Shouldn't he be wearing shoes?" Emile asks.

Where are those stupid velcro shoes of his? "They're in the caravan. Can you hold him a sec?"

"Why don't we just lay him on the bed?"

"But he has to walk."

Lucien lets go of my arm and reaches for the bed rail. He clutches it, then puts his other hand down next to it. Without any help from us, he shuffles one step, then two, around the foot of the bed. "Good lad!" Emile says.

"Pfff," Emile sighs once we've got Lucien onto the bed. "That was hard work. You're good at this, you know."

"At what?"

"Good with him, I mean. He trusts you."

"But he barely even walked!"

"A little further every day. Your brother needs to get used to things too." Emile wafts a cool breeze over his belly with the front of his shirt. "Shame about that photo."

"That was my gran."

"Your father won't like that much."

I shrug. "He only started calling her 'dear old mum' after she died. We only visited her five times in my whole life."

In my memory, smoke came out of her mouth even when she didn't have a cigarette between her lips. There was always something smouldering inside her. She sat there coughing and watching telly all day, especially the adverts. "Don't need that," she'd mumble, shaking her head. "Don't need that." And every once in a while, "Already got one of them."

"Dear old mum." Emile smiles. "Sometimes you appreciate people more when they're gone."

"How do you mean?"

"I have far better conversations with my father now that he's dead."

"Do you believe in ghosts?"

"No, no. But at least his gravestone lets me finish a sentence."

Emile sizes up our caravan.

"Don't you want to live in a house?"

"What's wrong with this place?"

"I'm sure there are agencies that could help. What, with you being a child."

"I suppose."

"A caravan gets pretty cold in the winter, I'll bet."

"It's not so bad."

"A house is nicer. Gives you more stability. More people your age in the neighbourhood. I don't see anyone your age around here. Or am I missing something?"

"They're all away on holiday now anyway. Besides, you live in a caravan too."

"Yes, but that's temporary. I'll move back into a house one day."

"Will you?"

Emile looks straight at me for a while, then catches himself doing it. He lowers his eyes. "At least I hope so."

21

An itchy cloud of mosquitoes is swarming above a mountain of car tyres. The sun has already dipped behind the treetops, but it's still warm enough for Lucien. Curled up on his side in his outdoor bed, skin shining. A sea creature washed up on the beach, panting for breath. His hair is wet from the shower but a smudge of tomato sauce still clings to his chin. He's lying on a couple of towels to stop the mattress getting too wet. "Let's leave him to dry in the breeze," Dad said when I started towelling him down. "Then all we'll have to do is give him a quick rub in a little while."

"How did you manage to get him outside anyway?" Dad asks.

"What do you mean?"

"He was out here when I got back but I left him inside with you."

"I lifted him."

"Alone?"

"No."

Dad looks over at the garage.

"The tenant gave me a hand."

"The tenant? You let him handle your brother?"

"Lucien's too heavy for me on my own. And you were gone all of a sudden."

I've never seen a back as white as Lucien's. The darker skin of his ball sack bulges between his legs and there's a kind of seam that runs through the tight clutch of wrinkles and disappears between his buttocks. I wonder if I'm going to get one of those. At least his dick has shrunk back to normal again, the size of a smooth pinecone. We both have black hair, though his is blacker than mine. Lucien's eyes are staring at nothing. The way he's lying deepens the long dent in his breastbone.

When he still lived at home, Mum used to bath us together. I had to squash up or there wasn't enough room for my brother to lie down. I used to sit with my bum on the plug and that metal thing in my back. "Stop moaning," Mum would say. "Be happy you can sit up by yourself." Bath toys bobbed around us. Lucien lay with his ears underwater, sucking on a flannel.

Whenever Mum left us alone for a bit, I would dunk the toy watering can below the surface and pour water over him to make a little pool in the dent in his chest. Then came the best bit. Lucien would hiccup and splash as soon as I started filling the watering can again, his toenails scratching the side of my bum impatiently. Then I let the water rain down on his willy, which stiffened and sent a fountain of wee over his belly and my squashed-up legs.

In the shower just now, Lucien's dick got bigger too. Dad didn't mention it.

He plops the top off a bottle of beer with his lighter. "I've earned this."

"Feffe, feffe," Lucien mumbles. A gust of wind sends a shiver up his back, all the way to his neck. Dad is leaning over the bed rail, middle finger stuck in the mouth of the bottle. That's how he always holds his beer.

"Feffe, feffe." Lucien begins to shake. "Feffe."

"Yeah yeah, son. Tell me about it," Dad says. He takes a long swallow.

Lucien's hands are like the grabber in a fairground machine. You never win a cuddly toy at the fair. But Lucien grabs the bottle in one go.

His eyes light up and his whole body shudders with excitement as he strains to pull his prize toward his chest. "Oh no you don't! Let go." Gulps of beer splash over Lucien's belly and his sheets. "Let go!" Dad commands. Rico and Rita spring to attention but can't figure out what they've done wrong. Dad tries to twist the bottle from Lucien's hands without spilling any more. "Let go, you little …!"

"FEFFE!" Lucien bellows. I stand there hesitating, wondering whether to help. "FEFFE!"

"All right, have it your way." Dad pulls Lucien's hand over the edge of the bed and tips the bottle until the rest of the beer spills onto the grass.

"Were you paying attention in the shower?" Dad nods at Lucien.

Did he notice Lucien's dick after all? I shrug.

"Then you can manage it without me next time."

"On my own?"

"What do you think?"

"Uh … together?"

"Together? We can't do everything together."

"Are you going to leave me here alone every day?"

"Your brother's getting cold." He tucks one of the towels around Lucien. "We'll put a clean nappy on him in a while. There's another thing you'll need to learn." So far I've managed make myself scarce when Dad cleans him. "Or would you rather leave him lying in his own shit whenever I'm away?"

"Of course not."

Our eyes follow the bee buzzing above Lucien's face. Just as Dad's getting ready to swat it away, it flies off and vanishes into a sandy tunnel in the grass, smaller than a mousehole. The entrance is dotted with orange-black bits of fluff, all dead.

"Do you remember that time with the bumble bees?"

"Huh?" I try to look puzzled but I know exactly what Dad is talking about. I like to hear him tell it, mainly because he always ends by giving my nose a gentle tweak. No idea why.

"We went swimming one afternoon, it was when your mum was still around. Over at the sand quarry, remember?"

"The one where the diver drowned?"

"Might be, yeah. You saw those little buggers flying around and asked 'Dad, are bumble bees fur coats for pixies?'"

"Did I really say that?"

"Ha! Bet your life you did. You were about this high." His hand pats my invisible head at hip height. "Genius! Give me a coat of bumble-fur any day." He slides two knuckles over my nose and tweaks.

"When's your birthday?" I ask.

"If you start skinning 'em now," Dad chuckles, "you could run me up a sleeve for my fortieth."

22

"What do you think you're playing at?" I hear Dad shout. "It's the crack of bleedin' dawn!"

"Any later and you'd have done another runner." Henri's voice. "Seems like you're hardly ever around these days."

"Some of us have to work for a living."

"Oh, is that right?"

"Damn right!"

"Even if it means leaving your youngest to take care of his own brother?"

"I can't be everywhere at once."

"First you have your disabled son shipped in and suddenly you're out working all hours."

"Only because you keep banging on about the fucking money I owe you."

"No need to play the victim, Maurice. You're months behind. And where's our share of the tenant's rent?"

"What share?"

"The tenant was supposed to cough up at the end of the week."

"I'm working on it."

"Listen, Maurice ..." Jean's there, too. "We gave you a chance ... two days ... to come and see us."

"About what?"

"That boy of yours ... for Brian we made an exception. But this ..."

"Where else is my Lucien supposed to go?"

"We made ourselves crystal clear ... and still you fetched him here."

I ease open my door. Henri and Jean are standing with their backs to me. Dad is pacing up and down in his underpants, scratching his arms like his tattoos are itching. "It's only for a few more days," he says to calm things down. "He'll be gone before you know it."

"Don't lie."

Dad's eyeballs just about pop out of his head. "I'm not lying!"

"A month! A fucking month, Maurice. That's what we heard."

Silence.

"That's … that is … not true."

"Oh no?"

"A week tops."

"And that bed is still being sold on at a profit?"

"Lucien's in it for now. Meanwhile, it's up for sale."

"Well, we're in the market. How much do you want for it?"

"No can do." Dad hesitates. "Already found a buyer."

"Liar!" Henri spits the word in his face. Dad reels from an unexpected jab to his shoulder and his head slams into a cupboard door. Jean reins Henri in.

"We're giving you one week, Maurice."

"For what?"

"To settle what you owe. Every penny."

"A week?"

"Plus our share from the tenant. If you're working as much as you say you are, that shouldn't be a problem."

"Or else?"

"You'll find out soon enough."

Dad clenches his fist and pounds his chest. "You two can't touch me."

"You heard, Maurice." The pair of them turn on their heels and march out. As they go, only Jean sees me watching. "Ten days!" Dad calls after them. "Give me ten days."

As soon as they've left, he dives into his clothes.

"Where are you going?" I ask.

"To work."

"Do you have any work?"

"Are you going to start on me now?" Dad checks his head's not bleeding.

"What are Jean and Henri going to do to you?"

"Nothing, nothing at all. People are all talk when they want you to pay up. They might tighten the thumbscrews, but that's it. Go too far and they'll never see their money again."

"Why don't you just pay the rent?"

"That's enough, Bry. And how do they know your brother's here for a month?"

It takes a second or two but I answer without blinking. "I don't know."

"Who else could have told them?" His eyes burn into mine.

"Emile," I say.

"The tenant?"

"Could be."

"What does he know about it?"

"He asked."

"Je-sus fuck-ing Christ." It sounds like a hunk of rock crashing down a slope. He slips into his flip-flops, fishes his keys from his jeans pocket.

"Where are you going?"

"To work. You deaf?"

23

"Can I use your phone?"

"Uh," Emile hesitates, surprised to see me standing in his kitchen. "I'd rather you waited outside till I invite you in."

"Okay," I reply. "But can I?"

"Is it an emergency?"

"No." All his dirty dishes have been washed and put away. The aluminium counter is shining like never before.

"Do you want something to drink?" He gestures to me to sit down. "All I have is coffee."

"No, I'm okay," I say, hoping that might help appease him. "Can I make a call?"

"Hmm ... the nature of your call is really none of my business. But I'm going to ask you anyway."

"A girl."

"A girl?" He slides the phone across the table toward me. "You can test to see if it's working. Or if it's only me no one picks up for."

It weighs less than a remote control.

I look at him. "Would you mind leaving me alone for a bit?"

That little smile of his pops into place. "Of course not." He looks around to see if he can leave things where they are, then grabs his keys and his puzzle book. "I'll wait in the car."

"It won't take that long."

"See how it goes."

I start keying in the number of the home, but by accident I wind up in a list of sent messages. To Louise. The last one is only a question mark. Sent late last night. The one before that is a question mark too. Sent a few minutes earlier. The message before that says *Call me. Please? E.*

The further back I click, the longer they get. *I know I don't have the right, but I'm worried about you.* The fish in the aquarium follow my every move with their tiny, glassy eyes.

Let me say sorry, please. Hear me out, just once. Don't punish me this way. E.

No reply anywhere.

Hate me if you have to. But give me a chance to do right by you. Please. Let me have that at least. E.

Suddenly the caravan door opens. "Can you manage?"

From fright, I drop the phone in my lap. "The line's busy."

Emile wipes his feet.

"Wait! Not yet. Let me give it one more go."

He turns around, thank goodness.

I key in the number again. "Hello, this is Selma's uncle," I repeat to myself. "I would like to speak to Selma please. I am Selma's uncle." The phone rings twice. My heart seems to be juddering instead of beating.

"Saint Francis Care Group. Esmée Dujardin speaking."

"Hello," I whisper.

"Pardon?"

"I am calling for Selma."

"I'm sorry, I didn't catch your name."

"I am her uncle. Could you ask Selma to come to the phone, please?" I try to talk louder, to sound like a grumpy uncle who's in a hurry and wants to ask a quick question.

"Certainly. If you could just repeat your name for me?"

"Emile," is the first thing that comes into my head.

"And your surname?"

"That is my surname."

"Oh, I see ... And your first name is ...?"

"She lives on the first floor," I interrupt.

"Yes, I know who Selma is. But I am afraid I can't connect you unless you tell me your full name."

"Maurice Emile." Hesitant, but I don't think she noticed.

"Maurice Emile. One moment please, just putting you on hold." *Beep* ... *Beep* ... I've done it. "Selma, it's me," I practise. There's a strange rushing sound in my ear. I look around the caravan. "Hello?" I ask, and hear my voice echo. *Beep* ... *Beep* ... Is someone listening in while I'm on hold? I focus on the sound when it comes again and realize it's my own breathing. "Maurice Emile," I repeat. Perhaps she's putting me through to the rec room on Selma's floor. Or someone is taking a mobile up to her. I'll have to tell her what to say so she doesn't give me away as a non-existent uncle. Tell her to say "Hello, Uncle Maurice." Then make sure she's alone before I let her know it's me.

"Mr. Emile?"

"Yes," I say, in my own voice by accident.

"Thank you for waiting. I've been through Selma's list of contacts. But ..." A tut, then a mouse click. "No, I don't see a Maurice Emile ... Could you be listed under another name?"

"As her uncle. Her mum's brother. And Selma has black hair. Down to her shoulders. And she only needs to come to the phone for a minute."

"I have several names listed here. Yours is not among them."

"I don't call often."

"But your name is not on her list of contacts."

"Well you should add it." Ha! That's a good one.

"I'm afraid that's not how it works."

"How come?"

"Only a parent or guardian can add a contact to Selma's telephone list."

"I told you, I'm her uncle. Just put her on, will you."

"There's no need to be so insistent, Mr. Emile ..." Her voice remains irritatingly calm.

"I want to speak to Selma."

"Mr. Emile, I am going to end this conversation. And to file a report, because I'm afraid I don't tru—" I press all the keys at once and a frantic orchestra of beeps blares from the phone. *Call ended*, the green screen says. One minute forty-nine.

The door opens immediately.

"Wasn't Selma there?"

I shake my head. Then I realize I haven't told him her name.

"Were you listening in?"

"It was hard not to. You were practically yelling down the phone."

Emile sits down across from me.

"I thought you were going to wait in the car?"

"Even there I could hear you." He wipes a greasy print from the screen. "Do you know her from school?"

The coffee rings on the tabletop look like they've been drawn with Spirograph. I trace them with my finger.

"I know her through Lucien."

"Do you mean she ..." Emile looks at me in surprise. "Is she a patient like your brother?"

"No, no," I say, determined to look back at him until I win. "I saw her a few times at the home. Her sister lives there."

"Ah, I see." A little smile. "Of course. And are you two an item? Or whatever they call it these days?"

I shrug.

"You can try again another time, if you want. What is it you like about her?"

"Don't know. I just do."

"Well, that's none of my business anyway. Does she ever come here?"

"No, she lives ..." I almost put my foot in it. "A long way away."

24

"How long were you in there with the tenant?"

I jump. "Not long." I had Selma on my mind as I walked back to the caravan, and didn't notice the pickup parked outside.

"Cosy little chat?" The cigarette between Dad's lips bounces up and down when he talks.

"Just normal."

"Normal?"

"He told me he was a teacher. English."

"Go over there a lot, do you?"

"No. First time. I bump into him now and again."

"That's odd."

"What is?"

"I never bump into him."

"He likes me, I think."

Dad looks at me like I've dried myself off with one of Emile's used towels and he can smell it on me. "From now on, stay out of his way."

"But wasn't I supposed to sort out the rent?"

"Sort out your brother. That's enough to be going on with."

"Why?"

"Be nice to the tenant, like. But any problems and you wait for me."

"I need his help to get Lucien out of bed."

"Keep him away from your brother. If something needs doing, wait till I get back."

"But that can take all day."

"Is that right?" It looks more like he's chewing on his cigarette than smoking it. "I'm here now, aren't I?"

I shrug and he thumps me on the shoulder.

"Well then, take a look what I wangled for you!" Petrol slops in the little tank he lifts off the back of the pickup. "You can finally give that scooter of yours a go."

25

"I have to go out for a bit." I ride a toy car along his arm, up his neck, behind his ear, through his black hair, and onto his forehead. I keep going until he hiccups with laughter. He keeps nudging my hand with his cheek so I'll stroke him.

"Back soon." I arrange the blanket so the cord won't show, in case Dad returns before I do. One last check—I slide two fingers between the cord and each of his ankles.

"Have an extra drink." Lucien sucks a vacuum in the beaker. "A bit more?" He twists his mouth away. His wrist pulls on the clear plastic cable tie I looped through a hole in the pallet just to be sure. "As long as you don't turn over, it won't hurt." I tied a sock around his wrist to cushion the plastic. "I'll be back before you know it," I assure him and leave the door open to let in some air. "Sorry, bro."

The saddle is so hot I can barely sit on it. I push my scooter through the grass, which is almost up to my knees in places. *I'll be back soon, I'll be back soon.* It's like a chant in my head. I slam my full weight down on the pedal and turn the right grip toward me. The scooter roars and roars again. It works! The pointer on the fuel gauge says the tank is half full. "Selma, Selma," I whisper. "It's all going to work out."

I want to feel the wind in my hair but it's a long drive to the home and I don't want anyone to notice me. The helmet is an old one of Dad's, the foam rubber lining crumbles to powder when you press it. At least the visor is dark enough to hide my eyes. The kickstand rattles along with the sputtering of the engine. I check the money in my pocket one more time, enough to get me home if I run out of petrol. The cans of energy drink in my back pockets dig into my bum. It's much too warm, but I zip up my jacket anyway. One last look over my shoulder at the curtains hanging limply in Lucien's window.

The first stretch is a bumpy ride across the grass, and I have to stick my legs out to keep my balance. Once I'm through the gate, I turn the accelerator all the way. After following the main road for what seems like ages, I turn off along the stony river, past the electricity pylons and the sawmill. At the concrete steps up to the bridge, I have to get off and push but it's much easier than I thought it would be.

I overtake an accelerating truck hauling a trailer stacked with tree trunks and find myself on a road I barely know, all dips and rises. Trees crowd in on both sides, sweating resin. I can't see beyond the next bend. The spruces look dead up to head height, their broken branches like the antlers of deer hiding in the woods.

Suddenly, I hit a road that looks familiar. The stream glinting up at me from the bottom of the slope is the same one that runs through our turf. The air seems to part and let me through. I lean forward in the saddle and all I can see is the trembling pointer on my speedometer and the asphalt ahead. The wind cools my knuckles, but my palms are sweaty. A car blasts its horn—I shouldn't even be on this road. *Selma, Selma, Selma.* I see us swimming in the stream. Our hands searching for each other underwater as she presses herself to me, the unexpected warmth of her belly against mine.

I'm worried someone will catch me if I drive up to the main entrance, so I leave my scooter in the cover of the rhododendron bushes by the bins. A shiver shoots up my back all the way to my damp forehead. Even my ears are slick with sweat. Through the branches, I can see the grey walls of the home. Now I'm not here to see Lucien, it looks like a whole different building.

"Selma?" I try again.

She is sitting no more than three feet from the television, staring intently at the screen. Selma's sharing now—there's a new bed opposite hers, another girl's posters on the walls.

With a tiara on her head and in clothes I've never seen her wear before, she could almost be someone else. Smaller than my thoughts had made her. I'm looking forward to her eyes, though she could still be angry with me.

"Selma?" Her neck has dipped between her shoulders. She doesn't want to miss a moment of the film. A clip-on earring sparkles beside her cheek. Her mouth mumbles along with the princess and hangs open whenever the prince speaks. Prince and princess say goodbye, tilt their heads and suck their mouths together. Selma edges closer to the screen and the credits roll. "The end," I say and tap her on the shoulder. "Did you like it?" Selma looks up, startled. "I've come back. For you."

She stands up so abruptly that she drops the remote control.

"Don't be scared," I stammer and pick it up off the floor. Selma retreats to a corner of her bed, gathers her dolls and hugs them to her chest. She puts her other hand over her eyes. "Don't be scared," I say softly. "I've come to say I'm sorry."

As gently as I can, I pull her hand aside. She fends me off with her elbow.

"I didn't want to be nasty to you the other day in the car park but I had to. Dad was there and he can't know that we ... Do you understand? I tried to call, but they wouldn't let me talk to you."

There's a click from the video recorder, and the tape whines its way back to the start.

"Look." I hold up a can of energy drink and sit down beside her on the bed. "A present."

Two fingers in front of her face scissor open.

"Do you want me to open it?" Her eyes follow my movements. A hiss escapes the opening and I rush the can to my lips to slurp the froth. "Oops."

Selma gives a little giggle. The tip of her tongue appears between the tight line of her lips. "For me?" She points a finger between her breasts. "No sharing?"

"Look!" I pull the other can from my inside pocket. "This one's for you."

Dolls tumble from her lap, their arms outstretched toward her. "No sharing," she says, shaking her head.

"It's all yours."

Selma squeezes dents in the can, froth fizzes over the rim.

"Are you still angry?" I ask.

After a couple of greedy swallows, a burp explodes from her throat. It makes us both laugh. "Look." She points excitedly around the room and for the first time I notice the decorations. Selma points at each balloon in turn. "Look! Look! Look!" The number 19 is written on them with magic marker. A fourth balloon has shrivelled into a little granny tit. "That one's nearly dead," she says and bops it with her hand.

"So you're nineteen now?"

She nods proudly, bobbing her chin three times.

"Really?"

"I really am," she says.

"I don't believe you," I say to tease her. "If you ask me, those streamers are for the new girl."

"I rea-ully a-ham!" She seems to see the fun in our bickering. "Want to see?"

"See what?"

With both hands she slides a belt bag from her hip to her lap. Her shirt bunches as she turns and I glimpse a patch of bare skin. I move a little closer.

Selma pulls out a plastic pouch and removes a few crumpled pieces of paper, which she unfolds and lays out on her bed. A photo of an old woman and Selma, cheering and throwing her arms in the air.

"Is that your gran?"

Another photo shows Selma on one of those horses that hobble up and down beside a supermarket copy machine when you drop a coin in the slot. Her bent knees are sticking out above the horse's head.

She tips her belt bag upside down and shakes furiously. It rains silver paper without peppermints, strands of dust, and a pen that writes in four colours. On the front, Minnie Mouse does a pirouette while a shamefaced Mickey spies on her from behind a wall. Selma pokes around in the empty corners, then swings the bag to one side. "Do you want to see?" she sighs.

"What are you looking for?"

"Promise?"

"What do you want me to promise?"

"Not to grab it!" she orders, wagging a finger at me.

"Okay."

"Thee-crit."

"Is it a secret?"

"Shhhh." Her fingers grabble among her things. An armband made of knotted string. Something shiny, which she hides under her pillow.

"Can I see it?"

"It was Gran's. Very precious."

"Look." She holds up a piece of paper. Before I can read it, that's disappeared under her pillow too. Next up is a season ticket for the swimming pool. "Look!" she cheers. "Told you." The passport photo is from a few years ago. No straight fringe but the same palm-tree ponytail. One of her eyes looks off to the side, more noticeable in the photo than in real life. *Selma Lena Lenoir.* The ticket has expired. Beside the photo is her date of birth, I do the arithmetic in my head. "Ha! You really are nineteen!"

"Kithy, kithy." She tries to press the season ticket to my lips, but her hand is too slow and I dodge it. She keeps on trying. My movements slice through air, while hers seem to push through water.

With another sigh she starts stuffing all the papers back into her bag, followed by the bits and pieces she hid under her pillow. There seems to be more of it now it all has to fit back in. "Do you want me to help you?" She doesn't let me.

"I'm thirteen," I say to the back of her head.

"I know that."

"How?"

"By looking." All at once, I feel exposed. I thought it was only me looking at her, that she looked back without really knowing what she was seeing.

"But how did you know?"

"Cause I know."

She leans so far forward that from where I'm sitting it looks like her head's gone missing. When she tugs the belt bag round to her hip, a stripe of her back is bared and her bum crack peeps above the waistband of her skirt. She sits up without straightening her top.

Selma doesn't jump when I touch her. The skin feels warmer than I expected. My pinkie bumps over the red ripples left by the elastic waistband.

Closer to her hip, the skin is colder. Selma's hands slide from her thighs and fall onto the bed, palms open. I try to read her face to see if this is allowed. "Selma?" I whisper. Her eyes stay closed.

I trace a triangle of downy blond hair, run my finger down a little further to stroke the hollow that becomes the cleft between her buttocks. My whole body has poured itself into the tip of my pinkie.

"My leg tingles."

"What?" I pull back my hand and tug down the hem of her top. Luckily there's still no one in the corridor. "What's the matter?"

"It tingles." She points, as if it's something to do with the people downstairs.

"Your leg has gone to sleep," I say, louder, as if we've been chatting. I didn't touch her. I was just straightening her top.

"My leg is napping." Selma giggles.

"Something like that, yeah."

I ease back to the edge of the bed.

"Ow," she groans, and turns away from her sleeping leg in the hope it won't prickle as much.

"Just wait," I reassure her. "It'll be better in a minute."

Her pained face softens and the corners of her mouth curl up again.

Selma slides off the bed and walks to the window, limping slightly. She takes a snow globe from the windowsill and sits back down beside me. "Look!" She shakes it. "For my birthday." Two tiny figures on a frozen pond kiss. "From Nino."

"Who's Nino?"

"My friend."

"Your friend?"

Her firm nod looks more like she's whacking something with her chin.

"What kind of friend?"

"*My* friend."

"Like Lucien?"

"My friend too."

"What am I then?"

Selma puts her hands on her hips. She studies my face, then my hands and my bare knees below my shorts. Her lips move as if to answer a few times, then settle on a smile. And just when I think she won't say anything, she says, "You're Lucien's brother."

"Is that all?"

Selma jiggles her snow globe again.

Without even thinking, I press my mouth to hers. Eyes tight shut. Her lips shape themselves to mine. I stick out my tongue. Inside our kiss it's wet and tastes of energy drink. I feel her teeth, warm emptiness behind them. Then we're apart again. Selma pants a little, as if she's been held underwater.

"Sorry," I stammer.

I stand up and smooth the wrinkles from the sheet. Selma doesn't look like a girl who's been kissed. More like someone who has smacked her head off a window. I grab my half-empty can and take a swig. A few birthday cards are pinned to the noticeboard.

"I promise I'll give you a present too."

"Present?"

"Next time I come. Would you like that?"

Selma nods.

"Here," I say, taking her can from the bedside cabinet

and holding it out to her. She takes a sip, then wipes her mouth.

"When's my present?"

"Next time."

26

Way down in my insides, there's a glow I've never felt. I French-kissed once before, with Nathalie. After a game of tag in the school playground. Kissing me was the booby prize. It didn't have to be a long one, but everyone stood in a circle and cheered, because it had to be with tongues. Afterwards it felt like someone had tried to knot my lips together.

On my way out, I nip in to see Henkelmann. His door is ajar and the blinds are closed. "Are you asleep?" The top end of his bed has been lowered and a blanket covers the shape of him. Nothing moves. Another bed has been parked under Lucien's paper birds, but it's still wrapped in see-through plastic.

"Got the place to yourself again. Did you scare everyone off?" The only sounds in the room come from outside. "Selma isn't mad at me anymore," I whisper. "We kissed. Tongues and everything." Henkelmann doesn't care what I say. "Do you know Nino?"

His eyes glimmer in the half-dark.

"Do you want to play our game? Henkelmann?"

His mouth is a round, dark hole.

"Don't jump. I'm going to switch on your bedside lamp." His eyes barely respond to the light. I notice his bed rail is down and step back instinctively. "You're a sly one. Trying to lure me in, Henkelmann? Get me to take one step closer and then ... waarrgh." My laughter falls flat against the walls. His chest swells and sinks inside his shirt.

"Henkelmann?"

His wrists are free of velcro. Hands loose on the sheet, palms open.

"Wait!" I see Zoubida passing the open door. "Henkelmann is lying in bed with nothing to hold him down," I shout. "The rail's not up. His hands aren't strapped."

"There's no need anymore."

"Is he on stronger medicine?"

"No, no," she says. "It's only a matter of days now, for Mathieu. A week at most."

"Until what?"

"We found him like this a few mornings ago. Since then, it's all been downhill."

"What happened?"

"We're not sure. Something in his sleep."

"Just like that?"

She nods.

"Does it hurt?"

"It's hard to know with a guy like Mathieu. He can't tell us. We're giving him painkillers just in case."

"Is he going to die?"

"We think so," she whispers, as if it's something she's not supposed to say.

"Are you sure?"

"Yes, we're sure." Zoubida rubs my arm. "It's just a question of when."

"Oh."

"Hmm."

Henkelmann looks more alone than ever, the way he's lying there.

"Does he have family?"

"I think an aunt came to visit him once."

The bedside lamp casts strange shadows across Henkelmann's face. "Shall we go over and stand beside him?" Zoubida asks. "Together?"

I nod.

His toothless mouth is an endless yawn.

"But if no one else comes, who's going to remember him after?"

"After?"

"When he's dead."

She doesn't seem to hear me. Her hand glides gently over the crocodile skin on his forearm. "We will," she says.

"What do you mean?"

"We can remember him. You and me."

In a greenish vein on one of his eyelids, I see the beating of his heart.

"Deal?" she asks quietly, as if we're not allowed to disturb Henkelmann while he's dying. I nod, and it's only then I notice her hand held out to me. It's warm and dry. She doesn't seem to mind that my palm is sweaty.

"He's lived longer than we ever thought he would."

She checks a bag of dark yellow piss hanging beside his bed. "Mathieu is a tough cookie."

"What age is he?"

"I can't tell you off the top of my head. But he was one of our first residents. He was here when the monks were still running the place." She places one hand on his neck and looks at her watch. "Come," she says to me once she's finished counting. "Shall I get you something to drink?"

"I'd like to stay a little longer."

"Okay."

Zoubida puts her hand on the back of my head and ruffles my hair.

"I used to play the biting game with him."

"That was nice of you."

Now that we're alone, it feels like death is hiding under his bed. Or behind the door. Or in the folds of the curtains you can pull round all the beds in this place.

"Henkelmann?" I tap his fingers and bring my hand to my chest. "I didn't know your name was Mathieu."

His dull eyes stare holes in the ceiling. "You're maybe going to die." When I brush his eyelashes with my pinkie, they flicker in slow motion.

"I'm sorry I was scared of you."

I bring my finger to his face, trace the ridge of his nose. Touch his top lip. "Bite me, if you want. Bite, it's okay." There is only the quiet heat of his breath on my palm.

When I'm leaving, I run into Zoubida again.

"What are you doing here anyway? Isn't Lucien at home with you now?"

"I had to pick something up. Medicine."

Zoubida looks at me for a moment, then nods. "Okay." Has she really not noticed my hands are empty?

"Are you coping all right? With Lucien at home?"

"Yeah, it's all going really well."

"Good. I'm glad to hear it."

27

Whew! Dad's not back yet. I don't take the time to kick down the stand, but let my scooter fall. The Astroturf hisses against the exhaust pipe as I leap into the caravan. "I'm back." Lucien is lying calmly on my bed.

I hug him so tight that his breath squeaks. "You're not going to die on us." My forehead pressed to his, I try to look him in the eye. "Promise?" He doesn't seem to notice the tears, probably thinks pressing foreheads is our new game.

"Selma's not angry anymore. That's something at least."

Lucien starts to rock again. "Selma," I repeat. He shudders so fiercely that I have to let go of him. I decide to keep quiet about Nino. He has managed to wrench one foot free, the other is still fastened. "We kissed," I whisper. "Tongues and everything."

His wrist is scored and bruised, despite the sock I tied around it. "Shit." I hunt around for a pair of pliers. "Selma is nineteen now," I say. "She let me feel her bum."

I grab the wrong end of the cable tie and accidentally pull it tighter. Quick as I can, I clip through the plastic.

Rico and Rita start barking and seconds later the pickup appears. "Shit ... your foot." Lucien strains to reach the spout of his beaker. "I'll get you a drink in a minute." Fumbling for the cord, I free his ankle and rub the red skin underneath. His foot lies slack and heavy. For a second I worry it might have gone dead, but a quick tickle on the soles of his feet jolts his legs back to life and

I stuff the cord down the side of the mattress. "Here you go." I stick the beaker in his mouth, upside down.

"Billy goats gruff!" Dad calls out to us. Rita and Rico follow him in, drooling. A plastic bag from The Snack Palace is dangling in front of their noses. "Grub's up! Get it while it's hot."

"Hang on a sec."

"Is Lucien dozing off again?"

"Just woken up." I slip the cable ties and pliers under the covers.

"Quiet afternoon?"

"Yeah, no worries."

"I got an extra sausage for your brother. Do you think he's up for that?"

"Sure, why not."

Once Lucien has emptied his beaker, Dad and I heave him to his feet and clamp his hands around our shoulders. Leaning heavily, he trails along behind us out of the bedroom. His nails sink into my skin. We lower him into the deep leather chair opposite the TV, the one he's least likely to fall out of. "Dig in," Dad says. "Or your chips will get cold. I've already pinched a few out of the bag."

"Don't you want any more?"

"Yeah, but let me feed your brother first. You've been keeping him entertained all afternoon."

Dad carves up the sausage with the side of his fork. Then he shifts the coffee table closer to the chair, sits on one corner and stabs the first chunk. "Fancy a bite?" Lucien's mouth opens wide.

"Do you think Lucien might die, just like that?"

"What's brought this on?"

"It happens, right?"

"No one dies just like that."

"They do," I say. "Boys like him do. They can't even tell you if something hurts."

"Don't start worrying about stuff like that." Dad puts down the sausage, grabs Lucien by the elbows and shakes him roughly, as if to make sure all his parts are still attached. A laugh gurgles deep in Lucien's throat. "Your brother here can take a knock or two."

"You really think so?"

"No question," Dad promises. "If there's anything wrong with him, we'll notice soon enough."

I drag a couple of chips through the mayo and ferry them over to Dad's mouth. "Here," I say. "For you."

"Nice one." He chomps them from my hand.

"We're a regular feeding machine."

"Indeed we are." Looking at Lucien, you'd never know I left him alone all afternoon.

"How's it going with his pills?"

"What do you mean?"

"You know, did you manage to work out that schedule?" Dad nods at the file on top of the TV.

I don't know what to answer.

"That was your job, wasn't it?" Dad asks.

"The pills, yeah."

"Brian, look at me."

"What?"

"Do you mean to say you haven't been giving him any?"

"Yeah, it's all fine."

Lucien lolls blissfully in his chair while Rico sits beside him, licking at his fingers.

"Was there any work going today?"

"Sure." His tongue flicks across his lips as he feeds Lucien the tail end of the sausage. "I'm making things happen. We're doing just fine, the three of us. If your mother could see us now, eh?"

28

We never missed a single Sunday. The closer we got to Lucien, the more Mum sped up, until she was half a car park ahead of me and Dad. At the electric doors, she would turn and wave at us to get a move on. We all had to walk in together.

"Ah, there's my little love!" Mum shouted when we saw my brother sitting there in the rec room. As always, he hid his face in his armpit when he heard her voice. "Not shy around your own mum, now, are you?" She tried to twist his mouth round to meet hers. "Now give me a kiss." He whacked the back of his head with the ball of his hand, trying to knock the words from his brain to his mouth. Zoubida held up the little tub of applesauce, almost empty. "I wasn't sure you were coming, so I started already."

"Well Zoubida didn't need to do that," Mum said to Lucien. "Mummy always comes, now, doesn't she?" She took the tub and the spoon from Zoubida and began to scrape together what was left.

"It was my birthday," I said to Zoubida.

"Was it?"

I turned my head so that she could see my earring. "My present." I was supposed to keep the stud in for another week, but Mum had already put in the ring by the time we found out.

"Well then, belated happy birthday," Zoubida said, and briefly patted the back of my head.

"I'm seven now."

"Wow, your little brother's getting big. Isn't he, Lucien?" My brother had never answered a question, but everyone always left a pause to give him the chance.

Dad toddled around the room looking at no one, and ferreted among the magazines to see if there was anything new. I was relieved to see Henkelmann hadn't shown up yet. All the tables were islands where parents and the odd grandma sat with a child in a wheelchair or lying on a bed with wheels. The residents no one came to see were parked around a table by the window. Sometimes they were allowed to join in someone else's visit.

Lucien's wobbly walk took him along at a fair old pace but only half as quick as me. He knew which door was his without Mum having to point.

Lizzy was sleeping with her mouth open. Her mother was thumbing through a magazine. As Mum passed they squeezed hands for a moment.

Dad lifted Lucien into bed; I helped with one of his legs. Mum took a close look at the skin on the inside of his elbows, so pale you could see all the veins. Then she felt the backs of his knees. If she found even one red dot she would go straight to the nurse in charge and demand to know who had given him an injection. And why.

"Can I give him his present now?"

"Oh yes," Mum said. "Fetch it from my bag, will you?" Whenever it was my birthday, Lucien always got something too. He growled at a corner of the ceiling, still a bit miffed that his walk was over. I placed the present on his lap and when he didn't react I was allowed to unwrap it for him. I picked at the bits of sticky tape one by one to make it more exciting. "For you!" I said, and walked the cuddly dinosaur up his cheek to his forehead and down the other side.

"That's enough, Bry," Mum said softly, so as not to wake Lizzy.

When I brushed the dinosaur below his eyes, Lucien began to sniff and flap his hands.

"No teasing." Mum pulled me away from the bed.

"I wasn't teasing. He likes it." Mum made me let go of the dinosaur.

"So," she said after a while. Dad had already headed for the coffee machine. "You sit here and keep your brother company. Mum's just popping out for a smoke."

I nodded.

"And no arsing about, okay Bry?"

"I won't, honest!"

Mum checked to make sure her cigarettes were in her shoulder bag.

"Shall we?" Lizzy's mother asked.

"I could do with one, that's for sure."

They usually sat in the smokers' room, leaning in close across the corner of a table. One nodding as the other spoke, because they were always in agreement.

They had only been gone a minute when Lucien began to flap around and call out in panic.

"Hey, don't worry. I'm here, okay?"

"Nging-nging-nging." He wobbled on his bum like a Weeble. "Shhhh, you'll wake Lizzy if you keep on like that." There was no calming him. "Mum will be back in a minute." I stroked his cramped pinkie. "Look. Just like Mum does it." Suddenly he grabbed my three middle fingers. I wanted to shout for help, but I knew a nurse would come and she would fetch Mum and Mum would have a go at me for not being able to leave me alone with Lucien for a minute. "Let go!" I tried to pry open his fingers with my free hand. "Stop!" With a quick twist of his arm he flipped me onto my back and pulled me onto the bed. I knocked the plastic lamp from his bedside cabinet. It fell to the floor and broke, his beaker clattering down behind it. Lizzy jerked awake and began to scream.

"Don't!" I shouted. "Let go of me!" He forced my fingers so far back that he almost tore them clean off my hand. A rumble came from deep inside his chest. "Stop, stop, please," I begged. "I won't ever touch you again." Lizzy fumbled for a tuft of hair to tug, but only found a bald patch above her ear. Lucien's mouth was at my cheek, his breath wet in my ear. For a second, I thought he was trying to say something. Then his teeth cut deep into my earlobe. I screamed. Wailed. Punched his face, his chest. I fought for all I was worth. "My ear!" Lucien held on so tight that I dragged him with me as I fell and slammed into the ribs of the radiator. Pain seared through my back. Lucien lay beside me on the floor, his neck at a strange angle. The floor was a frozen pond as he tried to scramble to his feet. He convulsed, twitched, kicked his legs. I crawled out of reach but couldn't lean on my hand. My fingers felt heavy and slack, like they weren't even mine. I hid under the table against the wall, stuck my pounding fingers in my mouth, blew on them. Pressed my other hand to my ear. Blood dripped onto my shirt. Lizzy's mother stormed into the room first. "What's the matter, love?" Then she spotted Lucien lying there and clasped a hand to her mouth. Mum was right behind her.

"Oh, no! Oh, my darling."

Zoubida and a male nurse came running in. All I could see were their legs moving fast.

"Darling, darling!" Mum tried to kneel down next to Lucien, but he kicked and snorted. Zoubida pushed Mum aside. "Out of the way, please."

"Oh, darling. Look at the state of you ..."

"Have you got him?" Zoubida asked.

"Yes," a man's voice replied. "One, two, three." They lifted Lucien back into bed.

"Ow!" Zoubida shouted. "Got me by the wrist."

"Should we get someone else in?"

"It's okay. It's okay."

They called for a third nurse anyway. "Oh, darling, oh my," Mum sobbed. Dad's work boots clomped into the room. "What's going on here?"

"Lucien ..." Mum cried.

"For fu— Where's Bry?"

"I don't know. He was supposed to be watching Lucien."

"I'm here." But Lizzy began wailing like a siren. The brake on her bed was kicked loose and her mum bumped her into the doorpost and out into the corridor.

"Where did all that blood come from?" Dad asked.

"We'll attend to that in a moment," the man on the other side of the bed answered. A trolley was rolled in. "Sedation," Zoubida commanded.

"What are you doing?"

"Giving him an injection to calm him."

"No!" Mum screamed. "No, no, no!"

She screamed in Dad's face as if he hadn't heard. "They're going to knock him out."

Zoubida had a different voice for everyone in the room. "Perhaps it would be better if you stepped into the hall for a minute," she said calmly.

"I! Do! Not! Want! This!"

"It's standard procedure," Zoubida said.

"You do this all the time? Whenever our backs are turned?"

"Easy now," Dad ventured.

"Do something, Maurice. They can't abuse my boy like this."

"We are not abusing your son in the slightest. This is purely to calm him down. For his own good."

"No, no, no!" Mum screamed. Dad steered her out of the room. The door slammed shut behind them.

I crept out from under the table, still unable to lean on my right hand. Then I saw Lucien. His wrists and his legs were strapped to the bed, held tight with velcro. He was struggling and twisting like a fish that has to flap back into the water or die on dry land. A little beard of blood ringed his mouth.

A syringe was pricked into the lid of a little bottle, the plastic tube sucked itself full and the needle was pulled out. The nurse held it in the air and tapped three times with her finger. Liquid shot from the tip. Lucien's face turned in my direction, but his eyes rolled back in his head. No sound came out of him when the needle pierced his skin. "Stop!" I cried. "You can't do that!" Two of the three backs turned to face me. "Where did you spring from, all of a sudden?" Zoubida picked me up and carried me out into the corridor, where my parents were standing. "And now this ..." I heard Mum say, and felt her hand brush my cheek. "What happened to you?" I heard her asking questions. Dad tried to take me from Zoubida's arms, but she said she could manage and carried me into a side room. Mum and Dad followed but stayed outside.

"What happened?" Zoubida asked.

"I was trying to calm Lucien down," I said. "After Mum left, he started shouting."

Zoubida walked over to the wash basin, squirted soap on her palms, let it foam all the way up to her elbows, then rinsed it off under the tap. "Where does it hurt?"

"My back. And he grabbed my hand." I held up my throbbing fingers, but you couldn't see from the outside how much they hurt.

"And your ear?" Zoubida reached for a metal cabinet. The front rolled open like a garage door. She took out an orange case, laid it on the desk, flipped the lid. From what looked like a box of tissues, she pulled two rubber gloves, flapped them about a bit, and pulled them on, letting go of the wrist with a thwack.

"Now, let's see ..." She rolled a stool toward me and sat down on it. "That doesn't look so good," she mumbled in my ear. "Where's your earring?"

"My earring!"

"It's been pulled out." In a flash, the pain got much worse. Zoubida stood up and went to fetch my parents. "You'll have to take this little guy to Accident and Emergency."

"Accident and Emergency?" Dad asked, examining the side of my head. "For a cut in his ear?"

"He'll need stitches to be on the safe side."

"Can't he get by with a dovetail?"

"I think the wound is too big for that."

"It hurts," I sobbed. "Where's my earring?"

"That'll cost us."

"Your insurance will cover it," Zoubida said.

"Yeah, only ..." Dad began. "We're kind of between policies for our Brian here."

"Oh," Zoubida said.

"But if it really needs doing ..."

Zoubida took another look at my ear. "Do you want me to see what I can do?"

"You sure you know how?" Mum snapped.

"I've done it all too often," Zoubida answered, as if she was letting us in on a secret. "We can't go running to A&E every time a resident has an accident. I should be able to patch this up neatly enough."

Mum and Dad seemed to think it was a good idea.

"Fine. If all goes well, you won't see a thing once it's healed."

"Oh God," Mum said as Zoubida ripped open a plastic wrapper and took out a curved needle.

"Perhaps it's best if you wait outside."

"I'm staying right where I am!" Mum bit back.

"I wouldn't recommend it," Zoubida said.

"I'll be outside with your mum, Bry." My father's hand on my shoulder. "Your ear will soon be good as new."

Mum continued to protest but I could hear in her voice that she wanted to be convinced. "Mum will be out in the hall," she said, out of nowhere.

The room went quiet. Only the low drone of Dad's voice through the door, and Mum's teary answers coming thick and fast. Zoubida gave me a shot to numb the pain. "Ow!" It felt like a wasp sting.

"That will take a minute to kick in. Shall I take a look at these in the meantime?" Her rubber fingers felt my own. "Are they throbbing? Tingling?"

"Can you tell just by touching the outsides?"

She smiled and shook her head. "Try moving them." She pulled each finger in turn, then gently bent all the joints in my hand. I yelped as quietly as I could so Mum wouldn't come charging back in. "Nothing broken," she concluded. "Just badly bruised."

"Bruised?"

Maybe I should have yelped louder.

Zoubida smeared ointment on my fingers, as thick as if I'd stuck them in the jar. Once they were bandaged, she told me I had to hold my hand up when I walked. I didn't feel the stitches go in at all. My bandaged ear made me feel deaf but I was pleased now everyone could see something bad had happened to me.

I thought it had gone quiet in the corridor because

Mum had let Dad comfort her. But the two bucket chairs by the door were empty. "Do you know where they went?"

"Come with me." Zoubida let me walk ahead of her as she guided me through the corridors. "Keep your hand up, remember."

"We don't have to go past Lucien's room, do we?"

"No, we don't." We stopped outside a grey door in a corridor I had never been down before. Zoubida let me knock.

"Then you shouldn't be sending interns to take care of him," I heard Mum say as we walked through the door.

"That is not the case," said a woman with black spiky hair who was sitting at the other side of a big desk. It was the nurse who had given Lucien the injection.

"Oh, my little lamb." I reached out to Mum, but she kept me at arm's length first to take a look at my ear. Then she tried to peek under the edge of the plaster. I gave a little moan when she touched it, though I couldn't feel anything much because of the anaesthetic.

"I managed to stitch it up nice and neat," Zoubida said proudly. Mum nodded, Dad thanked her. "It's just a matter of keeping it clean for the next few days. A cotton bud and a drop of Betadine will do the trick. And a fresh plaster every day. In two weeks' time you can make a doctor's appointment to have the stiches removed."

Dad took a look under the plaster too, as if he was peering into a long, dark tunnel.

"Ah, could've been worse," Mum sighed, and pulled me to her breasts.

"Ow ... My back," I groaned. She took a quick look under my shirt and spread her legs so that I could stand between them.

"See you next visit, Brian."

I waved Zoubida goodbye.

"All right then," said the woman across the desk. "Shall we continue this conversation with just the three of us?"

"Brian stays right here," Mum said. "He can tell us what happened."

"Fair enough," the woman said. "Okay, as I explained, this is not the first incident we've had."

"These are my boys. They like to play a little rough and sometimes accidents happen. Isn't that right, Brian?" She nodded so that I would nod too.

"I was only trying to stroke him."

"Brian will say sorry to Lucien in a little while and, as far as I'm concerned, that will be the end of it."

"Why do I have to say sorry?"

Mum acted like she didn't hear.

"Mrs. Chevalier, you are well aware that this is not an isolated occurrence."

"Those interns of yours," Mum interrupted, "think they're Florence bloody Nightingale, but they have no idea how to handle my boy."

"Our interns only fulfil a supporting role and are supervised by a member of staff at all times. And besides ..." The spiky-haired woman loosened the buttons on her cuff and rolled her sleeve up to the elbow. "We also need to discuss this." It looked as if a muscle was hanging off the bone. "This is what Lucien did last Tuesday, when we were bathing him." Four bloody crusts in a patch of greenish yellow. "And here. An earlier incident." Another patch, closer to her elbow, mostly yellow, topped by a little round scab. "I have worked here for twenty-three years, Mrs. Chevalier. I don't believe you can class me as an intern." Mum zipped her bag open, shut, then open again.

"And who says it was Lucien who bit you, and not one of the others?"

"I say." The spiky-haired woman did not blink or take her eyes off Mum's face.

"If you knew how to handle my son, things like this wouldn't happen."

"We are used to the occasional snap or nip from Lucien, but in recent weeks he has been biting as hard as he can. It's happening more often, to say nothing of the harm he can do with his hands. In years to come, his strength will only increase. A solution is called for and, in our view, he needs medication. It's an option we've discussed in the past; one you have refused to consider. But letting this go on until something even more serious occurs is a risk we cannot take. For the sake of his fellow residents," she counted on her fingers. "Our staff. And, of course, Lucien himself."

Mum rummaged in her bag. All three of us looked to see what was coming. A hanky. She clenched it in her fist as she zipped up her bag again.

"And so ...?" Dad asked, his lips so tight and narrow that only small words could fit through.

"What do you mean?"

"Your solution?"

"No drugs," Mum said, softly but stiffly. "At home he was always a sweet, calm boy."

"I am happy to believe that," said the woman. "But we have to base our conclusions on how he is functioning in this environment."

"You heard what I have to say," Mum said.

"There are very good sedatives available. Medicines that can also help improve Lucien's quality of life on a daily basis. That can ensure his safety. And the safety of our other residents."

"No," Mum said, as if she had taken a while to think it over. It came with a short, sharp shake of her head.

"Some parents prefer physical restraint to medicine, but that is not something we recommend. Many of the residents are afraid of Lucien at mealtimes, so we already sit him at a separate table most days. He currently shares a room with Lizzy, but she is a vulnerable young girl. In one instance he almost succeeded in attacking her."

"Almost ..." Mum repeated.

"And today he did succeed." The woman looked at me.

"That was just my boys and their rough and tumble."

"I was only trying to stroke him."

"Bry!" Her voice like the tug of a leash.

"Honest!" I shouted indignantly. "I was trying to calm him down. The same way you do."

The spiky-haired woman gave a condescending smile. "And what are your thoughts on the situation?" she asked Dad.

"God, well, uh ..." He rubbed the side of his nose. "It's her decision. But if it was up to me ..." He raised his hands. "There's a reason we brought Lucien here. On days when I wasn't home, there were plenty of times when she couldn't handle him either." Mum squeezed the blood from her knuckles.

"Our proposal," the woman on the other side of the desk said, "is first to see how Lucien responds to the medicine, then step it up to a dosage that has the desired effect."

"Never!" Mum leapt to her feet. "You will do nothing of the kind. He's my boy!"

"We are doing everything within our capabilities to take care of your son. I understand that this is a complex situation. It's the same for every parent."

"No, it isn't!" You couldn't hear it in her voice but Mum had started to cry. "Lucien's coming home with us today. And he will never set foot in this place again."

"I understand that you are upset, Mrs. Chevalier. But you cannot simply remove Lucien from our care."

"He's my son." Mum spat out her words. "I decide what happens to him."

"Of course you do. Which is why we are having this conversation." The woman signalled to Dad. "Mr. Chevalier?"

"Yeah, yeah," Dad said, and spread his arms as if Mum was a sheet of glass that could crash to the floor at any minute. "Easy now, Milou." Mum swatted his hands away. "Loulou!" Dad pleaded.

"It's your fault Lucien is in this place." She might have meant both of us, but she only looked at me. "And now this." Her breasts were trembling with anger. She walked out, slamming the door so hard that the filing cabinets squeaked.

"All right," the woman said after a few seconds. "It's all right."

The corridors that led to the exit all smelled of soup.

I looked up at Dad. "Is Lucien really coming home again?" I asked, trying not to let on that I didn't want him to.

"Lucien is fine where he is."

"But didn't Mum say …?"

"Your mum says a lot of things. Always wants the opposite of what she's got."

I had to do my best to work that one out. "So he's going to get the medicine after all?"

"Your mum is …" A shrug finished the sentence for him. "She wants people to think she's a good mum." He held his lighter in his fist and ground the little wheel under his thumb. Lucien used to love to watch the sparks.

"Of course he has to go on the medicine. But when

there's a difficult choice to be made your mum needs someone to blame. As long as it's not her fault."

I couldn't bring myself to ask if I was that someone now. When we reached the car park, Mum was nowhere in sight. I was allowed to sit in her seat up front. Dad didn't look around once, barely seemed to notice she wasn't there. We drove back, just the two of us. I have no idea how Mum got home that night.

In the days that followed, I let all the kids at school take a look under my plaster. That started the wound bleeding again. The plaster got grubby, the stitches began to throb. It even hurt when I chewed.

Eventually I ended up with three earlobes. No one at school believed I had been attacked by my dinosaur brother.

29

All the strips are still full of pills.

I twist the lid on every bottle. None of them have been opened either. “Shit.”

The table says Lucien should be taking twelve pills a day. I collect boxes and bottles from the plastic bag, one of each sort. All this rustling arouses Lucien’s curiosity. Two long pills. Four of the blue-brown capsules. Four white oval ones that melt and leave chalky marks on my sweaty palms. I’ve already fed him all the applesauce we had, so I have to find some other way of getting him to swallow them.

“Open wide.” Lucien turns his face away. With my fingers in his hair, I tilt his head back in the hope that his mouth will open all by itself. It does! “Here you go.” I pop the long pills in whole, though you’re supposed to break them down the middle. “Go on, crunch them to bits,” I tell him. He chews for a moment then sticks out his tongue to get rid of them. “Don’t … You have to bite them.” The half-chewed gunk is stuck to his chin. I grab the other pills, shovel them in, and hold my hand over his mouth like a lid. His tongue twists and tickles my palm. He breathes hard through his nose and gags, but slowly his teeth begin to grind.

“And now this one.” I clamp the bottle awkwardly against my hip and try to screw the top off. Rita has sneaked into the room. A couple of pills fall to the floor and she’s on them in a flash. I jump and the bottle slips from my hand. Pills roll and scatter in all directions. Rita chases them down, grunting and smacking her lips. "Leave them alone!" I roar and try to scoop them up, but she's too fast for me.

Lucien stamps his feet against the foot of the bed. I can't tell which one of us he's rooting for. Rita sneezes and shakes her head. "Shit." I've managed to recover three pills and there are two still left in the bottle.

Now Rico's found his way into the bedroom, too, and swabs his tongue over the places Rita has already licked clean. "Stupid fucking mutt." I drag her through the caravan by her collar. Her claws skitter across the lino and she braces her legs against every doorpost. Once we're outside I yank open her jaws. "Sick them up!" I order her. Grains of white are stuck to her gums and the roof of her mouth. The rest has disappeared down her wet, panting gullet.

"You've got to sick them up." I pluck a handful of tall grass and hold it to her mouth. She sniffs but she won't touch it. "Sick 'em up!" I shove the grass between her teeth but she shakes her head and growls softly.

As a punishment, I lock Rita in the cage, then pluck more grass and toss it through the bars. If we don't feed her anything else, she'll have to eat it.

Not long after, there's a timid knock at the door. In a flash, I picture Selma standing there. It turns out to be Emile.

"Hi there."

"Hello."

"I didn't see your brother outside on the bed. And with your father's car gone, I wondered ..."

"What?"

"If you needed some help lifting him." Before I can say anything, he's breezed past me into the caravan. "Are you managing okay?" He remembers the way to my room. The file is still open at the medicines page. Emile takes a look.

"It's a list of all the pills I'm supposed to give Lucien."

"Do you give him his medicine?"

"Yeah."

"That's quite a responsibility."

"Do you know about this kind of stuff?"

Emile picks up the file. "Hmmm ..." he says, studying the table. "From what I can gather, this is to protect his stomach lining." He points at the third row down. "It's the same one Louise used to take."

"What's wrong with Lucien's stomach?"

"No idea."

"So he might not have to take it?"

"Oh, he probably does. Drugs often have a harmful effect on the stomach. This one's probably to counter the side effects of the other pills he's taking."

"And this one?" I point to the pills that Rita's just gobbled down.

Emile shakes his head. "Doesn't mean anything to me. But then I'm not exactly an expert on this kind of terminology." He hands me the file and our hands touch briefly.

"But ... uh ... Do you think it would be a problem if he took a few too many?"

"Is that what's happened?"

"No." And when Emile keeps looking at me, "No, honest. But what if Dad already gave Lucien his pills this morning? I could end up giving him a double dose."

"In that case I'd wait till your father gets back. And you can always ask the staff at the home for advice."

Lucien has turned our way. "Nga-nga-nga."

"What's he trying to say?"

"He wants something to drink."

"Do you want me to ...?" Emile is already holding the spout of the beaker to his mouth. But that's something between Lucien and me.

"No, don't. He needs to take his pills first. Otherwise he won't be thirsty."

"Sorry." Lucien has already bitten down on the plastic.

"Oh well, leave it now or you'll make him angry. I'll give him his pills later."

"Sorry," Emile repeats. He runs his hand over Lucien's forearm and sees the bruises that the cable tie left on his wrist. Before he can ask, I slide my arm under Lucien's knees.

"Can you grab his shoulders?"

"Of course."

Carrying him is easier than last time. I already cleared away anything he might want to grab on his way past.

"Don't lay him on the bed," I say. "We're going to take a walk first."

Lucien has to get used to the sun's glare. While I shove the shoes onto his feet and velcro them tight, Emile asks out of the blue, "Do you think you might have left Lucien on his own too long the other day?"

"What are you talking about?"

"I heard you drive off on your scooter. And since there was no one else around, I went in to check on him." He looks so friendly that I can't quite bring myself to lie.

"I had to go somewhere."

"Does your father know?"

"No! And he mustn't find out."

"Did you go to see that girl?"

"How do you know?"

Emile laughs. "Your eyes gave you away." I look away, worried he might read all kinds of other stuff in my eyes too.

"Is it serious between the two of you?"

I shrug. "We kissed. Tongues and that."

"Hmm, that does sound serious."

I wonder if he knows what comes after tongues.

"How old is this girl of yours?"

"Selma? She's nineteen."

"Oh," he says. "Nineteen, eh? That's quite an age difference." He looks around for something else to talk about. "When will you see her again?"

"Soon. Maybe."

"If you go off again, I'd like you to let me know. So there will be someone to keep an eye on your brother. Strictly between us, you understand."

"And what if you have to go away, too?"

"Then I'll let you know."

"Don't you go to the shops or anything?"

"Since I arrived, I've been living off the tins and jars I brought with me." He rubs his forehead, ruffles the hair behind his ear. "I know this sounds ridiculous ..." He looks at me sideways. "But I don't like leaving the yard. It gives me the shakes."

"Like you're scared?"

"Yes, scared."

"But all you have to do is start your car and drive. Straight up the track. Keep right till you reach the petrol station and then follow the signs for Saint Arnaque."

"If only it were that simple."

Rita is yawning away on her usual spot in the cage. She hasn't touched the grass I tossed in. I got all worked up about nothing.

30

Chipped stones crunch beneath the soft tyre. Wasps zigzag all around us. Lucien kept grinding to a halt every few steps and trying to pull me in another direction, so I sat him in the wheelbarrow. The further up the rutted track I push him, the heavier he seems to get. Thank goodness we're almost at the top. Then all we have to do is cross the road and from there it's only a little way down the slope. You can almost hear the stream from here. Suddenly Lucien gets all antsy. "Feffe!" he shouts.

"We're almost there," I say. "Keep still."

He's wobbling so much I can barely keep the wheelbarrow steady.

"Did you get stung?" I set the barrow down, but Lucien is rocking so much he tips the whole thing over. *Clang* goes the metal tub and he's face down in the dirt. Motionless, like he's listening to moles tunnelling below. "Are you okay?" I kneel down beside him, try to look into his eyes. For a moment I'm afraid he's broken something, or even that he's dying. I brush a few chippings from his cheek. "Feffe!" he croaks.

I pull him up by his arm.

"Feffe!"

"You have to sit still in the barrow. Or this is what happens."

"Feffe! Feffe! Feffe!"

Luckily, he's not bleeding. Maybe I should make a kind of seat belt for the wheelbarrow, or strap him in with a bungee cord.

Lucien rocks from side to side, his nappy is a kind of cushion beneath him. "Feffe! Feffe!" It's the bottle bank that's got him excited.

"Come on!" I try to get him to his feet and hold the wheelbarrow steady with my other hand. Lucien shuffles away from me. "No! Don't!" I yell. "Come and sit down. Here ..." I kick the tub, so he knows where he's supposed to go. "I'm going to show you the stream." Lucien's feet keep moving and the only way to stop him falling is to walk with him over the prickly grass.

"Leave that alone! It's dirty." Lucien bends to pick up an empty bottle. I tug at his arm but he jerks my hand away with so much force that I stagger forward. "Fuckin' hell." We lie next to each other. Lucien's limbs flatten the grass around him and he presses the bottle to his chest. "Come on," I sigh. "Let's get you back to bed." Lucien sinks his teeth into the blue bottle top. "Yee-uch, don't put that in your mouth." I try to take the bottle off him. He resists with cold, dark eyes.

"Okay, you win," I concede. "Keep it if you want." I prop him up against the bottle bank and go over to fetch the wheelbarrow. I turn to see that Lucien has taken a step or two, close enough to latch onto the filthy opening. A wasp flies out of the hole, spoiling for trouble. "Watch yourself."

Lucien doesn't let go, but tries to peer down the hole. I can almost taste the sour, musty smell.

"Feffe!" His shout echoes inside the metal shell. He's got the bottle by the neck and bangs it on the side. I steer his hand toward the opening. "Go on, chuck it in." With all his strength, he slams the bottle into the hole. It smashes and shock takes hold for a second. Then he doubles up laughing, whacks the back of his head, and stamps the grass flat.

I can't help laughing too. Someone has dumped a bag full of empty jars and wine bottles in the long grass. "Do you want another go?" I grab the first jar to hand and hold it out to him. "Feffe?" I ask. His mouth twists in concentration. All he can see is the jar I'm holding out, a clump of mould floating on the dregs at the bottom. I help him clamp his fingers around the lid, and guide his hand to the rubber flaps at the opening. *Clang!* Shock. Then a fit of laughter that turns to coughing.

"Here you go." An empty ketchup bottle. No lid this time and a wasp inside, ticking against the glass. I want to swap the bottle for another one, but Lucien won't let go. "Careful."

He blinks and looks away.

Slam.

Clang.

Silence.

Hiccupping with laughter until he starts to splutter.

A car grinds up the track. It's Emile. I hand Lucien a new bottle. Behind us I hear the creak of a handbrake as the engine dies. "Thank you!" Emile shouts, brighter than I've ever heard him.

"For what?"

"I'm off to the supermarket. When you gave me directions, all of a sudden I couldn't understand what was holding me back." Is it all some kind of joke? I still can't believe he was too scared to leave the yard.

"What are you two up to?"

"Throwing bottles."

"Oh."

"Watch." Lucien is already blinking like mad and wallops in another bottle. It smashes into pieces.

"Looks like your brother's found his vocation." Emile's elbow is resting in the open window. His hand pats the car door.

"Do you know if they sell prepaid cards at the supermarket? I'm nearly out of credit on the phone."

"Was it my fault?"

"You only called for a minute or two. No, don't worry about it."

"Maybe at the cash desk. If not, you could try the petrol station. Or the *tabac* opposite the church." I could buy two phones and give one to Selma. We could call each other without anyone knowing.

"How much does a phone like that cost?"

The thrum of an engine. Our pickup turns onto the track.

"You have to go!" I shout.

"What?" Emile makes as if to get out of the car.

"No, get going! Now!"

Emile turns the key in the ignition and his car rolls a little way down the slope when he takes off the handbrake. Dad advances toward him, painfully slowly. Emile's car finally starts and he has to step on the gas to make it up to the road. His tyres don't find their grip straight away.

I wonder if Dad has even noticed us by the bottle bank. He only seems to have eyes for Emile, who shoots uphill in a cloud of dust. Dad turns to watch him go, before the pickup bumps its way down the track.

"Come on," I say to Lucien. "Time to head home."

Back in the yard, I can't find Dad straight off. Lucien cooperates for once and I have no trouble getting him out of the barrow and into his wheelchair. I buckle the strap around his chest. His knees are supple and it's easier to wedge his feet onto the footrests.

"What did *he* want?" Dad asks, appearing from behind the caravan.

"Who?"

"Didn't I just see you talking to the tenant?"

"He wanted to know if you were around."

"And?"

"I didn't say anything."

Dad picks at something stuck between his teeth.

"Just that you weren't home." My lies sound better when I'm doing something else, so I go and get a rabbit for Rita. She is still dozing on the same spot in the cage. Dad follows me round to the side of the caravan.

"What did he want with me?"

"How should I know?" A cold mist rises from the freezer. "I didn't talk to him." I grab a rabbit, let the lid fall shut. "Just like you told me."

"Bry, Bry. You did good. But ..."

"What?"

"It's a bit odd, don't you think?"

"What is?"

"The guy talks to you, but never to me."

"I can't help that, can I?"

Dad tags along behind me to the cage. I stick the frozen rabbit between the bars. Rico sinks his teeth into the frosty ears and pulls the rest of the steaming coat inside. Rita doesn't move. I click my tongue to get her interested.

"Has he been over here?"

When I don't answer right away, he makes me look at him.

"No!" I shout. "He was asking for you. I keep telling you that."

"Yeah, yeah," Dad says.

"What's that supposed to mean?"

"If our gentleman lodger needs to speak to me that bad, why would he race off as soon as I get back home?"

"I don't know."

"Well I do."
"Then tell me."
He shakes his head. "Call it fatherly instinct."
"Rita?" I try to rouse her again. She lifts her head at last.

31

By late afternoon, a film of pollen is floating on Rita's water bowl. That and a dead fly. She hasn't drunk anything. I rattle the cage door and watch the rhythm of her breathing in the skin that sags around her nipples. She doesn't even try to shake off the flies buzzing around her ears.

"Dad?"

"What?"

"I think there's something up with Rita." I say it as casually as I can. "She's just lying there."

"Must be the heat." He kicks a steel toecap against the bars, then sticks his fingers in his mouth and whistles. Only Rico responds.

"Hey, little doggy?"

I squeak open the door. Dad worms his way inside and kneels down next to her. "Jesus. Get some water, Bry. Quick."

"Here." I snatch Lucien's beaker and twist the top off. Rita licks at the water, but soon starts to splutter and choke.

"Out of the way." Dad lifts the weight of her limp body out of the cage, hurries past the bed, and steers her sideways through the door. Inside, he lays her down on his television chair.

"Wet towels," he orders. "She's been in the sun too long."

"She might have swallowed one of Lucien's pills."

"This is no time for jokes, Bry."

"One of them rolled under his bed."

"And she ate it?"

"She maybe ate three."

"It's the heat, Bry. If only you'd given more of a fuck about that. A pill or two can't hurt her."

We lay the wet towels on her belly. Dad tries to pour a few sips of water into her mouth, but most of it runs down her teeth and out the sides.

"Should I get the electric fan?"

"Top up that bucket."

We soak the towels again, dab her neck, her belly. "You'll be all right, girl. It's all right," Dad almost croons. He feels her ear. "She's cooling down."

There's a trembling in her legs, then a sigh. Deeper than before. I only notice because after that she doesn't breathe at all. Her head slumps sideways and her tongue twists out between her teeth.

"What's she doing?"

"Aw no, poor old girl," Dad stammers. "Dear old girl." He stays on his knees next to her chair, barely moves. "It's okay, girl. Let go."

"She's dying! Do something." I thump his shoulder.

"On you go, girl. That's right, let go."

"You can't just let her die!" I shout in panic. A dark trickle of wee comes from between Rita's hind legs.

"Do something. You've got to do something."

Dad strokes her belly, where the hair is thinner than the tough coat on her back, then buries his face in her neck. He wraps one arm around her and pulls me to him with the other. "Dear old girl ..." Rita's wee drips from the chair onto the floor. The bitter, salty smell is prickly in my nostrils.

"Is she dead?"

I didn't know my dad could cry. His finger traces the curls on her front paw. It feels like a pin is pressing into the hollow below my Adam's apple.

"You let her die."

"She couldn't have had it any better than she did with us."

"It was the pills."

He doesn't seem to hear me. With the greatest of care, he plucks a speck of hay from her coat.

"Dad?"

"An animal has to die sometime, Bry. You just have to let it happen. A pill or two can't do that much harm. Take my word."

"Bury your sorrows right away."

More hacking than digging, Dad makes a hole with his field shovel. He hits more stones than soil, has to pull them loose by hand. His shirt is dark with dirt and sweat.

Rita seems heavier now that she's dead. Dad has laid her out on the grass so he can see how big the hole needs to be. A fly crawls over her ear and I chase it away for her. Death has made her more beautiful somehow. The depth has gone from her eyes.

Rico sniffs at Rita. Nudges her jaw a few times with his muzzle. He barks, jumps at the sound he's made, then slinks off and lies under Lucien's bed.

"Moo-wah-wah." Lucien sticks his arm through the bars all the way up to his armpit, but Rico won't come out to lick his fingers.

"It wasn't my fault," I say to Dad.

"I know that, Bry."

A carousel of sentences race around my head. There was nothing I could do. Rita ran in before I could stop her. I tried to feed her grass. I told Dad she swallowed the pills. There was nothing I could do …

When the hole is finally deep enough, Dad leans against the edge, puffing, before he pulls Rita toward him and lays her on the bottom.

The first shovel of sandy earth dirties her coat. "Wait." I take off my T-shirt and cover her head.

"That's kind of you, Bry." It feels like he's accusing me of doing something good.

We shove the dirt into the hole with our feet until she is completely covered. I throw the stones into the bushes. A bare, sandy rectangle in the trampled grass is all that's left. I can't believe she's there beneath the ground.

32

"Maurice!" Henri leans in through the door. "Is your dad not around?"

"Rita's dead," I say, but Henri doesn't hear.

"Maurice!" he bellows again. He bangs his fist on the open door a few times. "There's someone on the phone for you."

"Who?" Dad shouts, but stays in his room.

"Damned if I know. Umpteenth time he's called."

"What does he want?"

"Ask someone who gives a toss. He's looking for Mr. Chevalier. You gave him my number."

"Mr. Chevalier? That'll be the lottery."

Dad emerges, steps into his flip-flops, and scuttles past Henri, out into the sunshine.

"This joker says his name is Santa ..."

"Santos?"

"This is the last time I play messenger boy, Maurice. The next caller gets told you've kicked the bucket. That should shut them up."

"Come off it, how often does anyone call?"

"You heard me. Sort out your own phone."

"I've got things on my mind, Henri. I lost a dog today."

"What?" Henri's voice turns friendlier. "Which one?"

"The bitch."

"Dead?"

Dad nods solemnly.

Minutes later he comes stamping back in a rage.

"Who do you think gave our man Santos a call?" Dad snorts. "Your mum, that's who!"

"Huh?"

"To ask how Lucien's doing."

"Mum's a cow!" I shout, to make him feel like I'm right behind him. Or on his side. Or wherever he wants me to be. "What did she do that for?"

"We're not going to let this throw us, Bry. I'm going to fix this." He pulls me to his chest.

"What did she say?"

"That I can't be relied on. That my home's not a fit place for Lucien. That ... that ... God only knows what else. Flipped her lid, he said. And now Santos has called me in for a little talk. It's either that or they send someone round. I'm not letting them take my son off me again."

"So Mum's back from honeymoon?"

"Nah. Thinks she can pull the strings from the deck of the fuckin' Love Boat. Not if I have anything to do with it."

"And now?"

"Nothing."

"Do we go and see Selma?"

"Who?"

"Santos," I gasp. Lucky for me, he's so angry he's only half listening. "You said he wanted to talk?"

"And you think I'm going to let him boss me around? Is that what you think?"

"No."

"Well then."

Dad spends the rest of the afternoon tinkering with the truck. At least now he's madder at Mum than he is sad about Rita.

"Go and wake your brother up!" Dad shouts when dinner's ready. Another round of spaghetti with ketchup and mince. Lucien's been out for the count all afternoon. A second trip to the bottle bank saw to that. With one hand clamped on my shoulder, he shuffles into the living room. "Look," I say to cheer Dad up. But he doesn't notice that I've managed to get Lucien out of bed by myself. "We're practising walking."

"That's great, son," he says flatly.

"We walked outside the other day. To the fence and back."

Through the window I can see the sandy rectangle in the grass.

"Can't we buy a new dog?"

"Your food's getting cold."

"Do you want me to turn on the telly?"

"No point."

"Why not?"

"Those fuckers have cut the power again. Not an ounce of feeling between them."

Rico is lying by the window with his back to us. His tail sweeps across the floor. Not because he's in the mood to wag it, just because he can't keep it still. I pick up the plate of spaghetti to feed Lucien.

"This is right, isn't it?" Dad holds out the back of a used envelope. He's scribbled a bunch of numbers on it.

"What is it?"

"Just check it for me, will you?"

When I don't start straight away, he thumps me on the shoulder.

"Come on, your dad asked you a question. Divide that top number by seven."

Two hundred and twenty-eight divided by seven should be a little over thirty.

"Looks right to me."

He thrusts the envelope into my hands. "Work it out properly, there's a good lad."

I put down the plate and do as he asks.

"Thirty-two point six."

"Well, what do you know? Almost three euros more than I thought." Dad snaps his fingers. "So it's that times the number of days he's here."

"Is that the money for Lucien?"

"In two days' time we're off to the bank. Then we'll have the money to get those fuckers off our backs."

Lucien is still sitting with his mouth open wide, like he's afraid I won't know where the food goes otherwise.

"Won't the rabbits in the freezer start to stink if there's no power?"

"With the lid shut, they'll be cold enough for now. And if they start to rot we'll hide one in Jean's caravan. That'll teach him not to mess us about."

33

Somewhere in the night, I wake with a shock. My scalp is itchy with sweat. It's dead quiet. "Lucien?" Without the glowing red numbers on my radio alarm, the room is darker than ever. I switch on the bedside lamp, but of course that's not working either. I feel my way across the mattress to Lucien, touch his arm, then his throat. "You still alive?" I have to lean over him before I hear his shallow breathing. "Lucien?" Just to be sure, I give him a good shake. No response. I go on shaking until he makes a grumpy noise. "Sorry," I whisper. "Go back to sleep."

Among the folds of my sheet, I find something round. It's a pill Rita missed. I see her lying in that hole, coat dirty with the sand we threw over her.

When Dad leaves in the morning, my bedside lamp flickers on and the freezer under the bedroom window begins to hum again. My radio alarm flashes zero-zero-zero.

I've figured out that when I give Lucien a toy car in each hand, it's easier to grab him by the wrist and pull him to his feet. He stands beside the bed, panting, his forehead against mine. Deep in the colours of his eyes, I see the universe. That's what Mum used to say. There's a lot our Lucien can't do, but he's got the universe in his eyes.

"Good morning." Emile's voice goes up at the end, like he's not sure there's anyone home.

"We're coming."

"Is your brother already out of bed?"

"Yeah, you don't need to help anymore. I can do it on my own."

By the outdoor bed, I push Lucien forward onto his mattress. He tries to catch the air as he falls. I lift his legs on after him, shove him to the middle of his bed, and pull up the rail. It will be another half an hour before the sun leaves him in the shade.

There's something in Emile's expression I don't understand.

"Why are you looking at me like that?"

"Louise called."

"Really?"

"It was a brief conversation."

"Does she want you to come back?" Even as I'm asking, I hope the answer is no.

"Actually, she called to tell me she never wants to speak to me again."

"So you're staying?"

He nods.

"Why is she so angry?"

"It's a grown-up thing," he sighs. "I don't think you'd understand."

"If you don't tell me, you'll never know." I resolve to understand everything he's about to say.

"You're a child. I can't go burdening you with ..."

"Are you getting a divorce?"

Emile rubs his chin.

"Did you cheat on her?"

"I hurt Louise, hurt her very badly."

"Did you hit her?"

"A different kind of hurt. She's ill."

"Ill?"

Emile nods.

"But that's not your fault, is it?"

Emile gestures that he's had enough of my questions.

"Want something to drink?"

"No, I'm fine."

Looking at his sad face makes me feel uncomfortable. Lucien has worked himself up onto his elbows and, to get away for a minute, I go inside to get him some bread and pour myself a glass of cola. I watch Emile through the little kitchen window. He rubs his eyes and leans against the bed rail. Maybe I can buy his phone and give it to Selma now he doesn't need it anymore.

His smile pops into place as soon as I come back.

"That's nice of you," he says, and takes the glass of cola meant for me.

He nods at the rectangle in the grass.

"Did one of your dogs die?"

"Rita."

"I saw you and your dad yesterday and thought as much. Did you have her long?"

"A few years. Got her from animal rescue. Rico was already here at the yard when we came. Dad used to breed dogs on and off, till he met Mum. She wanted nothing to do with them."

Emile takes a sip of my cola. He taps his lips with his finger a few times, smiles when he notices me watching him. "Would you ever want to live with your mum again?" His question is so unexpected that I don't know what to answer.

"I can't," I say at last. Then I shake my head. "Mum isn't Mum anymore."

It dawns on me that my mum's looking at things too, right this very moment. That she's awake. Breathing. That her heart is still beating. That when I'm somewhere, she's somewhere else at the same time.

"But would you like to, if you could?"

I shake my head. "She's mad at me."

"Oh."

"Because I didn't want to visit Lucien."

"Is that the only reason?"

"You'd need to ask her that. We were going to visit Lucien, but Mum stayed at home under a blanket on the couch because she couldn't stand to see him after they gave him the new medicine. And I begged her to let me stay at home with her."

Swallows peep and Lucien turns to see their nest, his neck twisted so far that it must really hurt.

"That's not so strange. You were only a child. Still are, in fact."

I tug at Lucien's T-shirt to straighten it and hold his beaker up to his mouth. There's still some water left from yesterday.

"I went with Dad in the end. Even in the car, I kept moaning that I didn't want to go."

"And then?"

"Then nothing."

"And that's why your mother doesn't want to see you?"

I shrug.

"Parents sometimes do things that are impossible to understand." He runs his hand across my back, rests it briefly on my shoulder. "There's nothing you can do about that."

"How do you know? You don't even have kids." The words make me jump as soon as I've said them. But they don't make him angry.

"That's true. But I know what it's like to have parents."

34

When Dad and I came back from seeing Lucien that Sunday afternoon, I gave Mum a drawing. A purple dinosaur on the back of a paper placemat. With lots of scribbles around it, because most of the felt-tip pens had nearly dried up. "Did you make this with Lucien?" She ran her fingers over the scribbles. "For me?" She asked about our visit. Dad told her Lucien had said "Mama." *Mama. Mama.* Mum pulled a face like she was trying to hold something sad inside. "Really?" She leaned into Dad. "Did he really say that?" Now she was asking me.

The way Dad told it, we sat with Lucien in the rec room and did the drawing together, and that was when he said "Mama." So I answered, "Yes, that's what he said. Really." She pulled me into their embrace, planted a kiss on my forehead. I wiped it away because I didn't deserve it. I was ashamed, afraid Mum would see that my drawing had been done on a placemat from Chez Pierre. "Next week, Mum will come too, I promise. Your mum will be back to her old self by then."

Saturday evening rolled around. She grew restless, collecting all kinds of things for Lucien, things he didn't need. Took a long shower, as if she wouldn't have enough time next morning. Smoked cigarettes until the filter began to smoulder.

Sunday came. It was almost noon and Mum was still in bed. She called me to her. With her sleepy breath she said,

"Will you go with Dad to see your brother? Please, will you do that for your mum?"

This time we sat at a different table. Everyone who came into Chez Pierre said hello to us or raised a hand. New faces asked, "Is that your boy, Maurice?" I didn't know so many people knew my dad. The television above the bar was showing a mud-spattered bike race.

Dad gave me a five-euro note to change. He took his beer over to the fruit machine and plonked himself down on a barstool. Then he sat me on his lap. I leaned into him and it felt like a hug. His fluorescent yellow jacket was creaky and smelled new. It was back when all the cross-roads were being turned into roundabouts and he used to direct the traffic. He had high-vis trousers too, but at weekends he only wore the jacket. I felt proud because he looked kind of like a policeman.

"Having fun?" he asked.

I nodded. "But Lucien's all alone."

"Do you think your brother notices if we skip a week?"

"I don't know."

"Take it from me, he'll be asleep most of the day. Not much point hanging around watching him snooze all afternoon, is there?"

"But what if he wakes up?"

"Here." He gave me a coin to shove into the slot. The lights on the fruit machine all started flashing at once. "Do you want to press the button?" he asked and put his hand over mine. We pressed it together. And won nothing. I was lifted from his lap and deposited on the floor. I thought of the rec room and hoped Lucien had been parked among someone else's visitors. And that he couldn't tell they weren't us.

"But aren't we letting Mum down? I mean, didn't we promise her?"

"Well she's not visiting either, is she?"

Dad went over to the bar for another beer and returned with a placemat and a box of felt tips. "Time to draw your mum another masterpiece."

At home we told her Lucien said "Mama" again. And I said he had burst out laughing when I tickled him. Dad slipped me a wink. Mum called us sweethearts and promised that next week she really would come with us. I didn't know what else to say, just watched her standing there by the window. It was like looking through the wrong end of binoculars. The harder I tried to see her, the smaller she became.

One afternoon a few weeks later, the school bus dropped me at the end of the street as usual. I rang the downstairs bell, but Mum didn't pick up the intercom. I rang again. Luckily, someone with a key came along and I was able to slip in behind them. I didn't want to wait for the lift, so I ran up the stairs and sprinted to the end of gangway. There was no string hanging out of the letterbox for me to open the door. I rattled it angrily and shouted that I was going down to play football. Peering through the slot, I saw that the hall was full of things. Some of them were broken. I stood on my tiptoes and looked in through the window. All the kitchen cupboards were open. She had left empty spaces on every shelf.

Later we found out Lizzy's mum had called to see if anything was wrong at home. It was so long since anyone had been to visit Lucien.

35

With the shower head aimed at the wall and the tap on full, I wait for the water to warm up. As long as Dad's not home, the power stays on and the boiler works. Stripped to my underpants, I hold Lucien upright on the white garden chair in the shower.

"Don't panic," I warn him and spray his whole head as quick as I can. Lucien gasps and snorts in all directions, tries to hide his face from the water. I run my fingers over his scalp, feel sand under my nails, avoid the cuts. Squeeze shampoo on his head and rinse it straight off again.

Lucien wants to rub his eyes. As the water flows over his neck and shoulders, he tips his head back and calms down. "Does that feel good?"

Then I point the shower head at his legs. The soles of his feet are brown, but he won't let me clean them. Same goes for the dark rims under his toenails.

Lucien licks the water from his chin. I push him forward. His bum is caked in shit all the way round to his balls. Most of it rinses off in little flakes that disappear down the drain. His skin is pinkish up to where his nappy reaches.

Then it's time to do his front.

The pale skin between his legs looks thin enough to slice open with your thumbnail. His pubic hair is a nest of wiry curls, his dick sticks up like a periscope. "Sorry, but I have to," I say, mainly to myself, and aim the full force of the jets at his crotch. Lucien doesn't seem that bothered, just sits there lapping water.

In next to no time, Lucien is lying face down on the bed, dried off and naked. He lifts his bum enough to slide one hand under him, then raises it a little higher. "Are you wanking off?" The noises he's making sound like an argument going on inside his mouth. His body starts to shudder. Even my bedside lamp rocks along. I tug at his cramped elbow. "Stop that!" Lucien doesn't give an inch, his breathing only gets heavier. I wonder if it's Selma he's thinking of.

"Go on then," I sigh. "But don't be long. I'll wait outside."

I sit on the aluminium threshold, my feet on the Astroturf. The poplar trees behind the caravan are rustling, but I can't feel the breeze. Jean is lugging a cardboard box into his own caravan. Behind me I can hear Lucien's noises.

Maybe I could bring Selma over here on the back of my scooter for her birthday present. Take a ride together.

Lucien is lying still on the bed, eyes half closed.

"Finished?" Carefully I roll him onto his back. His dick is flattened against his belly and a spatter of white snot glistens among his pubes. He's made a stain on the sheet. It smells of swimming pools, just like when I do it.

I bunch my pillowcase into a big ball and wipe his belly clean. Then I drag him back over to sit in the shower. Sliding my hand under one buttock, I ease him off the seat and work a clean nappy under him.

"Where are my billy goats gruff?" Dad shouts. I didn't hear him coming back. Quick as I can, I stick the tabs of the nappy in place. "Hey, something smells good around here. Shampoo!"

Dad leans forward and pokes Lucien in the ribs a couple of times.

"He doesn't like that."

"Ngang-ngang-ngang."

"Ha, see! Our Lucien's always in for a bit of fun," Dad smiles. "Everything okay around here?"

"Nothing out of the ordinary," I shrug.

My radio alarm is dead again. I try the light switch, but that's not working either.

"What do you say the three of us go for a drive? Get some shopping in? We can call in at the bank. Maybe get ourselves an ice cream on the way."

36

I wheel Lucien down the aisles of the supermarket while Dad fills the trolley. As we roll past the soft drinks, I don't see my brother's outstretched arm until it's too late. Seven bottles of orange cordial spatter across the floor tiles.

At first, they want to make Dad pay for the damage, but when the manager sees Lucien in the wheelchair, he changes his tune. "Sorry," he mumbles. "My apologies." And he lets us get on with our shopping. Next stop, the bank.

I look out at myself and Lucien from the front seat of the pickup, reflected in the bank's bronzed windows. First off, Dad tried to withdraw money from the cash machine. When that didn't work, he had to go inside.

Lucien keeps bashing his knees on the glove compartment. Every time he moves, the plastic raincoat Dad put on him crinkles.

A man shuffles past in bedroom slippers, braces strapped over a white shirt that's way too wide. A bag of bread rolls clutched in one hand, he drags a limping Scottie dog behind him with the other. He stops and stares at Lucien, then jumps when he sees me sitting beside him.

"Come any closer and he'll bite your head off."

The man tugs the leash like it's the dog that made him gawp.

Dad made me sit in the middle, in case Lucien lunged at the gearstick. Or pawed at the steering wheel and sent us hurtling into a crash barrier.

At long last the door of the bank swings open.

"Not a penny." Dad gets behind the wheel, fuming.

"How come?"

"Madam in there claims no money's been transferred. I know for a fact it was due in today." As soon as he starts the engine, Lucien starts ramming his knees against the glove compartment again.

"Bry?"

"What?"

"I can't cope with that racket right now."

"What do you want me to do about it?"

"Think of something. He's your brother."

I try to hold his knees still but that only makes him ram all the harder. "Hey, what's this?" I take a toy car from my trouser pocket. It does the trick. Especially when I do hairpin bends on his shoulder and loop-the-loop around his ear.

"Have we got any money left?"

"Spent the last of it on the shopping."

"But you've got work, haven't you?"

When the silence turns prickly, I try to fill it up quick. "I can pay you back for those cans of energy drink."

"Sure, that'll make all the difference."

"So what do we do now?"

"Wait till Monday," Dad sighs. "We've got enough food to tide us over." Before we set off, he peers through the steering wheel at the fuel gauge. "Just as well Benoit works Mondays."

37

"What's up with you?"

"Nothing," Dad grins. "Can't I smile at my boy once in a while?"

I can feel him angling for my attention, but every time I look his way he looks back at the TV. It's not even on. Lucien is lying on his outside bed, chewing a toggle on the hood of his yellow raincoat.

"Tum-ti-tum," Dad says.

"What?"

"What do you mean 'what'?"

"You tell me."

"Tell you what?"

At least the twinkle is back in his eyes. The same twinkle he had in the supermarket car park, before we drove to the bank.

I go outside to give Lucien his beaker. "Shit." Lucien's brandishing the handle for winding down the car window. "How did you get hold of that?"

"Check his pockets while you're out there!" Dad yells.

"What for?"

"Just do as you're told, will you?" Dad insisted we put the raincoat on Lucien before we went into the supermarket. In case he caught a chill from the aircon and the freezer units.

"Well?" Dad shouts.

"He's all sweaty," I say and stuff the handle under his sheet. I lift Lucien's shoulder and tug at one of the sleeves.

"Here's your beaker. Drink it all down." He can lift the spout to his lips now, with only a little help from me.

"Well?" Dad asks, peering impatiently through the kitchen window.

"What's the matter? Have you lost something?"

"Might have."

I pat one of the deep pockets and pull out a wrench. Followed by a cloth hanky and a broken lighter. "You mean this?"

"Try the other pocket."

I feel a flat square of plastic and fish it out. Razor blades.

"Well, I never. That brother of yours ..." Dad sticks his hand through the window to grab the box. "And my brand to boot! Go on, have a good feel in the other pocket."

"Do it yourself."

He comes out looking all pleased with himself and fishes around in the pocket I already looked in. "Hey, it's Christmas come early." He holds up a little pack of thin batteries. "Expensive little buggers."

"Did you slip all this stuff in his pockets? What if they'd caught him?"

"Ah, but they didn't."

"Yeah, but if ..."

"He's a spaz in a wheelchair, Bry. Do you really think they're going to frisk him? And even if they did, all I have to say is 'Bad boy, Lucien! Shame on you!' And lay the stuff on the counter, nice and decent like. And off we toddle into the sunset while your brother waves the bottles goodbye."

A thump on my shoulder.

"And if they had tried to detain us, your brother would have kicked up a shitstorm and the blokes from security would have been all too happy to see the back of us."

Lucien has drained his beaker and is mainly slurping air.

"Bry," Dad says, milder now. "No one in their right mind is going to call the police over what some spaz has in his pockets ... Get it?"

"Stop calling him a spaz."

"Okay, okay."

"You nicked that stuff. Not him."

"Don't be so uptight. Christ, it's like being back with your mum." And he gives my shoulder another thump. Without thinking, I lash out and whack him full on the cheek.

"Fuck's sake." His fists clench in a reflex, but slacken just as fast.

"Sorry," I say. "I was aiming for your shoulder."

Dad runs his tongue along his teeth.

"What if they had reported it and the police had carted him off?"

"Okay, say they had ..." he sighs, summoning the last of his patience. "What are they going to do? Take him to court? Throw him in jail?"

I say nothing.

"Boys like your brother can't be punished. He's had a life sentence since the day he was born. What else can they do to him?"

But Dad must feel like he owes me, because after a while he says, "Why don't you take your scooter for a spin tomorrow?"

"Who's going to look after Lucien?"

"I will."

38

His fingers stink. He's spent half the night scratching at the wallpaper and sucking on them. As I try to wrestle him into clean clothes, Lucien twists and slams his knees against my shoulder. "Cut it out!" Not caring if it hurts, I pin him to the mattress. "Cut. It. Out!" But as soon as I let go, his knees shoot up again. "Ow!" I shout, more in anger than in pain. "Put your own bloody clothes on." I fling the T-shirt in his face. Lucien thinks it's all a game. "Drop dead."

Dad left three hours ago. Last night, all I could think of was seeing Selma again. And I don't dare ask Emile to look after Lucien.

His nappy is a soaked sponge that gets squeezed every time he moves. Drops of piss seep along his legs. Lucien doesn't seem to mind, so I pull a blanket over him. "Dad can do the rest when he gets back." The cans of energy drink in my pockets have gone lukewarm, so I put them in the freezer compartment and decide to wait five more minutes. When they have ticked by, I wait another three.

Lucien's eyes are staring past me in a weird kind of concentration. He's having a shit. "Jesus! Hold it in, will you? Wait till Dad gets here." Mum always used to say with a kind of pride in her voice that she never let Lucien lie in a dirty nappy for more than five minutes. "Not like some mothers ..." she'd tut, with a shake of her head.

"Okay." I relent and pull a clean nappy from the pack next to the shower. "But you'd better cooperate." Lucien lies there, unexpectedly calm all of a sudden, so I pick open the tabs and fold down the heavy piss flap. His dick springs to attention. By accident, I smear shit halfway down his leg. "Oh fuck ..." Rico starts barking and Lucien turns to see, spreading the contents of his nappy across the sheet. "Fuck, fuck, fuck." Quick as I can, I shove the clean nappy underneath him. A brown splodge sticks to my hand. The nappy's on crooked but it's the best I can do. "You'll just have to lump it. I'm off to see Selma." That starts Lucien shuddering again.

I take my two cans out of the freezer—not much colder than when I put them in—then wash my hands and run outside. Rico rears up against the bars of his cage, tongue lolling. "Moo-wah-wah!" Lucien shouts, and Rico's tail wags twice as fast. He barks three times, short and sharp. "Come on then." I slide open the bolt on the cage. Rico trots around the party tent and the outdoor bed, slips as he leaps onto the step, and scampers inside. I make a grab for his collar and miss.

In the short gap between my door and the bed, Rico manages to pick up speed. He jumps up beside Lucien, who wallops him in a mixture of alarm and enthusiasm. "Here!" I command, but Rico's not going anywhere. He licks Lucien's face and stretches out beside him. "Have it your way," I mutter. "Just make sure you look after him."

39

We down our cans of energy drink in no time. Selma still hasn't asked me for her present.

I move two of her dolls and slide to the foot of her bed, tucking my legs under me so that I'm leaning against her cupboard, below the poster of scooter boy and his girlfriend. Out of sight, if anyone walks past.

"Can you do belly-belly?" Selma asks.

"Belly-belly?"

Her ponytail swings in time with her nodding head.

"What's that?"

Her finger makes a dent below her navel. "Belly's here."

"Do you mean *doing* it?"

Selma nods.

Sliding off the bed, she wobbles herself upright and heads for the door. "Come on." She looks over her shoulder and beckons me like I'm a dog.

A girl is scurrying about at the far end of the corridor, stopping and shaking her head like she's got water in her ear. There's no one else around.

We walk side by side.

"Here." She opens a wide bathroom door. The tube light flickers on. There's a bath on wheels, waist height, made of thick tarpaulin. The kind they use to take stranded dolphins back to the sea. "Come on, come on," she says, until I squeeze past her.

Two parked wheelchairs with ripped seats. White kitchen cupboards with timetables in plastic sleeves stuck to the doors. A big bag of nappies on top, torn open. A green trickle from a block hooked under the rim of the toilet bowl. Selma turns the lock with both hands and tries the handle twice to make sure the door doesn't open.

She yanks up her top. "You too."

I whip off my T-shirt. Selma bends forward, the neck of her top keeps catching on her ponytail. Her backbone is a valley down the middle of her back. "Help." Before I can touch it, her top falls to the floor with a clumsy shake of her shoulders.

Static strands of hair dance around her head. I don't know if I'm allowed to look. Her breasts are heavy in her bra. Red dots on her arms. Uneven white stripes score the bulge of her belly, like rips in her skin that have grown back together. Her navel is a secret tunnel.

"We're nearly bare," Selma giggles. "You're Brian."

"And you're Selma."

"That's not allowed," she whispers, suddenly serious as she runs a finger down the zip on her jeans. "That way you get in trouble."

"But I thought you wanted to do it?"

Her hand reaches for the light switch.

"What are you doing?"

"Come here," she says and points to a spot in front of her on the tiled floor. "Here."

I do as I'm told.

Click. The light hums and ticks, and it's a few moments before the blue fog in the tube fades to black. A strip of light seeps under the door. To my right an alarm button glows red. A fluorescent cable runs around us to a second alarm button on the other wall.

"Tell me where you are," Selma commands.

"Over here." I stick out my hands, reach up, feel hair. And one ear. "Here I am."

"I am, too," Selma says.

Now that I can't see her, it feels like this is not quite happening. "Belly-belly." Her fingers climb to my shoulders and force me to bend my knees. "You're tall," she complains.

Suddenly, she presses her belly to mine. A pillow of soft skin shifts from side to side, so slowly it dizzies me. Something on her bra scratches my nipples. I move with her. To and fro, to and fro. A caress as soft as Mum's bathrobe, the one I put on as a kid. Way softer than the velvety red insides of the box she kept her specs in. Or the fur of that dead baby rabbit I found, so soft it almost hurt.

I can no longer feel where my belly ends and Selma's begins. Her breath merges with mine.

My tongue swims restlessly through my mouth, I want to bite into something. My dick tingles, my fingertips are all pins and needles. I think of candle wax, warm and squidgy, of sinking my nails in. Of tonguing tepid cream against the roof of my mouth. I stick out my belly, but softer feels better as it rubs against hers. I gulp at her warm breath but my kiss misses. The next kiss grazes her nose.

I stop trying and drift to the bottom of a pool that is thicker than water, pulsing me gently from head to toe. I feel close to somewhere no one in the world has ever been.

Then it's gone.

"Selma?" I follow the sound of her in the darkness, my hands reaching for her hips. The tube light flickers, hums, floods the room with light. We both stand there blinking.

"Why did you stop?" I ask. "Did I do something wrong?" Selma yawns without putting her hand to her mouth, her pupils dark and wide. Her fingers brush her hair behind her ears and, without a word, she bends to pick up her top, stepping her feet a little further apart to keep her balance. Our bellies are our own again.

"Just a bit longer," I plead, and try to press my hips to hers. Selma fends me off.

"Have you got something to do? Work or something?"

She shakes her head all the way to the left and all the way to the right.

"Then why stop?"

I hold up the key to my scooter.

"I still have a present for you."

"Present?"

I pull on my T-shirt. "You can ride on the back of my scooter."

Selma squeals so loud we both jump.

"You can wear my helmet, but you can't tell anyone you're going for a ride."

"Can't tell anyone," she cheers and throws her arms in the air.

I turn the lock. "Quiet now. Maybe we can ride all the way to see Lucien."

"Lucien?" Her eyes widen. "Where is he?"

"At home. With us."

A boy is standing outside the toilet, glaring.

"Nino!" Selma guides his hand to her shoulder, takes his face in her hands and begins to stroke it. His eyes look away, but he brings his high forehead close to mine. A threat. His breath smells of liver pâté.

"Is this Nino?" His haircut is like tufts from different brushes stuck to his scalp. He must be a lifelong teeth grinder. Even his front teeth are slanted and worn.

"Is he angry?"

"Nino is kind."

"He smells of pâté."

Suddenly, all the anger seems to melt from Nino's face and he gazes toward the far end of the corridor. There's nothing there but an empty bed. Before I can ask what he's looking at, he starts shaking his head.

"Can he talk?"

"Come on," Selma says. "To my room."

"Can't he stay here?"

His shins are scratched, the sole of his left shoe is at least an inch thick.

"Come on," Selma says. Nino follows her and she gives an awkward hop-skip.

"But I thought you were coming with me. To see Lucien."

"Lucien?"

"On the back of my scooter."

"Coot-aah!" She turns and heads for the main entrance.

"Wait! I know another way."

"Door's that way."

"Yes, but there's one here, too." I take her hand.

When I arrived, the woman at reception stopped me and asked me who I was visiting. Before I could even think of an answer, I was out on my ear. But at the other side of the building, it was easy. The third door I tried was unlocked and opened into a room strewn with rubble and grit. Out in the corridor, all I had to do was peel away a big sheet of plastic and there I was, at the bottom of the stairs.

The helmet is so tight it makes her pout. "Ow." Selma shakes and jerks her head, then fiddles with the buckle that's digging into her neck.

"Stay still and you'll get used to it. Or do you want me to loosen it for you? Then it won't hurt anymore." Her throat is the same kind of soft as her belly. I slide the buckle along a notch. "Better?"

She tries to stick her whole hand under the helmet to scratch her ear.

"You can take it off as soon as we're through the gates." I show her the footrests. "Put your feet on those. And hold on to me, nice and tight."

"Look," she says, pointing to our upside-down reflection in the headlight. Spindly little bodies with massive heads.

Nino gawps and glares. He looks down the drive and shakes his head. "Nino," I say. "You stay here and keep a lookout." Nothing about him shows he understands. I can't stand it that he's followed us all the way down here. "NINO!"

"Dafty," Selma says. "He's got no ears."

"Is he deaf?"

"He's nearly got no eyes."

"Does he understand that he can't come too?"

Selma nods.

"Okay ... This is the exhaust pipe, it can get very hot," I warn her. "Understand?"

Her nod is a headbutt in thin air.

"You mustn't touch it. Not ever."

I'm already in the saddle. "Come on then."

Selma leans heavily on my shoulders, pulls at the side of my neck. The springs by the back wheel groan. I strain to keep the scooter upright. She's in place, her breasts and belly a firm cushion against my back.

"Now put your arms around me."

"Don't hurt me," she mumbles.

"Of course I won't hurt you."

Her fingers settle once they're clasped around my navel. We sit like this for a moment.

"We're my poster," she says softly. I nod but I'm scared to look back in case she lets go when I move.

"Ready?"

To keep the scooter under control, I have to lean forward. Selma moves with me and the visor of the helmet scratches my neck.

"No need to be afraid. I'm going to start the engine." I press the button next to the horn and turn the throttle. Selma hugs me tighter. I try to rev in short bursts, so she can get used to it. "Hold on tight."

The first stretch among the bushes is strewn with twigs, and steering is tricky. We reach the asphalt driveway without falling and head for the gate—even riskier, because someone might spot us. The pointer on the speedometer nudges twenty.

"Don't squeeze so tight!" I shout over my shoulder. I take one hand off the handlebars for a second to loosen her grip and we wobble.

We can stop for a swim when we reach the stream, strip down to our underpants. They'll dry in no time when we drive on. Maybe Dad will let her sleep over because she's Lucien's girl. I can sleep in the outdoor bed, and once Dad starts snoring, I can sneak in to see her. She'll lift up the covers and I'll slip in beside her. Her belly already bare. And in the morning, before anyone's missed her, I can take her back to the home.

We skirt past the bins. Almost at the gates.

Suddenly Selma's hands fly loose. She paws my face and tries to turn me round in the saddle. "Don't!" I brake but Selma falls back and the scooter shoots out from under me. I aim for the grass and jump clear. The scooter rides on for a few yards before the front wheel swivels and it hits the ground.

"Are you okay?"

Selma is sitting on the ground just as she was sitting behind me—arms in front of her, knees bent. "I'm not allowed," she says, pointing at the gates. "I'm not allowed."

I unfasten the helmet. Her palm-tree ponytail droops limply over her head. Nino is still propped up against the tree at the start of the drive, exactly the way we left him.

"But didn't you want to see Lucien? On the scooter? It's my present for your birthday."

"I'm not allowed," she sobs.

"Easy now, take it easy. You don't have to." I want to help her to her feet, but sadness makes her heavy and feeble.

"Not allowed," she stammers.

"Will I take you back to Nino?" Now Selma lets me pull her up. I brush blades of grass, pine needles, and twigs from her back and her bum. She wipes her nose on her sleeve.

"You don't have to come," I reassure her. "I thought you wanted to, that's all."

I take hold of her warm, clammy little fist to stop her crying again. Our arms swing awkwardly as we walk back, like we're singing the same song but in a different time.

"Belly-belly with you was nice," I say.

Selma smiles again.

40

Shit. Shit! Dad's back already.

I let my scooter fall in the grass and pull the helmet off my head. Clicks and buzzing from under the bonnet of the pickup. He can't have been home long. "I'm back."

"For Christ's sake," Dad snorts. "Where the hell's your brother?"

"In bed. I just ..."

"Fucking hell, Bry."

"Isn't he there?" I rush inside. The bed is empty.

"What do you think you're playing at, leaving your brother alone?"

"I wasn't gone long," I say, looking behind every door. I can hardly say Rico was supposed to look after him. Dad yanks open cupboards. Shelves collapse. He dashes outside.

"Lucien, Lucien!" he calls in all directions. Emile's curtains look as closed as they were this morning. His car doesn't seem to have moved either. Dad catches me looking. "Does that scumbag have anything to do with this?"

"No," I burst out. "No way."

"So your brother the cripple climbed out of bed all by himself?" He grabs my cheeks and pinches viciously. "Well?"

"He can do more than you think."

Dad shoves me away.

"Lucien!" he screams, so loud that everyone must have heard. "Lucien!" His trot turns into a gallop, heading straight for Emile's. "Lucien!"

"What about Rico?" I call. Dad isn't listening.

I stick two fingers in my mouth and whistle. Rico answers straight away. The barking is coming from behind our caravan. I run over.

"He's here!"

Lucien is caught between the pallets and our freezer. Arms and legs splayed like tent poles after a storm. "Here!" I shout. "He's here!" Thank God he's still breathing. Burst blood vessels in his right eye. Camouflage stripes on his face—green mould from the side of the freezer. My brother looks smaller than ever, but somehow huge at the same time. Rico stands with one paw on Lucien's calf, as if he has cornered a runaway shoplifter for us.

The insides of Lucien's elbows are flecked red with nettle stings. There's one on his neck, too. And they're all over his calves. "Sorry. I went to see Selma." He doesn't seem to hear. "Selma!"

"Where is he?" Dad yells.

"Here. He's okay."

"How could you leave your brother?" Dad pushes me aside. "Bloody hell, look at his arms!"

"You were away all day. And you told me you were going to look after him."

Dad plucks a few dock leaves from beside the freezer and crushes them. He kneels down beside Lucien and dabs the red welts. They turn white when the leaves touch his skin, then flare up again.

"Where were *you* all day?" I ask, and kick his knee. "Well?"

I flinch when he stretches his arm. But it's only to pull more leaves from the ground. He rubs them between his hands until his palms are green with sap, and smooths the mush over the nettle stings. "Poor sod."

"What do you care if it hurts?"

"Shut your mouth."

"You only brought him here for the money." I want to kick his stupid head in. "This is your fault!" I spit. "Rita, too. She's dead because of you. You fuck it all up, leave everything to me." If he looks up at me now, I'll break his nose with one jerk of my knee. "I hate you!"

He lifts Lucien off the ground.

"And Mum hates you too. She never wanted you back. And I don't want anything to do with you either!"

"Then fuck off back to your mother," he says, calm enough to scare me. His elbow knocks me to one side. "Oh no, wait. Your mother didn't want you. She chose your brother."

Lucien scratches Dad's face.

"Keep those claws of his out of my face," Dad commands.

"Do it yourself."

"Bry!"

"Then you'll see what it's like to be alone with him all day!"

Dad kicks Rico out of the way and boots the door open. He tries to switch on the light in my room, but the power's off again. "Jean and Henri are right. You're useless." Dad puts Lucien down on the indoor bed. "If you're out working all the time, how come we've got no money? How come we can't even live in a normal house?"

"That fuck-ing does it!"

His explosion makes my blood run cold. Lucien screams and hits himself hard on the back of the head.

"Who makes sure you two get fed of an evening?" There are sparks in his eyes. "You miserable little traitor."

Rico stands outside barking but doesn't dare to come in.

Dad grabs me by the neck. "Come here, you." He marches

me out of the bedroom. "So your father's a sad old bastard, is he?"

"Let go of me."

"Shut your mouth!" He throws me into the leather chair by the television and digs deep in his pocket. "What do you call this?"

He pulls out two fifties. I don't know what to say.

"How much is this? Cause maybe I'm not seeing straight."

"Hundred euros," I stammer. "Sorry, I didn't know you were really working."

He crumples them in his fist. "Why is our tenant paying twenty euros extra all of a sudden?" His voice is quieter now. "Where do you get the fucking nerve? I'm out there busting a gut every day of the week and meanwhile my own flesh and blood is stealing from under my nose."

"I knew you'd never give me anything."

"How dare you call me a fuck-up?"

"I didn't mean it." I take all the money I have left out of my pocket. "Here."

Dad slaps my hand and it all falls to the floor.

"I'll earn it back, I promise."

I try to stand up but he pushes me down so hard that the heavy chair scrapes across the floor. Without another word, he storms out and drives off.

41

It's a deep, dark night outside. I pull my pillow under the covers and rub it gently against my belly. It feels good for a while but then it starts to burn. My fingertips feel best, stroking around my navel, skating across my skin. I see Selma's face. The little brown fleck in her eye. She whispers in my ear. "Belly-belly?" A tingle courses through my dick and down into my legs.

A smack of the lips tells me Lucien has woken up. Selma's face is gone, the tingle too.

"I went to see Selma." He rocks gently from side to side. "We danced. Belly to belly."

"Selma," I whisper her name again, taste it. Saying it out loud feels good, as if she's in here with us. "Selma is so sweet." Lucien wobbles wildly and the whole room seems to shake. "Sorry I was so pissed off with you this morning. Sorry I left you alone."

Dad is asleep on the other side of the wall. No idea where he was all night. By the time he got back, we were in bed. I pretended to be sleeping but I needn't have bothered. He stumbled into his own room and kicked off his boots without looking in on us.

42

Last night's fight has fizzled out. As long as we keep our mouths shut. When we talk, I still feel the heat behind his words.

He was away all day again. Now he's slumped in his chair with a can of beer on his belly. Rico noses around in the hope of a pat on the head.

Two Mercedes rolled into the yard a while back, one with a German number plate. Brown Henri's brothers is my guess. The dusty bulbs strung along the garage roof ever since we moved here are lit up like Christmas lights. "They must have something to celebrate," I say. A fire is blazing in an oil drum but no one's standing round it. The flames colour the front of the garage a flickering orange. "No invite for us."

"Did you want one?" Dad asks.

A bloke comes wandering out of the garage. The construction lamp snaps on of its own accord and he looks up mid piss. Sparks spin in the smoke above the fire.

Dad has heaved himself out of the chair and is peeking in at Lucien. "Looks like he's out for the count."

"We were walking all afternoon."

"Good for you."

"Honest. It went really well."

"Come on then."

The construction lamp snaps on again. A bat flutters into the circle of light with us and shoots off into the dark.

No one looks up when we appear. Only Emile raises a hand to greet us. What's he doing here? Henri turns in his garden chair. "Well, look what the cat dragged in."

"Fun times," Dad says, and his eyes dart across to Emile.

"They were till you showed up." The brothers around the table snigger in chorus. Three versions of Henri that shrank in the wash. Each with a different moustache so you can tell them apart.

"Sounds like we're not wanted, Bry." Dad shoves me toward the door.

"Pull up a seat, Maurice. Might as well, since you're here."

"No, no."

Brown Henri drags over an empty crate and Dad makes a show of refusing.

"Watch yourself ... Watch yourself." Jean bears down on the table with a grill tray of hissing meat. He doesn't seem to notice that we've gate-crashed. I sit down as far away from Emile as I can. "Rrrr-righty ho," Jean says. I take the paper plate he hands me. "A nice bit of cheek ... for you." With Jean you never know what you're eating. Once Dad swore he was eating rabbit, until Jean revealed we were chowing down on muskrat. Even brought out the head to prove it.

The grill tray is a jigsaw of charred meat. I recognize a jawbone by the pointy teeth, another bit looks like a two-prong socket roasted brown. Must be piglet. I grab a bread roll from an old laundry basket on the table. "Sauce?" Jean asks and squirts a blob of mayonnaise onto my plate. "You know where to find the cans." Jean thumbs in the direction of the fridge.

One of the brothers is in full flow. Emile nods along with his story as he takes a plate of piglet and thanks Jean politely.

"Beer, Maurice?" Brown Henri says. Dad gets a cold bottle in the neck.

"For fu—" Dad splutters and fends him off a little too fiercely.

"Come on, Maurice. Just kidding around. Here."

Dad takes the beer, cracks open the bottle on the edge of the table, and slurps at the foam welling up. Pallet wood crackles as it's thrown onto the fire outside.

"The beers in your fridge must be room temperature by now, eh, Maurice?" Henri asks when the conversation around the table falters. Henri's brothers chuckle and stamp their bottles on the table, their applause for every joke.

Emile, Jean, and Henri have slipped me separate winks, like they all have a secret Dad's not in on.

"What's the big occasion?" Dad asks between gulps.

"Just having a few friends around for a beer."

"Friends? Is he one of the gang now, too?"

"Who?"

Dad nods at Emile.

"Why not?"

"Oh well, it's your party."

Another brother has launched into an anecdote that makes no sense. Emile listens. His smile makes it look like he's part of every conversation he's watching, but I can tell he has no idea what the guy's yakking about.

"When's your son leaving?" Henri asks Dad across the table. "A week he was here for, wasn't it?"

Dad drains his bottle in one go so he doesn't have to answer.

"Pay-up time tomorrow, Maurice?"

Jean signals to Henri to keep things friendly. I sink my teeth into the piglet's cheek. Someone must have cracked another joke, because they bang on the table again until the necks of their bottles start to foam. "Another round everyone?" Jean asks. Only Emile gestures that he's fine with his cola. No one asks me anything.

"Let me get 'em," Dad says, pushing Jean back into his chair.

"Well, well, what a treat ... Waiter, six beers for table two." No one watches Dad except me. He crouches at the fridge, takes out seven bottles and puts seven warm ones back in their place. He drains one in a single swallow and slots the empty in the crate.

Returning to the table with two fistfuls of beer, he barges in so that Emile has to lean back and bangs his head on the post of the hydraulic lift.

The beers are passed around and opened. Bottle tops roll over the ground. Emile joins in the toast with his cola. I keep myself occupied with my pork cheek and chuckle along when they laugh. When it's time for the next round, Dad repeats the same routine. Come the third round, he hooks a bottle of vodka toward him, unscrews the top, and carefully tops up his beer.

"Paws off," Henri grunts and yanks the vodka out of his hands.

"Your beer's too watery for me," Dad mutters.

Henri screws the top back on the bottle. "If you're here to cause trouble, Maurice, you can fuck off right now."

"And what's this?" Dad drags a bottle of Pernod toward him.

"Present from the tenant. You can keep your paws off that an' all."

"Present from the tenant, eh? Fancy."

"Mind if I join you?" Emile is standing at my elbow, holding his chair. Jean shoves up to make some space.

"How much longer till you're back at school?" Emile asks.

"Week or two."

"And then?"

"New class."

"That must be daunting. Or not?"

"Not specially."

"I was going to come over and help with Lucien this morning, but I saw you were managing fine on your own."

Dad is grinning along while one of the moustaches spins another yarn. I don't know if he can hear us.

"Where's Lucien now?"

"In bed."

"He must be wiped out after all the walking you've done."

I want to snatch the words from the air and cram them back in his mouth. Emile has put his cola down next to mine. I don't know which can is whose and I don't want to drink out of his.

"That fence you've built around your brother's bed means nothing much can happen to him."

"Even if he falls out, it's not so bad."

"Oh?"

"The state he's in, there's not much damage left to do." Dad must be tuned in after all, because a little smile appears on his face. That line is one of his.

"Where are the ferrets?" I ask Jean's back.

"We moved them. If there's too much commotion, they start gnawing at each other."

"By the way, I have something for you," Emile goes on.

"For me? I don't want anything."

"Just a little something. To say thanks for helping me make it to the supermarket."

Dad heard that. I can tell.

"As soon as I saw it, I thought of you. Because you were taking such an interest in your brother's medicine."

Dad gets to his feet suddenly. I'm the only one who flinches.

"Everyone in for another beer?" he asks.

"No, thank you," Emile answers. But Dad wasn't asking him. Emile leans toward me. "How's things with that girl of yours? Is she coming to visit? You're welcome to call her again. Knock anytime you like."

Dad taps my shoulder with his beer bottle. He wants to swap places. Now I get to sit on the crate. When I don't move fast enough, he bumps me off the chair. "That's more like it," Dad grunts, spreading his legs and blanking Emile.

"Eat! Eat!" Jean holds up a dish of sputtering sausages. Rolls are ripped open and squirted full of sauce. Brown Henri stuffs a sausage in every roll, blows on his fingertips before grabbing each one.

"Reminds me of my ex," says one brother, holding his roll aloft. "She could take two bangers no trouble." Howls of laughter, the table almost gives way under the hammering of beer bottles.

"On second thoughts, hold the ketchup!" Brown Henri shouts.

More howls.

Emile clings to his can with both hands. He shoots Dad a sideways glance.

"That's nothing on Brian's mum ..." Dad says.

"Da-aad." I know what's coming and I don't want to hear it. But everyone's already listening. "What about her?" Jean asks. Dad takes another gulp of beer, gestures that the punchline is on its way. But he stretches it too long. "Don't tell me you had yourself a real live woman?" Another roar around the table.

"That mother of his was dry as a bone," Dad does his best to drown them out. "Had to cry me a river before I could stick it to her." Dad thrusts his can in the air, laughs louder than the rest put together.

"Says more about you ... than it does about her."

More hammering of bottles.

"And still two sons?"

Dad takes a bow. Luckily, no one cracks a joke about Lucien.

"Where there's a will, there's a way," Dad says. "You want to know how ...?" But no one wants to know. They've all tuned in to another story.

"And how about you?" Dad bellows.

Emile jerks to attention.

"Did your little fishies swim over the dam?"

Everyone falls silent.

"Or don't they have what it takes?"

Emile stares at the ground.

"Hey!" Dad whacks him on the shoulder. "Why so quiet? You're always eager to talk to our Brian here."

"Maurice," Jean tries to call him off.

"I can ask your new friend a question or two, can't I?"

"I don't have any children, if that's what you mean," Emile says in a clear voice.

"Goes by the name of Louise, that bird of yours?"

Emile takes another swallow from his can. I will him to look at me, so I can give him a sign that there's nothing I can do about this.

"Dumped you good and proper, if I'm not mistaken?"

Emile puts his can on the table and gets to his feet. "I wish you all a pleasant evening." He nods to everyone in turn. Everyone but me. Without a backward glance he walks into the night. I want to go after him but I don't dare.

Dad has keeled over by the fridge and heaves himself back onto his haunches. Takes out another bottle, fumbles with the bottle top against the aluminium edge of the fridge, has to sink to his knees to pry it off. Jean puts his arm around me. "Maybe it's time for you to get some sleep," he says.

"But what about Dad?"

"I'll keep an eye on him."

Dad has started moving in slow motion. He doesn't so much turn as reel.

"Gents," Jean says. "Our Brian has decided to call it a night."

Thumbs-up all round. A pat on my shoulder. "Hands above the covers, mind," one of the moustaches quips.

Dad sticks a crooked thumb in the air and presses a few times on an invisible doorbell. He leans in close to my ear. "Bastards, this lot. Every last one of 'em. One more drink, and I'll be right behind you." He rubs his rough hand over my bare forearm. "You're a good lad," he slurs. "A proper good lad." He wobbles unexpectedly and grabs my shoulder to steady himself, spills cold beer on my T-shirt. "Lemme say a few words ...!" he shouts. No one pays us any attention, so he tosses an empty beer bottle high in the air. It shatters on the concrete. Now everyone's looking.

"Yeah, yeah," he says. "This little fella here ... an un-be-liev-ably good lad. Good to his brother, too." His eyes go teary. "And nothin's gonna come between us. Nothin'." He nods to show how much he agrees with himself. "My boy." He pounds a couple of dents in his chest.

"To Brian," Jean says.

Brown Henri pulls Dad down into the chair vacated by Emile. "Now, what do you say we pipe down a bit, eh, Maurice?"

"But I'm allowed to say ... That boy there, he's my son, you know?"

“Of course you are, of course. He’s a good lad, through and through.”

Dad sticks a warning finger in the air. “Well then.”

Henri slaps a bottle of beer into his hand. “This one’s for the road.”

“Sleep tight, Brian,” Jean says.

43

No boots kicked into the corner. No clothes on his chair. "Dad?" I ease his door open a little further. Nothing but a mattress and a tangle of sheets. Behind me, Lucien flexes his knees. "About-turn," I say. "We're going outside." He clamps the spout of his beaker between his teeth and we negotiate the doorstep together.

"Dad?"

Every time I shout, Lucien groans an echo.

"Dad? Where are you?"

The pickup is parked where he left it. The moon is stamped pale on the morning sky, the cold, dewy grass makes my flip-flops stiff and slippery.

After last night, I was worried Emile might have taken off, but his car is still there. For the first time, his curtains are wide open.

Smoke is still snaking from the oil drum outside Jean's place. Most of the blue paint has flaked off, the metal flecked from the heat. "Dad?" I call.

"Bry ..." A dusty croak. I can't work out where it's coming from.

"Dad?" Is he lying in the bushes?

"Bry?"

"Where are you?"

A retching cough. "In here. With the dog."

He's a heap in the corner of the cage. "What are you doing in there?" His face is crumpled, his cheek dirty. Lucien leans on my shoulder and we edge closer. Only then do I see the blue-red blister below his eye and the raw skin under the dirt on his cheek.

"Moo-wah-wah." The beaker drops from Lucien's mouth and he bends his knees excitedly a couple of times.

"How did you end up in there?"

A chain lock is looped through the cage door and the bars.

"Who locked you in?"

Dad shifts his weight, blinks.

"Where's the key?"

"Those fuckers are more worried about a Dad taking care of his son than a scumbag tenant."

"Why didn't you call me?"

"You were already asleep." The thought that I could leave him locked up like this triggers an uneasy feeling in my stomach.

"Where's Rico?"

"Knocking about somewhere." Dad sticks his fingers in his mouth and whistles. The weeds by Emile's caravan sweep aside and Rico comes bounding toward us.

"Moo-wah-wah."

"Do you want me to get the angle grinder?"

"It's been sold for a bit."

"Sold for a bit?"

"Pawn broker's. Till your brother's money arrives, then I'll buy it back."

"Why didn't you say something?"

"Shut up about it, will you!"

"But you could have pawned some of my stuff ..."

"I'm not flogging anything that belongs to my own son." That's exactly what he did with all my birthday presents these past few years, without asking. The dragon castle that was way too big for my room. The electric go-cart. The second-hand keyboard without an adapter.

"Jean? Henri?"

Flies swarm around gnawed bones and open sauce bottles. Broken glass and trampled sausages litter the concrete floor.

"Feffe ..." Lucien puffs, out of breath from walking.

"Henri?" I shout. "I need the key."

"Feffe, feffe." Lucien sinks to his knees and reaches for the glass splinters on the floor.

"No, no ... Here." I hand him a bottle. He grabs it and smashes it. Shock first, then a whinny of laughter. A pigeon up in the rafters flaps and resettles.

"Hey! There's a deposit on that bottle ..." Brown Henri appears wearing only his underpants, rubbing finger and thumb together.

"You can get the ten cents off Lucien."

"Brian!" Jean greets me as he comes trundling out with his oxygen tank. "I was just about to look in ... on your dad."

His eyebrow is swollen, blood sticky among the hairs.

"What happened?"

He dips his fingers into the breast pocket of his shirt and pulls out a ring of three identical keys.

"Tell him I never want to see him here again."

"Tell him yourself."

"Already have and I'm not going to ... waste my breath on another warning."

"Feffe ... feffe ..." Lucien is straining to reach the bottles that are still on the table.

"What happened?"

They both start scratching at the same time. Jean his throat, Henri the side of his belly.

"You promised you'd keep an eye on Dad."

"And I did. Sent him packing because he'd had ... enough to drink. And then he lost it."

"You know we gave him a week to come up with that money," Henri says. "And he lied about your brother only staying a few days. Well, now we find out he's been pocketing our share of the tenant's rent. Nothing but trouble, that dad of yours."

"Started hurling abuse," Jean chimes in. "Calling us ... filthy bastards. Calling the tenant ... a pervert. Threatened to ... set off fireworks ... under his caravan."

"And did he?"

They shake their heads in unison.

"That's when we dragged him over to the dog cage."

"And what happened to your eye? Was there a fight?"

"Let's just say he didn't ... go quietly."

"But by the time we threw him in there, he was already well gone."

"Feffe ... feffe ..."

"Watch out," Jean warns, but Lucien has managed to grab another bottle and proceeds to smash it on the floor. He has stepped in broken glass and his foot stamps blood on concrete. He doesn't seem to notice. "Here." Jean tosses me the key ring. "I want them back."

Henri starts sweeping up the splinters. "It's nothing against you."

"What does that mean?"

Jean looks at Henri. "We're sorry, Brian."

"What?"

Lucien is getting impatient.

"Your dad is going to pay what he owes us. And then he can clear off out of here."

"Where to?"

"You'll have to ask him that. The three of you have got to go. This is no place for you and your brother."

44

As soon as I helped him out of the dog cage, he jumped in the pickup and drove straight to the bank. The slamming door when he got back told me all I needed to know.

"Nothing on my account. Zero!"

"How can there be nothing?"

"Santos promised me the transfer was on its way. So where's the bloody money? Riddle me that."

He flings open the kitchen cupboards and grabs an old food mixer. Blows dust off a couple of bowls.

"What are you going to do now?"

"There's a car boot sale in a village the other side of Saint Arnaque." He picks up Lucien's box of Duplo.

"Wait! He likes those cars, they help calm him down."

But Dad's already out the door, box under his arm. He comes back for the drill. And the old bread box that holds the drill bits.

"But you only borrowed that ..." I say, trying not to rile him.

"Yeah, from those fuckers."

"Do we have to move house?"

Dad scans the contents of the cupboards under the sink.

"They told me we have to clear off."

"Not bloody likely. I've been sent packing once too often in my life."

He dangles Rita's collar from his pinkie for a second, then tosses it back onto the kitchen counter. Sees Lucien's bedpan and shoves it in the bag with the drill.

"But that's not ours."

"What's not ours?"

"The bedpan."

"They gave us a bedpan?"

"You ticked it off on that list."

"Lucien wears nappies. What do we want with a bedpan?" I follow him into our bedroom. He snatches the radio alarm clock. The cable swings behind it like a tail, whacking the plug against everything it passes. His eyes settle on Lucien.

"How much could we get for him?"

Dad doesn't think it's funny. "I'm doing what I can here, Bry."

I stand in front of my desk to hide my comics. Dad charges into my room and his eyes flit across my things. He picks up my old Olympique Lyonnais shirt from the floor and stuffs it into the bag with the bedpan. Catches sight of my old football boots. "Aw, Dad, no ..." I plead. He's already carried them off. Not that they fit me anymore, but they were the last birthday present from Mum. "From Didier too," she said when she gave them to me. He was outside in the car waiting for her.

Nothing in Dad's room is worth shit, but he looks anyway. On his way out the door he pockets Rita's collar after all. "I'll be back around noon."

"Can't we come with you?"

"Your brother's bad for sales."

"I'll keep him quiet, promise. I could take him for a ride in his wheelchair."

"Half the customers will be too busy gawping at Lucien to buy anything. The other half will look the other way."

When Dad's gone, I hope the power will come back on, so I can take a warm shower. It doesn't.

45

"Look. Lucien's walking."

"All the way over here?" Emile acts like he cares, but he won't let us in.

"His foot's bleeding."

Emile opens his door a little further. "Show me." Like an old nag in need of shoeing, Lucien lets me lift his foot.

"That doesn't look good."

"He stood on some glass. I was hoping it might heal by itself."

For a moment I'm afraid Dad has doubled back, but the sound of the passing car dies away. Emile comes out of his caravan holding a toilet bag and pulls out a roll of bandage. "Shouldn't he be wearing shoes?"

"Yeah, I forgot."

He takes a close look at the sole of Lucien's foot. "This doesn't look good at all."

"It's my fault, I wasn't paying enough attention."

"I don't think you could have prevented this."

"Why not?"

"You do what you can. A boy like your brother hurts easily. It would take a thick coat of fur to save his skin. Without you, Lucien would have been all cuts and bruises by now."

He goes back inside for a bowl of water and a towel. We rinse Lucien's foot clean and pat it dry. "This is going to sting," Emile murmurs and sprinkles a few drops of Betadine on the cuts.

"I'm sorry about last night."

Emile acts like he hasn't heard me.

"For what my Dad said to you."

From a side pocket of the toilet bag he removes a roll of sticky tape the colour of plasters. He tears off an awkward strip.

"I said I'm sorry."

"I heard you."

"Well?"

"I don't want to talk about it."

"Suit yourself."

Emile focuses on taping up Lucien's foot, then says, "I told you those things in confidence."

"What happened to 'I don't want to talk about it'?"

All the fiddling with his foot is starting to make Lucien restless.

"I expected better of you. And your father seemed very ..."

"What?"

"Perhaps it's time to find myself another place."

"I said I was sorry. And Dad was drunk."

Emile checks that the bandage is tight enough.

"Besides, you said things too. Things you weren't supposed to say. About Selma. And that you helped me with my brother."

He looks me in the eye for the first time today. "I thought your father knew all that."

Lucien shakes his taped-up foot. The bandage seems to bother him more than the cut did.

"So does that make us even?"

"I apologize. I didn't give it enough consideration."

Emile holds out his hand and I shake it.

"I still have something for you." He goes back into his caravan. He must be the only tenant we've had who wipes his feet every time.

With no warning, Lucien grabs my ear and twists it hard.

"Let go, let go, let go!" It hurts all the way down to the roots.

From inside the caravan, I hear a dull thud and a cupboard door slam.

"Ow!" I have to bend Lucien's wrist to breaking point.

Emile reappears just as Lucien lets go. "Are you okay?"

My ear throbs to the touch.

"Cartilage can usually take a bit of punishment." He takes a closer look. "From what I can see it's still firmly attached."

Lucien's attention has wandered again. He's spotted the aquarium through the caravan window and seems to be hypnotized.

"Your opened your curtains."

Emile nods. "Here. For you." He hands me a square parcel. "As promised."

"For me? So you're not angry anymore?"

"Go on, open it."

It's tightly wrapped in coloured paper. He's even written my name on it, like he's got a bunch of presents tucked away and needs to tell them apart.

"Looks like a book," I say. "But that's not a present ..." I tear off the paper.

"I saw it on the shelf and I thought of you."

"Pocket Medical Dictionary," I read aloud.

"You were asking me all those questions about Lucien's medicine and I didn't know the answers. If you don't like it, you can give it to someone else."

"No, I do, I do." I want to act like I think it's great, so I flick through the pages looking for something nice to say. "It looks really, really interesting."

Emile jumps. Lucien's hand is grabbing at his shoulder.

"If he's annoying you, just push his hand away."

"No, no. It's no problem. Took me by surprise, that's all."

Lucien pulls us over to see the aquarium. He bangs the window so hard I'm afraid he'll smash it.

"Maybe we should take a walk."

"Yes, let's," Emile says.

"Do you want to come?"

"If that's okay?"

Dad hasn't been gone long, so I'm not afraid to risk it.

"Where would he want to go?" Emile asks.

"Just for a walk. Anywhere, as long as it tires him out."

Once we've put his shoes on, Lucien steers us toward the bottle bank. Emile looks at Lucien's hand on his shoulder.

"Is he hurting you?"

"His nails need cutting."

Lucien pants and plods behind us, like he's forcing two grouchy donkeys up the slope. We reach the bottle bank and let him chuck in a few bottles we find under the bushes.

Emile laughs along with Lucien's high spirits.

"Did *you* find out he likes this?"

I nod.

"That's quite something."

"Do you want to go a little further?"

"You think your brother's up to it?"

"We can give it a try. Otherwise one of us will have to wait with him while the other one fetches the wheelbarrow." The transistor at the top of the electricity pylon buzzes like a wasps' nest. "There's a stream across the road. I know a good place there."

You can see the water glint among the trees. Lucien is caught up in the rushing sound. Most days it's a tired old trickle, but upland rain swells it into a stream that makes your heart race.

"How about we go down this way?"

"I can see fine from here."

"We can walk a bit and then go down. It's not as steep further along."

"I'm not sure that's such a good idea, Brian. Especially not with Lucien."

I hold down a slack stretch of barbed wire with my foot. The rusty barbs poke through the sole of my flip-flop.

"Why don't we look for a shady spot by the road? We'll have a nice view from there."

The grassy verge is newly mowed. Emile sits down and Lucien slumps to his knees.

"Some parts are deep enough to swim."

"Do you come here a lot?"

I nod. "But with my brother I never got this far."

Lucien is lying on his back.

"Did you mean what you said just then?" I ask.

"What?"

"About leaving."

Emile squints into the sunlight. "I'm thinking about it, yes. To be honest, I was biding my time until Louise told me I could come back. But now she's laid it on the line, I realize that chance has gone."

"Can't you decide for yourself whether to go back or not?"

Emile shakes his head.

"What's she so mad about?"

Emile smiles again, he thinks I'm asking too many questions.

"But you're a really nice guy," I say.

He puts his hand on my neck, brushes something away.

"What are you doing?"

"I thought I saw a horsefly." Emile carves his thumbnail into the heel of his shoe. "You're the only one I talk to about these things ..."

"Even then, you don't say much."

"Remember me as you know me now. That's what I'd like best."

Just as I'm about to ask why, he starts talking again.

"Louise has every right to never want to see me again." He shields his eyes with his hand.

We sit quietly for a while. Lucien rolls around and rubs his back on the grass. His face is a wide grin. His arms and legs furry with short, yellow blades.

46

I peer at my shoulder in the mirror above the wash basin. The crescent left by Lucien's nails looks like the bite of a gap-toothed animal. The surrounding skin goes from blue to murky yellow.

I can't find the nail clippers. But I do find Dad's razor. Shaving foam. And a red bottle of aftershave that's evaporating little by little. Dad says he saves it for special occasions. And for the ladies.

Next to that, there's a jar of condoms. Dad takes it out and shakes it every now and then. "Oh yes," he chuckles, with a nudge and a wink, as if the jar contains all the sex he's still got coming. "Pulling the birds" he calls it. The number of condoms never changes. It used to be ten, until I nicked one and took it to school with me. Blew it up like a balloon at breaktime. The boys from my class all laughed and acted the tough guy, but a few of them came up and whispered in my ear later on. I charged them a euro to try it on in the toilets. Made them rinse it under the tap, dry it off, and roll it up again.

I slip a condom into the pocket of my swimming trunks and shake the jar so it looks like there's still nine.

"And?" I ask. "Sell anything?"

Dad whips out two tenners. And I can hear small change jingling in his pocket. He doesn't notice Lucien by the outdoor bed, standing with no help from me. Even Rico is wagging his tail proudly.

"Look, Lucien's standing by himself!"

"That's nice, Bry."

I want to tell him about Emile. The words are set to burst from my mouth, but I'm not going to betray him a second time.

Together, we carry everything back inside. That's the saddest thing about car boot sales. Not the way our stuff lies on the road beside the truck like it's spilled out of a torn rubbish bag. But this. The things that come back home with us, looking even more forlorn now they've been disowned and no one else wanted them.

"Didn't you sell anything at all?"

"Of course I did."

"Then what?"

Dad glances at the garage.

"Got twenty for the drill."

47

A car slows in the distance and for a moment I think it's Mum and Didier. That any minute they might drive through the gate, looking for us. Mum would get out and plant a kiss on my head before giving Lucien a hug. And I would tell her everything was fine. And show her how we walk together. And how Lucien can do more when I help him. Things he can't do without me.

They would want to take Lucien home alone at first. But he would start screaming and flailing when he realized it meant leaving me behind. So Mum would let me come and stay for a while. All I'd have to do is grab some clothes. Maybe not even that. I could hop right into the car and we'd buy new ones on the way. And when Didier turned to look at me from the driver's seat, he would have Dad's face.

Rico sits up in his cage and barks a warning. The distant car really is coming closer. When I hear tyres crunching down our rutted track, I jog over to the gate to take a look. It's a police car, the copper with the tough-guy sunglasses at the wheel. I dive into the bushes and watch as he eases into the middle of the yard, pulls up outside the garage, and kills the engine. The doors swing open and a copper I hadn't spotted gets out of the passenger side. They check their belts, straighten their berets, size the place up. The copper with the sunglasses disappears into Henri's shed. The other one circles round the back.

I sprint back to the caravan.

"Dad? Police!"

"Shit."

We peer out between the slats of the kitchen blind.

"What are they doing here?" Dad mutters.

"It's the same copper who stopped us the other week," I tell him. "Yves."

"Do you think they've come looking for the tenant?"

"Why?"

"How should I know? Because he's been up to something."

The coppers reappear. Before they get in, they start a conversation across the roof of the police car.

"No, no, no," Dad tries to will them away. But the car heads in our direction and rolls to a halt beside the pickup.

"Fuck … fuck."

"Did you sort out that paperwork, like he said?"

"When the fuck was I supposed to do all that? Well?"

Yves gets out of the car. Rico is barking non-stop.

"Do you think your mum's behind this? Or that Santos fella?"

"Have they come for Lucien?"

"Whatever they've come for, I'm not here," Dad whispers fiercely.

"What about me?"

"Go and talk to them. Tell them I left. Now!"

Yves removes his shades. Examines the back of the pickup. Sees Lucien's bed in front of the caravan.

"Dad's not here," I call over. He turns and looks at me.

"Do you live here full-time?" he asks in a friendly voice.

"How come?"

"Just asking."

"None of your business."

"All right, less of your lip. And who sleeps in this bed?"

"No one."

"Then what's it doing here?"

"Did my mum call you?"

"I'd like a few words with your dad. Get him for me, will you?"

"Told you, he's not here."

"Is that right?"

"Yup."

"Well that's funny. Because the gents across the way told me he's home."

"Then they're lying."

Yves hooks his thumbs through his belt loops and kicks a hunk of rubble sticking out of the ground. "What's his truck doing here?"

"Dad decided to walk."

"Maurice!" he calls. "We need to talk. I've had another call about you." Without asking he mounts the step and tries to push past me. "Bugger off!" I shout in his face. A tiny spit bubble lands on his cheek.

"Watch your mouth, sonny."

"You can't come in here unless we say so."

Yves stays exactly where he is, much too close. He's put his shades back on. I stare at my reflection in the lenses and inhale his chewing-gum breath. His forehead is shiny from the heat. He purses his lips, runs the tip of his tongue between two teeth, and takes a step back. "Tell your father I dropped by." He tries to peer through the window above Lucien's bed. "On second thoughts, don't bother."

"Why not?"

"Maurice! I'm assuming you heard me."

As soon as their car is through the gate, Dad emerges from the caravan.

Henri and Jean appear at the entrance to the garage. I expect them to come over to see us. But they don't. They just stand there. Looking.

"Trust those fuckers to tell the cops I'm home."

Dad starts banging on about Yves and who might have called him. "It wouldn't be that fucking tenant would it?"

"Why would he do that?"

"God knows what kind of information he's managed to worm out of you." Dad glares at Emile's caravan like he wants it to burst into flames.

48

I finger the little plastic square around the condom in my pocket. The deeper the sharp ridges dig under my nail, the calmer I become. I'm stuck in the car with Lucien until Dad gets back. He's gone inside to track Santos down. Lucien is dozing and I check to see if his seat belt is fastened. There's no way he can loosen it himself. If I run at top speed, Dad won't even know I've been to see Selma.

"Now!" I say it out loud to give myself courage. "Back in a bit." But before I'm halfway across the car park, Dad comes marching out the main entrance. In even more of a state than when he went in. I act like I was on my way to meet him. "And?" I ask, cool as I can.

"That mother of yours ..." he growls and shakes his head. "Thanks to her, our man Santos is sending an inspector over. And if I don't play ball, no cash." In the car he slams the steering wheel with his fists and stares into space. Then the engine roars.

It's dark by the time we lurch into the yard. We've been driving around for hours and I didn't dare ask why. Until the pointer on the fuel gauge slid into the red zone.

I help Lucien out of the truck. His hair leaves greasy streaks on the passenger window. Dad is first to notice the plastic bag in the middle of the outdoor bed. "What's this?"

"Beats me."

It's a bag of empty bottles. "Is this some kind of joke?" Dad pulls out a piece of paper, turns it over, and starts reading. I stare at my name in block capitals on the other side. Dad shoots me a look, his pupils sharp as darts.

I want to snatch the note from his hands but he scrunches it into a ball. He storms inside and grabs a torch. "Come with me, you."

"Why? The bottles are for Lucien."

He grabs me by the elbow. "You're always up for a chat with the tenant, right?"

Dad bundles me in front of him. I try to trip, but he holds me up as he propels me along.

"Don't hit him," I groan. "He hasn't done anything. All we did was take Lucien for a walk."

I think I see Emile's curtains twitch when Dad shines his torch on them, but it's only shadows retreating into the folds. Instead of barging into the caravan, he stops outside the door. "You are going to back me up," he says, tugging my T-shirt straight, his voice so low I can barely hear him. "It's time you and me had a little chat with your pal."

Hesitantly, Emile opens the door of his own accord. "Is something wrong? There's no rent due, as far as I'm aware."

"We've come to see you," Dad says. His sudden friendliness gives me the creeps. "Or is Brian the only one welcome around here?"

"No, not at all. It's just that I wasn't expecting anyone at this time of night."

Dad sends me over to the table. A dark wave rolls through the aquarium as we sit ourselves down. Fish eyes twinkle among the plants.

"Something to drink?"

"We've already had coffee. Isn't that right, Bry?"

"For Brian there's ..." Emile holds up a can of energy drink.

"Brian's not thirsty."

"Oh." Emile hesitates and puts the can back in the fridge.

"What was it you took over to Henri and Jean's little shindig last night?"

"Pernod."

"I'll have some of that."

Emile looks for a glass.

"Are your fish asleep?" Dad shoves past me, puts his nose to the tank, and raps it with his knuckles. "Little buggers must be worn out, all that swimming around."

Before Emile can answer, Dad straightens up and looms over the kitchen counter. "Now isn't this a fancy little glass."

"Just had my nightcap." Emile's smile twitches into place. "It's a glass I'm rather fond of."

"Ooh, I'll bet, I'll bet," Dad says and makes a show of picking it up by the stem, between finger and thumb. "Always extra careful with pretty things, aren't we, Bry?" He pings a fingernail against the rim. "Crystal, am I right?"

"It's a family heirloom. Belonged to my grandfather. A gift from my grandmother when they got married."

"Oh my," Dad says. "An heirloom. First thing you take with you when you make a hasty getaway."

"Would you mind if I offered you another glass?"

"This'll do just fine."

Much too fast, Dad slides the glass to the edge of the table. "Fill her up, why don't you."

Emile hesitates, then slowly begins to pour.

"Speed up, man." Dad gives the bottle a nudge. As much Pernod glugs onto the table as ends up in the glass.

"That's more like it. A bit of hospitality." He bends and slurps the puddle from the table. "Not having one yourself?"

Emile sits down across from us. I try to catch his eye but he's staring straight ahead. The reflection from his watch face quivers on the ceiling.

"Well?" Dad asks.

"Pardon?"

"No hassle from Jean or Brown Henri?"

"Uhm. No."

Dad weighs up what Emile has said.

"Why would there be any hassle?"

The glass is almost empty.

"Things got a little out of hand after you left last night," Dad says.

"What happened?"

"How can I put this? You've got a few tongues wagging." His hands flit invisible rumours through the air.

Emile looks at me like he wants a translation. I start nodding.

"I warned you to stay away from those two," Dad says.

"They invited me over. I saw no harm in that."

"No harm, eh?" He twirls the empty glass by the stem. The cut crystal sends coloured chips spinning across the tabletop.

"That's right."

"Okay, let me be very frank with you." Dad shifts in his seat. "Something's started smouldering in those tiny minds of theirs. Get my drift? They egg each other on, those two."

"What did they say? That wasn't the impression they gave last night."

"Listen." Dad hunches over the table. "You're a man alone. Holed up here in your sweaty little lair, curtains drawn. Money's no problem, yet here you are renting a caravan in the arse end of nowhere. And every time I drive off, they see you getting pally with Brian here. It all starts to add up."

Emile swallows. "I paid what you asked. I don't owe anyone an explanation."

"That's what *you* think. But once people get an idea stuck in their head just you try and get it out again." His knee bumps mine under the table. "What do you think, Bry?"

I don't want to nod, but I do.

"In a bind like that, it can be useful to have some help around."

"Help?"

"Someone to keep their ear to the ground." Dad pulls an invisible fuse from the side of his head. "To suck the filthy air out of their little fantasies. Before they really start to fester."

Emile fiddles with the clasp on his watch.

"Wouldn't it be better if I had a word with them myself?"

"You're right. That wouldn't be better."

"Last night they seemed perfectly fine."

"Let us take care of things for you."

"I'm sorry, but this is complete nonsense ..." Emile stammers. "Brian?"

"Leave my son out of this."

Dad grabbles in his breast pocket. Takes out a screw and stands it on the table.

"It's time I found somewhere else."

"No, no." Dad gestures to Emile not to get up, though he hasn't even tried to. "No need for that."

"Don't leave," I blurt out and shake my head.

"I'm sorry, Brian. But I think it's best if I go."

"You're not going anywhere," Dad says. "We're going to help you."

Dad presses the tip of his index finger on the point of the screw. He stares at it, presses harder, then raises his hand until the screw falls of its own accord and clatters onto the floor.

"Are we agreed?" He holds out his hand to Emile, who doesn't move a muscle. "Well?" Dad asks, a pinpoint of blood glistening on his fingertip. "Deal?"

Emile puts a hesitant palm to his.

"That's more like it," Dad says. "Soft hands you have." When Emile tries to pull back, Dad holds on tight. "Let's say a hundred euros to start with."

Emile tries to twist free, but Dad has him by the wrist. "A hundred." The friendly threat in his eyes holds steady. "A week."

"Okay," Emile caves in.

Dad loosens his grip but doesn't let go. "How about you fetch it now?"

49

Tiredness burns behind my eyes. Lucien has been rocking and humming, begging for my attention since the sun came up. I'm not bothered. Today I'm going to see Selma. I'm already dressed but it's only seven, too early to leave.

To keep Lucien occupied, I brush his teeth in bed. He bites down hard on the plastic bristles. I put a toy car in each of his hands. "Come on then, let's get you up." Even putting on his shoes is easier these days.

Every few steps he flexes his knees, like an old man doing his morning exercises. While I hunt for my flip-flops, he fiddles with the socket by the doorpost. Before I know it, he's pulled the socket out of the wall, along with a length of wire.

"Hey, leave that alone!" I whack it out of his hands. "Go outside. Rico's waiting."

But Lucien remains obsessed with his latest discovery.

"Moo-wah-wah is outside. He's waiting for you."

While I try to jam the socket back in place, Lucien makes his way into the living room. Dad is sleeping in a chair, face as pale as the soles of his bare feet. Lucien slaps himself on the back of the head with the ball of his hand. Dad struggles to open his eyes, coughs, and dozes off again.

"We're going to go feffe," I whisper.

"Moo-wah-wah!" Lucien shouts.

"Yes, Rico's coming too."

I have to make sure Lucien is worn out so he'll sleep the rest of the morning. There's no way I can count on Dad to look after him.

By now, Lucien knows the way to the bottle bank. He practically leads me there. Even so, I take the wheelbarrow along in case he suddenly refuses to take another step. The bag of bottles Emile gave us clink in the tub. Emile is awake too. The hatchback on his car is open. I want to go over and see him, but with Dad still around I don't dare.

Rico trots along a few yards ahead of Lucien, then stops so we can catch up. And when Lucien stops to gaze at something in the air, Rico sits and waits.

Our stash disappears down the hole quicker than I expected. "All done," I say once he's rammed in the final bottle.

"Feffe! Feffe!" he nags.

"All done, I told you."

He pulls himself up on the filthy mouth of the bottle bank. "Feffe!" he shouts inside.

"No! Don't stick your hand in. There's broken glass down there." Suddenly, he's off again, walking without my help. Up toward the road. "Careful!" I hurry after him. The tub of the wheelbarrow echoes every bump and pothole. "Trucks come past here, you know." We cross the asphalt together.

On the other side, his hand reaches for my shoulder again and his eyes light up as he sees the stream, a good ten yards below us. Rico is already bounding down through the trees. Lucien wants to follow. His leg presses against the rusty barbed wire and I remember Emile's warnings. Rico barks up at us.

"Okay, but hold on tight."

As we stagger from tree to tree, I'm glad I put on his proper shoes. My flip-flops keep losing their grip on the ferns and mossy stones. Not to mention the loose slates somebody tipped down the slope.

Rico has already plunged into the stream. He leaps out of the water in high arcs, barks at us to get a move on, and goes chasing after a dragonfly.

Lucien heads straight for the water too. "Wait, let me go first. Then I can catch you." The bitter cold swirls around my legs. I try to find my footing on the uneven bed while keeping Lucien on the bank. It takes too long and I can feel him wanting to fall forward. "No, don't. Sit down first." I tug him to his knees, pull one leg then the other over the edge of a flat stone so that his feet are dangling. His shoes fill with water and his face contorts. "Cold, eh?" I ease him off the stone until we are standing face to face in the stream. The water reaches to just above his knees. Normally I have to fight to control Lucien's hands, but now he is clinging to me. He kicks to shake off the cold, while Rico dives and splashes all around us.

Lucien tries to sit on the water. His nappy dips below the surface a couple of times. I can tell by his breathing that he's scared, but his hips sway like there's fun to be had. Then again, he might just be trying to shake the cold from his bum.

Suddenly his full weight is hanging from my arms. "Easy does it, I can't hold you up like this." He tugs hard at my shoulder and we fall. Underwater I can still feel his arms, the clawing of his nails, the soles of his shoes. I surface with the taste of the stream in my mouth. Water churns all around me. "Don't drown!" I call out to him and graze my knee on something sharp. Thank Christ, I manage to get him back on his feet. "Are you okay?"

Lucien is okay.

"We have to get back to the caravan." I feel like I've pushed him to a cliff edge in his wheelchair and then let go. "This wasn't such a bright idea." His hands crab their way up my wet back. He clamps his body to mine, a hug that pins my arms to my sides. "Don't hurt me," I shout fiercely and wriggle my arms free. Lucien lays his head on my shoulder. I can hear his teeth grinding much too close to my ear. "No biting!"

He shivers, he drips, he pants. I put my shaky arms around him. Feel his spine beneath his wet shirt, the knotted bones stacking up as he straightens his neck. To be sure, I nestle my fingers in the hair on the back of his head so I can rein him in if need be. "In case you can't help biting after all," I whisper. Rico has climbed onto the bank and is shaking himself off among the ferns.

I run my free hand over Lucien's back. He lets me stroke the hollow of his neck and his weary head clunks against mine. I hold him tighter and his breath comes more easily.

There we stand.

Anyone passing on the road could look down through the trees and see two boys knee-deep in a stream. And it would look like they were hugging.

"You are my brother," I tell him. "We are brothers."

50

Lucien is fast asleep, beaker of water by his head. Dad drove off without saying where to. He didn't even notice our sopping wet clothes. Lucien's shoes are drying in the grass. The rest of his things lie dripping on the dog cage.

There's still enough petrol in the tank to get me to Selma and back. I start the engine, clamp my helmet between my knees, and bump the scooter across the grass to Emile's caravan. "Hiya!" Emile comes out. I want to say something about last night but I don't know what. "Hiya!" I say again and rev the engine a few times to make it clear I'm not hanging around. "I have to head off for a bit."

"Oh ..."

"So my brother's alone now. But he's sleeping."

"Are you sure he'll be safe? No chance he might go wandering?"

"Can you keep an eye out? You won't have to do anything. I walked him till he was dead beat."

Emile shakes his head. "I don't think it would be wise. Not after what your father said last night."

"Dad will be away all morning. And Lucien's sound asleep. Promise. We chucked your bottles in the bottle bank. And we even made it down to the stream. It wasn't dangerous at all." It's only now I notice the coffee maker on the back seat of his car, next to the pendulum clock. There's a pillow too, and a removal box with its flaps open.

"What are you doing?"

There's another box waiting in the caravan. His aquarium is still on the table.

"I'm leaving."

I kill the engine. "Leaving?"

Emile nods.

"Is it because of last night? I didn't want him to say those things. I didn't tell him what you said about Louise."

"I know."

"I promise you'll get that money back."

"That's not the point."

"But you can't go. I like you being here. We can go for more walks if you want."

"That's nice of you, but my mind's made up."

I pick at the foam rubber in my helmet.

"And the fish? Are you leaving the aquarium behind?"

"No, that will be the last thing I pack."

"So I'll never see you again?"

"Of course you will."

I know he's lying but it feels good to believe him. We share a silence.

"Did you want to visit that girl of yours?"

"I promised her I would."

Emile sighs. "I can wait a little longer."

"For what?"

"For you. Till you get back."

"And you'll keep an eye on Lucien?"

"Only if you tell me exactly what to do."

I feel like hugging him. I restart the engine and put on my helmet. "Just take a look every now and then. From here. Through the window. That's all. And if he does come out, go over and put his hand on your shoulder, so he'll follow you. Have you got any empty bottles left?"

Emile shakes his head. "And what about your father? I really don't want any trouble."

I rev up the engine before he can change his mind.

"I'll be back before he is." I hold up two fingers and spit between them in the grass. "See you later."

51

Selma is standing by the entrance. "How did you know I was coming?" I look around reception, the chair behind the desk is empty. If we hurry, no one will know I'm here.

"Thee-crit," she whispers.

"What?"

"In the toi-let."

Nino is lurking nearby.

"Can't he wait somewhere else?"

"Nino's ma friend."

"I've come specially to see you. Not him."

I have a hard time believing he's blind. Those angry eyes are drilling holes in my skull.

As we pass Lucien's old room, I take a quick look inside. Henkelmann's bed is empty, a kind of parking space between two bedside cabinets. But his luminous little Christmas tree is still glowing. "Did he die?"

Selma doesn't seem to hear. The lift doors slide open, someone must have taught her how to work the buttons. Nino stops short at the threshold. "Come, come," Selma says, and yanks him into the lift like a reluctant pony. The doors close. There are only two buttons but Selma hesitates. I press the top one quick, before the doors can open again.

Maybe Henkelmann's not dead. Maybe they moved him to a quieter room to keep him out of death's way. Or he made an unexpected recovery. But when we get out of the lift, there's a card with his photo on the noticeboard.

Strange hands pressing a guinea pig to his cheek. Almost identical to the photo of Lucien on the magnet board by his bed. Might even be the same guinea pig. Mathieu died just shy of his fortieth, the card says. *He will be sadly missed.*

Selma is impatient. I let her drag me over to the bathroom.

"Are we going to do belly-belly again?"

She's already through the wide door. Nino follows.

"Can't he wait outside?"

"Nope," Selma says resolutely.

I press a sly heel on Nino's toes so he can feel that I don't want him there. He doesn't get the message.

I squeeze the plastic square in my pocket, feel the rubber ring slide about inside its wrapper. When I promise to bring her a can of energy drink next time, she finally agrees to make Nino wait outside.

As soon as the door shuts behind him, I pull off my T-shirt. Selma keeps hers on. "Touch me," she says. First she wants me to stroke her belly. I knead the cold skin above her hips. "Don't."

"What's wrong?"

"Touch me here." She steers my hands toward her navel. "Can you feel it?"

"Yes." I say, and feel the softness of her skin. My fingers circle, brush the edge of her bra. "Not there, dafty. Down be-lo-ho."

"Here?"

"Mebbe ..."

"What about here?" I inch closer and hope we'll soon be belly to belly.

"Feel it?" Her eyes are squeezed so tight that I can barely see her lashes. "It's the-e-ere."

Nino growls from the other side of the door.

“What is it? What do you want me to feel?”

The door handle wags up and down.

“Shhh,” she says, arches her back, curves her belly bigger. “Babies.”

“What?” My hands shoot back, as if I’ve been zapped by an electric fence. Selma looks frightened. Then she smiles—a wide, happy grin. “Dafty ...”

“No!” I blurt out. “That’s not true!”

“Yes it is, dafty.” She twirls a half pirouette so that I can admire her.

“How can you have a baby in there?”

“Belly-belly. Twin babies.”

“Belly-belly? But you can’t have babies unless you *do* it. Without a condom.”

“No-ho. Babies are in here ...” She jabs a finger next to her navel and giggles. “Cause of the bellies.”

“Did you do it with someone else? With Nino? Is that why he’s your friend?”

“No, dafty. With you.”

“Let go of me. There’s nothing in there. They would never let you have babies.”

“Would too!” she shouts, her voice shaky. “I can feel them.”

“Did you tell anyone else?”

“Everyone.”

“Everyone?”

She starts her list of everyone. “Nino. Computer lady. Thoo-bi-dah. The man that takes us walking ...”

I’m not even listening. “Selma, we can only be together if no one see us.”

“Be kind,” she pleads. “Be kind.” I smell the shampoo in her hair, feel the warmth of her belly against mine, push her up against the toilet door.

“Plea-ease?”

"You're a ..." I don't know what she is anymore. "I don't think you can even have kids."

Something hard raps the door. "Who's in there?" Another rap. "Everything all right in there?"

Selma jumps.

"Can you come here a minute?" the voice outside calls, this time to someone else. "Look after Nino for me, will you?"

"Yeah, yeah ... coming." Squeaking shoes, mumbling. "Let me past, Nino."

"Are you in there, Selma?"

"Yes," she answers, so softly I can barely hear her.

"Shhh," I hiss.

"Selma? It's me, Zoubida. Can you open the door, please?"

Silence.

"Are you alone, Selma?"

There's no other way out. The cupboards are too small to hide in. "Everything's fine." I try to sound as stern as possible. "Selma's not here."

"I'm coming in. Now." Jingling keys, fumbling at the lock.

"No, don't come in!" But the door swings open.

Zoubida looks at me first. Then she sees Selma, her top pulled up over her bra. Selma looks scared, staring at the floor like her head is too heavy for her neck.

"I was on the toilet and she came bursting in. Like you, just now."

"Keep your lies to yourself," Zoubida snaps.

"I'm not lying."

"Do you always pee with your shirt off?"

I look down at my bare belly.

"So it was you!"

"What was me?"

"Selma's been talking about babies for days. Babies and a secret brother. You crossed my mind, but I didn't think you were the kind to do something like this."

Selma rubs her eyes with trembling fists, then falls against Zoubida. "You're not allowed to do this, honey. You know that, don't you? We had a deal, remember?"

"We didn't do anything. She started it."

"Shut your mouth!" Zoubida pulls Selma's top into place and leads her into the corridor. "And put your shirt back on."

"It was her idea."

"Get over here. We have some talking to do."

Selma is standing against the wall, still staring at the floor. The toes of her shoes point at each other. Tongues of velcro curl at the edges.

"She likes me too."

"Of course she likes you."

"She's nineteen."

"It's different for girls like Selma. Surely I don't have to explain that to you?"

"She's not like other girls."

"Well then, you know exactly what I'm talking about."

"No, I mean ... she's ... Selma. She's just Selma."

"This is unacceptable behaviour. And that's all there is to it."

Residents the length of the corridor poke their heads out from behind their doors, none of them try to hide their curiosity. The swing doors at the far end fly open and Thibaut comes striding toward us.

"From now on, you stay away from Selma. Understood?"

"Say something," I beg Selma. "Tell them." A drop falls on the linoleum at her feet. Then a few drops more. They are not tears.

"Can you take Selma back to her room?" Zoubida asks Thibaut, over her shoulder. "She needs a clean pair of pants."

"Of course." Hiding her face in her hands, Selma lets herself be led off.

"I never want to see you anywhere near that girl again. Do I make myself clear?"

"But can't we ..."

"No," she interrupts. "And don't even think about coming back here for the time being."

"But I didn't ..."

"No buts. One more word and I'll tell your father."

"You do that and I'll tell everyone how you kill people here!" I am screaming at her now. "How you kill them with all the pills you give them. Henkelmann ..."

"Now you listen here ..." Zoubida says.

"Why should I listen? Lucien is never coming back here again."

"Nino-o-o-o!" Selma turns and cries out to her friend, who is standing a little way down the corridor. She shrugs off Thibaut's hand. He wants to go after her, but Zoubida signals to let her be.

Selma takes Nino's face in her hands. Runs her thumbs below his eyes, then presses him to her while he glares at the ceiling. Nino stands there, motionless, speechless, and comforts her.

A minibus full of residents blasts its horn as I swerve through the gates and off the grounds. The pointer on my speedometer quivers its way to thirty. I ran all the way from Selma back to my scooter. Handlebars gripped tight, I lean into the wind and grit my teeth, willing myself to go faster. The road is a blur of tears but I don't dare wipe my eyes.

The stretch through the woods feels far longer than it did on the way to see Selma.

Big trucks come thundering in the opposite direction, then a van. Then a pickup. Our pickup. The shock sends me veering to the sharp edge of the asphalt but I manage to steer back into the middle of the lane. Thank Christ Dad didn't see me. At least I think he didn't.

Tyres screech behind me. The pickup bumps onto the verge, then turns and gives chase, like a monster set on flattening me. I pray for a track that peels off into the woods. *Faster, faster.* But thirty's as fast as my scooter can go.

Dad is alongside me now, yelling something I can't understand. *Eyes on the road. Keep your eyes on the road.* I glance to the side, can't help myself. All the anger inside him is burning in his stare. The pickup shoots ahead of me.

"Da-a-ad!" I yell after him. "I had to go," I lie to myself. "I went to get more medicine but they wouldn't give it to me." The tremor and catch in my breath makes it feel like I'm not alone inside my helmet. "I went to get Lucien's money. I was trying to help you."

If I can turn onto the firebreak and cut through the woods, I might still make it home before he does.

52

The pickup is parked outside Emile's caravan. I race over there. Lucien is slumped on the grass beneath the window. No sign of Dad. I jump off the scooter and pull the helmet from my head.

Raised voices inside. Dad and Emile.

"And I'm supposed to believe that?"

"Ask Brian when he gets back."

Lucien's forehead is grazed where he keeps banging it against the side of the caravan. I try to pull him away but he won't budge. It's like he has to hurt himself.

"I only touched your son to make sure he didn't come to any harm. He wanted to see the aquarium."

"Yeah?" Dad's laugh mixes mockery with rage. "Told you that, did he? 'Please mister, can I see your aquarium?'"

"Be thankful I was looking out for him. It's more than I've ever seen you do."

Lucien's forehead is bleeding. With every thud of his head, blood smears the caravan. "Don't do that," I plead with him. I'd rather he hurt me than hurt himself. But he won't let me hold him.

"What kind of father are you anyway?"

"Stay out of my life. And stay away from my boys."

"Then take care of them. Why do you think Brian wants to talk to me? You're a worthless father."

"The fucking nerve ..."

"Don't touch me!" Emile shouts, but I hear a scuffle inside. "Let go, let go!"

"Keep your hands off my boys. Or you're a dead man."

"That's the last time you threaten me," Emile says. "I'm leaving. This minute."

"You're going nowhere."

A stomp. The crack of wood. "No, not ..." There's panic in Emile's pleading. A crash and the heavy slosh of water. I burst through the door as Emile's back slams into the table. It's already hanging off the wall. No aquarium, only flickering blue light.

Dad's fist comes down hard.

"No!" I shout. Emile paws at Dad's face, tries to fend him off. "Leave Emile alone."

"Outside, you!" Dad bellows. "Take care of your brother."

I grab the rinsed-out bottle from the counter. I want to hurt Dad now. Cut him down, force him to his knees. Make him let go of Emile. I shut my eyes and swing the bottle. I'll keep pounding until he begs me to stop, until he gets up and throws his arms around me. But he doesn't. Dad grabs me, shoves me back. Only his nose is bleeding. Emile's hair is dark and sticky, blood dripping from his ear, head hanging to one side. Did I do this?

Everything goes quiet.

Even the bleeding seems to stop for a moment. Only the fish move, flapping in the puddle of glass and water on the floor. Emile's hair turns blacker, blood seeps into his shirt.

"Lose the bottle! Now!" Dad barks. "You've killed him."

"No!"

"Oh fuck ... Bry. For fuck's sake, Bry!"

"I didn't do anything," I stammer. "It wasn't me." I let the broken bottle drop. Suddenly Henri is with us in the caravan.

"What is this, Maurice?"

Dad swallows, shakes his head. "Nothing. A spat that

got out of hand." He tugs at Emile. "It's all over now. Go! Keep out of it!" Emile's blood stains Dad's shirt.

"Out of my fucking way!" Henri shoves Dad aside. His shoes splat fish on the wet floor.

"He's going to die," I sob. "I know he is." Henri kneels over Emile, presses two fingers to his throat.

"Still alive." Henri shifts Emile carefully until he is lying on his back. His eyes roll back in his head. "We have to get him to a hospital."

"No," Dad says. "We can't."

Jean arrives. He and Henri carry Emile outside. His head is hanging back like his throat's been slit. Lucien's legs jerk as he scrambles around on the grass. Jean and Henri try to lay Emile on the seat of our pickup, but his body leaves no room behind the wheel.

"The back of his car," Henri orders. He digs a hand into Emile's trouser pocket and pulls out his car keys. Now it dawns on Dad that something has to be done.

"Yes, get him into the car," he says. "We need to get that guy out of here."

"Open the back door!" Henri shouts at me.

"No, no," Dad interferes. "The bloodstains will show."

"Shut up, Maurice!" Henri lowers his backside onto the back seat, drags Emile behind him into the car. I run round and open the door on the other side. A removal box is booted out, then comes the tuneless ding-dong of the clock, then the coffee maker. Henri comes crawling out after them. Emile fills the back seat, his knees jolt and shake.

Jean leans panting against the door. Henri grabs Dad by the throat. "Sort this, Maurice!"

"How?" Dad yells, like they've asked him to blow out a fire. "How can I?"

"Drive him to hospital, you idiot."

"I didn't do anything."

"And never come ... back here again," Jean puffs. "You're finished, Maurice. Tonight ... you pack up and leave. And never ... come back."

"Or what?" Dad stokes his anger again.

"Take the man to hospital, you dumb fuck!"

"Or what?"

"Or we'll torch your caravan if we have to. Make damn sure you have nothing to come back to."

I can't hear Dad's answer. Lucien is calmer now. With Jean's help, I get him into the passenger seat. We pull the seat belt tight across his chest. Dad steps back from the car but Henri forces him behind the wheel. "Anything happens to the tenant on the way and I'll drag you into the police station myself. I'm calling the hospital in Saint Arnaque to tell them you're coming. You've got ten minutes, Maurice. One minute late and I call the coppers. They won't need a description." Dad's hand shakes as he tries to slot the key into the ignition. I lift Emile's feet and slide onto the back seat.

"Go!" Henri yells. The engine screams into life. Dad struggles to get the car into gear.

Jean and Henri back away. Suddenly Rico leaps up at the window. I don't understand where he's come from. He tears after us, stands barking at the top of the rutted track as we pull out onto the main road. Emile's legs feel strange and heavy on my lap.

"I'm sorry," I tell him. "I didn't want to hurt you."

"Fuck," Dad spits through clenched teeth. Lucien thumps his head against the window.

"Emile?" I squeeze his hand but there's no response.

As Dad takes the bends, Emile's head lolls and stains the grey fabric of the seat.

"Listen, Bry."

"What?"

"Your brother can help us out here."

"Lucien?"

"I can't lose you, Brian. I can't lose you. I only went in there to put the wind up the tenant. But you smashed his head in, Bry. They'll lock you up for that."

"It's all your fault. Emile was only trying to help me."

"You're not even fourteen." He blasts the horn and cuts in at the roundabout. "If I take the blame, they'll take you off me and you'll end up in a children's home. Or a foster home. I'm not going to lose you." Lucien is slumped in his seat, wrestling with the belt under his chin.

"Here's what we'll do ... listen ..." But he doesn't say anything.

"What will we do?" My voice is shaking.

"Lucien did it."

I don't understand what Dad's saying.

"I'm the only one who saw it happen. You were outside. You didn't see a thing. Lucien grabbed a bottle. Hit Emile from behind."

"That's a lie. He didn't do anything. I'll tell them the truth. Tell them I did it."

"You do that ..." Dad looks at me in the rearview mirror, "... and I'll tell them you're lying. Lying to protect Lucien. Because you're a good lad."

"But what will happen to him?"

"Nothing. He'll go back to his old bed at the care home. Back to his paper birds. His applesauce. His pills. Everything he needs. That's where your brother belongs. Not with us." Emile's head looks like it's stopped bleeding. His chest heaves, his breath comes in short bursts. "We'll say the tenant tried to interfere with Lucien, that your brother flipped his lid."

Dad tries to pull Lucien straight in his seat. "Let him do this for you, Bry. For us. Let him give us something back for once. Who do we have if we don't have each other, eh? No one."

"Lucien didn't do anything."

"We can visit him every week. As often as you like. I promise."

Dad steers past a waiting car, bumps up onto the pavement.

"And if they find a way to punish Lucien?"

"There is no punishment for your brother, Bry."

"Yes there is!" I scream. "There is. He belongs with us now."

We drive into the shadow of Accident and Emergency and everything in the car changes colour. Two white coats are waiting with a stretcher.

The car doors fly open. A man with a buzz cut asks me if there's anything wrong with me. I shake my head and he pulls me from the car. I don't want to let go of Emile's hand, but I have to. Someone leans in through the other door. "Sir? Sir, can you hear me?" His hands feel Emile. "Pulse!" They slide a plank with handles behind the front seats. Someone has clamped a collar around Emile's neck.

"Sir?" A nurse comes hurrying out through the sliding doors. "Sir? Are you family?" She is talking to Dad, who stands hunched over the bonnet of the car. She taps him cautiously on the shoulder. "Are you family?" Dad shakes his head slowly and his red eyes appear from behind his hand.

"Can you tell me what happened?"

Dad looks at me, then at Lucien. A tear tries to slip unnoticed down the side of his nose. "Yes," he says. "Yes, I can."

53

There is hardly anyone out in the grounds.

The rain came last week and the grass is turning green again. The orange sunshades have been pulled in, the blinds thrown open. The building is wide awake and keeping tabs on me. I made it over the fence, now I'm sneaking through the bushes.

A workman rinsing out a paint roller in a cement bucket turns to look at me, but he doesn't say anything. Through every window I pass, I see residents lying in bed. Some spot me, one even waves. Most of them don't notice a thing.

I start to worry they might have moved Lucien to another room after the renovations. If he's on a higher floor, my trip will have been for nothing. Dad swore he would visit my brother now that I'm not allowed. Afterwards he told me Lucien was doing just fine.

"And? What else?"

"Nothing. Fine is all."

Bastard. I eventually got him to admit that he wasn't allowed to visit either. Mum saw to that.

I arrive at the window to Lucien's old room. There he is! Seeing him is a shock. His bottom lip is sticking out more than it ever did. He is sleeping. The wound on his forehead has healed to a patch of pink. His hands are limp but peaceful on the sheet. Is he doing okay? Is he sound asleep because he walked all morning?

The magnet board with photos is propped up on the

shelf above his head, still waiting to be hung on the wall. He can't see it from where he is lying. In the middle there's a new photo of Mum and Didier. Faces snapped in close-up, Mum kissing Didier's cheek. The cuddly dolphin at the foot of the bed must be a present from them.

Above Lucien's head, the paper birds sway gently in the breeze coming in through the little top window. Someone has put Henkelmann's glowing Christmas tree on the sill. The needles turn slowly from red, to green and white, and back again.

"Lucien?" I tap a fingernail against the glass. "Lucien, it's me. I'm sorry. Zoubida says I'm not allowed in."

Nothing moves but the breath in his chest. I climb onto the ledge and pull myself up on the frame of the open window.

"Lucien!" His eyelids quiver and his fingers dig into the sheet. "I couldn't come any sooner. Dad and me live kind of far away now, in the city. Lucien?"

I hope he will look at me, if only for a second. I want him to know I haven't forgotten him. I want to see in his eyes if he is mad at me, if he remembers what happened to Emile. Part of me is afraid they will burn hotter than the sun. Hot enough to hiss a hole in my eyes, to leave a black fleck on everything I see. But when they open at last, they are dull. Lucien has been folded up and tucked away, somewhere deep inside himself. Everything we managed to do together was taken from him when they wheeled him back into this place. He stares at the birds on the ceiling.

"Bro?" I tap the glass again. "It's me." I'd like to hold him, just for a moment. Take his hand and put it on my shoulder. Walk with him. Chuck a few bottles.

I take a toy car from my coat pocket. "Remember?" I worm my hand through the gap of the open window and throw. "For you." It lands beside the dolphin at the foot of his bed.

Lucien flinches and his eyes roam around the room. It takes him a while to see me at the window. "Moo-wah-wah," he says softly.

"Yes!" I nod. "It's me. And Rico's at home. He's sleeping."

"Moo-wah-wah."

"Rico misses you too. It's no fun without you." I shut my eyes for a second or two. Close them tight. "I'll make it up to you one day, bro."

A wasp shoots past my cheek and in through the open window, circles Lucien's open mouth. "Look out!" His fingers clutch the air, he twists his head away. "Where is it? Did it fly into your mouth?" I yell. "It'll sting you." Someone has to help. "I'm coming!" There it is, crawling up his arm. I thump the window. A shiver runs through Lucien's body, and the wasp takes to the air again. It hovers around the spout of his beaker, then disappears through the open door and into the corridor. As far as I can tell, Lucien hasn't been stung.

"Feffe," he says, with lazy lips.

"Yeah! Feffe! Do you remember?"

I wish Mum had seen our summer. That she knew what her two boys had done together. I don't think she would believe me if I told her. Perhaps if she heard it from Emile. But I have no idea where he went after they released him from hospital.

Lucien is getting restless. It won't be long before a nurse comes in and finds me here. "I have to go, bro, but I'll be back." I hope Zoubida will let me visit before long. "When I'm old enough, you can come and live with me. I promise. And I'll make sure you never have to take those pills again." I drop from the ledge. "See you next time."

Now that I've woken my brother, I don't want to leave

him behind, awake and alone in bed.

Then I notice a greasy mark on the windowpane. And below it a spot that's been licked clean. I look closer and see her nose stamped from one side of the window to the other.

Lucien has turned his face toward me.

I flex my knees, press my nose to the pane, and lick the glass. He smiles and begins to rock gently from side to side. It's still there. Lucien still has the universe in his eyes.

First of all, I would like to thank my editor, Ad van den Kieboom. You alone are reason enough to write another book. Thanks to Judith and Sander for your meticulous and painstaking reading of the drafts. Huge thanks to Nele, Jill, and Welmoed for your trust in me. The same goes to Paulien, Nathalie, and all the Singelaars. Thank you, Neeltje-Roos. And to everyone who spoke to me so openly when they heard what I was writing about. My loving parents, thank you for making me, for taking me with you, and for teaching me to look. And above all, thanks to my favourite human being, Suus.

DAVID DOHERTY studied English and literary linguistics in the UK before moving to the Netherlands, where he has been translating all manner of Dutch texts since 1996. He was commended by the jury of the 2017 Vondel Translation Prize for Marente de Moor's *The Dutch Maiden* and Jaap Robben's *You Have Me to Love*, and was runner-up in 2019 for his translation of *Monte Carlo* by Peter Terrin.

On the Design

As book design is an integral part of the reading experience, we would like to acknowledge the work of those who shaped the form in which the story is housed.

Tessa van der Waals (Netherlands) is responsible for the cover design, cover typography, and art direction of all World Editions books. She works in the internationally renowned tradition of Dutch Design. Her bright and powerful visual aesthetic maintains a harmony between image and typography and captures the unique atmosphere of each book. She works closely with internationally celebrated photographers, artists, and letter designers. Her work has frequently been awarded prizes for Best Dutch Book Design.

The letter used on the cover is Fonseca Black, a recent all-caps family with simple straight geometric forms, designed by Indonesian letter designer Nasir Udun. The width of this font enables the letters to form their own distinctive word image that fills the entire surface: text becomes image. The author's name acts as a breathing space between the two words of the title. The bright colors have been chosen for their association with sun, flowers, and summer.

The cover has been edited by lithographer Bert van der Horst of BFC Graphics (Netherlands).

Suzan Beijer (Netherlands) is responsible for the typography and careful interior book design of all World Editions titles.

The text on the inside covers and the press quotes are set in Circular, designed by Laurenz Brunner (Switzerland) and published by Swiss type foundry Lineto.

All World Editions books are set in the typeface Dolly, specifically designed for book typography. Dolly creates a warm page image perfect for an enjoyable reading experience. This typeface is designed by Underware, a European collective formed by Bas Jacobs (Netherlands), Akiem Helmling (Germany), and Sami Kortemäki (Finland). Underware are also the creators of the World Editions logo, which meets the design requirement that "a strong shape can always be drawn with a toe in the sand."